Dedicated to Ernie Adams

Chapter One
A Case of Mistaken Identity

Monday 6th September 1982

James repeatedly pushed at the sleeves of his jacket in front of the hall mirror. "I'm not going Mum, I look stupid!"

His Mum entered the hallway from the kitchen and, as she watched her son stand in front of the mirror, she bit her bottom lip. "Come on James, we've already gone over this. Trust me, everybody in the first year are in the same boat. Besides which, by the time you get to the end of the year, those sleeves will be halfway up to your elbows, and believe me, at what that cost me, it's going to have to last you the whole year."

He fidgeted uncomfortably and she hid her sympathy and remained resolute, her face fixed, almost stern, and he looked back, searching for the merest opportunity for his mother to relent.

A knock at the door broke the stand off.

"That'll be Richard. You got your bag? Hurry up, I'll get the door." She bit her lip once more as she took in the sight of Richard in his tailor-made school uniform, or at least it appeared that way. "Hello Richard, he's just gone to get his bag. Ooh, isn't it exciting?"

Richard shrugged his shoulders. "Suppose so," were the only words he could muster as an affirmative response. He was several inches taller than most in his year and could have easily passed as a third year. A shock of red curly hair framed his freckled face as he stood facing Mrs Simpson on the doorstep.

James arrived with his bag on his shoulder and she bundled him through the door with a quick kiss before he could raise another protest about his oversized blazer.

His very first registration and assembly at Middle Hardwick Comprehensive served to ease his and all the other first year pupils' nerves and angst, and before he knew it he was settling down into class for an hour of History and then onto lunch break. However, as opposed to his earlier class, Miss Kelly was intrigued to find out a little more about her new cohort. She worked her way through the register, listening to banal answers to her equally banal questions. Finally, as if a shaft of sunshine entered through the window, her face lit up.

"James Simpson?" she asked inquisitively. She raised her head, lowered her reading glasses to the end of her nose and searched the room.

James raised his hand and coyly responded, "Miss."

"Do your Mother and Father have an interest in History, James?"

"Err dunno Miss."

"The reason I ask is that you have a very interesting historical middle name. Would you like to share it with the rest of the class?" The question was of course rhetorical, he had no choice.

He squirmed on his seat, wishing his oversized uniform would swallow him up. Inside he was shaking and his heart began to pound on the inside of his chest. "T-t-tiberius, Miss."

Somebody in the room sniggered, and soon after the whole class erupted in laughter.

"Ok settle down. That's enough." She used enough authority to stem the laughter. "James, what can you tell us about the name?"

He froze, the only answer he could offer was so absurd that it would be better to remain mute.

"Come on James, why do you think your Mother and Father gave you the middle name of Tiberius."

Again, he did not answer.

The girl in the seat behind raised her hand. Miss Kelly acknowledged the girl and checked her seating plan before addressing her. "Yes Wendy."

"Is Tiberius a robot Miss, because I think you've broken him, Miss." The class erupted into laughter again. She kicked the back of his seat with a clear intent of animosity.

At this point Miss Kelly released the full venom of her wrath and the class silenced immediately. "I wasn't going to set any homework today, but I'm sorry to say that I'm disappointed with you all. You are to write an essay on the life of Tiberius Claudius Nero. I shall be expecting no less than five hundred words."

James shrunk as much as he could in his seat as the rest of the class sneered at him, and at that very moment the lunch bell rang in the corridor and the focus was drawn away from him to the more urgent matter of hungry tummies.

James was slow to clear his books, deliberately so. The last thing he wanted to do was the walk of shame passed the angry mob of his new classmates. One boy held back, hovering with as much deliberate effort as James.

Miss Kelly could not look at the scrawny specimen in front of her as a feeling of guilt washed over her; instead, she pretended to scrutinise a piece of paper that had nothing on it. She knew that he would be the subject of torment with his new cohort and that she was responsible.

Once James thought it was safe and the coast was clear, he made his way to the door. The other boy caught up with him in the corridor and James clenched his fists ready for whatever the other boy had him in for. James wasn't going to go down without a fight. As the other boy's footsteps closed in on him, James's breath quickened and his heart began to pound again. He stopped and turned abruptly.

The boy stopped dead as he turned and raised both hands, palms out. "Whoa! I don't know what you think I'm here for, but it's not a fight. It's my sister, Wendy, she was the girl taking the mick. I've come to say sorry. I know what she's like. Trust me, she's evil, if it wasn't you she'd have found somebody else to pick on."

James's breathing steadied and his hands relaxed from the tight knots they had assumed seconds earlier. "Is she your stepsister? She doesn't look anything like you!"

"No, she's my twin actually, but we're from different eggs, obviously."

"Huh. Oh, yeah of course!" James's quizzical expression cleared as he came to terms with his own stupidity. They continued in the direction of the food hall and the boy lurched forward as another boy slammed into him from behind. He turned, his face an expression of bewilderment, until he saw who it was. "Jack! What is it with you? Why can't you just catch up with us normally like anybody else?"

"Where's the fun in that? Besides, I need you for a game of football."

"When?"

"Now, in the playground, five-a-side. Steve Jones challenged me. There's a frozen Mars bar at stake from the school tuck shop."

"Who else you got?"

"Mick Brownlow. Just need two more with you on board, Peaty boy."

"You up for a game err T-i-b-er-i-us. Sorry, I've forgotten your first name."

"It's James."

"Tiberius. I'm sure that's what our next door's cat's called. I hear the old lady in the backyard calling him Tibbsy or Tibbs, something like that. Anyway, if you're in we need one more for my team."

As they pushed through the double doors at the end of the corridor leading to the schoolyard, James stiffened his neck and bobbed onto the balls of his feet like a dog searching for something in the long grass. "Thought so." He spoke to himself and then shouted, "DICK!" and waved his arms above his head.

Richard acknowledged him from the far side of the schoolyard, turning to beat his way back to James.

Mick Brownlow was already there setting up some makeshift goal posts with his duffle bag and blazer. The rest ambled up and followed suit.

"Might have known it, Steve's gone and roped his brother in to play."

Mick gestured at a big stocky lad loitering around menacingly.

Jack spun round, measuring up the giant, and then picked out his opponent. "Steve, who the hell's he?"

"My brother. I don't remember saying we all had to be from the same year."

Jack looked back at the giant, granted he was intimidating, but from the way he was moving while they warmed up he was clumsy with it. He watched his own tribe knocking the ball about. James was the most nimble and agile. He called his boys over and set them in their respective positions, pitting James against the giant.

In the beginning Jack's plan was working. James's first touch was to turn and shield the ball, trying to pick out a pass when he heard, "Tibbsy!" being yelled from behind his right shoulder, and released it instinctively in the direction of the yell straight to Jack's feet.

The giant carried on into James's back, forcing him to the ground. Jack had a shot at goal which was parried away, and this time it was the opposition's turn to make the attack. James assessed the graze on his hand, feeling its burn, and once again his attention was caught.

"Tibbsy, Tibbsy get up!" Mick pointed to the charging giant making good progress up the pitch, and James was the only player that could thwart his advance.

James made it onto his feet only to be barged off back to the ground and the big lad slammed the ball home past Dick, straight into the goal mouth. From those very first touches of the ball, as far as anybody was concerned, James was no longer James. He was Tibbsy.

Dick rolled the ball out to him from the goal calling, "Tibbsy!" much to James's surprise. Dick had been his friend since their first year of primary school, and before this day he had only ever known James as James, but now in the space of ten minutes the handle of Tibbsy seemed to be nailed on.

Mick monitored the team's progress, which wasn't good. They were two goals down and destined to lose unless something changed. James was being out-muscled, and without a bona fide referee, the consistent fouling was going unchallenged. He called out to James. "Tibbsy, you swap places with whats-his-name in goal."

"It's Dick."

"What?"

"His name, it's Dick."

"Look, I don't really care about that right now, just swap places with him."

James turned to make his way to the goal, dusting himself off and assessing the grazes and yellowy green bruises developing on his arms.

"Hold on a minute, who made you Captain?" Jack marched up to Mick, facing up to him square on. "Look, in any other football match with a referee you'd be right, but this isn't one and Tibbsy over there's being muscled off the ball. So, put our biggest lad against theirs and fight fire with fire. Use James's agility in goal. Do you want that frozen Mars bar or don't you?"

Jack stared back at him defiantly, but as much as he wanted to face him down he knew he was making sense. "Ok, do as he says, but if we lose you owe me a frozen Mars bar." Jack jabbed his finger at Mick as he made his way back to position.

As Mick had promised the game turned. Dick had enough strength to hinder the larger of the Jones's brothers and James was quick enough to deal with most of the other team's shots on goal. Jack's team pulled the score back to an advantage of three goals to two. He was beginning to allow himself to savour the thought of chomping down on one of the tuck shop's fabled frozen Mars bars.

It wasn't to be the case, however, as the bigger of the Jones' brothers managed to round Dick and, without any finesse, he threw all his weight behind the ball at the goal mouth.

James froze with his hands and arms held defensibly in front of his body and his eyes closed. The ball hit him square on but the force threw him back into the goal with the ball following behind, and with that the bell rang for the end of lunch break.

Jack turned to Mick and barked, "You owe me a frozen Mars bar."

"Get stuffed! We only agreed on that if we lost, and we didn't lose. We drew, so do one."

James lay on the floor struggling to draw a breath, winded by the force of the blow.

Peter came to help him to his feet and the rest just cleared off, apart from Jack who pressed onto James after his altercation with Mick. He looked down at James as he lay in the foetal position. "You owe me a frozen Mars bar!"

James couldn't respond, he could barely breathe. Peter reached his hand down to James which James took, and Peter hauled him back to his feet. "Good, isn't he? At footy I mean."

"Who Jack? Yeah, they won't get him into the team though. I'll guarantee they'll try to get him into the school team, but they won't get him."

"Why not?"

"He won't say. He just clams up and won't talk about it."

Jack entered his kitchen making a beeline for the biscuit barrel. "Hi Mum." He stretched his arm to reach for the barrel but a short sharp tap on his wrist changed the trajectory of his hand.

The ninja-like reactions of his mother didn't even distract her from the steaming saucepans on the hob. "Your tea's nearly ready. I won't have you ruining your appetite."

As he stood at the kitchen window he watched his neighbours tabby cat gingerly make his way along the top of the fence, two paws on the top of the feather boards and two on the cant rail a few inches below. "Mum, what's next door's cat called again?"

"What, Mr Tibbs you mean?"

"Yeah, strange name for a cat."

"Do you know what, I'd never thought of it like that. Oh well, it takes all sorts. How was your first day at school?" The lack of an answer was enough to draw her focus away from the pans to see the kitchen door swishing closed. She raised her voice to a shout. "I've got an extra dance lesson scheduled for you on Saturday."

James stealthily let himself in through the front door, a barely audible click from the latch as he opened the door and carefully closed it behind him. He tiptoed through the hallway and upstairs to get changed. Whoa betide his Mum should see the state of his heavily scuffed uniform. As soon as he was changed he buried his shirt in the wash basket. He would brush off his trousers and repolish his shoes later that evening.

He slouched into the kitchen as his mother prepared tea.

"Ooh, you gave me a shock. When did you get back? I didn't hear you come in."

"Oh, 'bout ten minutes ago."

"Come on then, how was it?"

"How was what?"

"Your first day at the big school, silly!"

"Oh, you know, ok I guess."

"Will you be down for eight?"

"Duuno, I've got a load of homework to do, why?"

His mother clutched a tea towel to her chest and looked up at the ceiling as if she were staring at a beautiful star in the night sky. "The Beeb are showing some reruns of Star Trek. I can't wait. I love it. You just don't get hero's like that anymore. Captain James Tiberius Kirk. Ooh!" She swooned as she lost herself in her fantasy.

Chapter Two
Life Choices

Thursday 12th August 1989

"So, remind me, what did you get again?"

"Come on! Stop rubbing it in."

Peter nursed the pint of bitter in his hand, took a sip and placed it back down on the beer mat with as much of an innocent expression he could muster, his eyes wide and searching.

James scanned his face, slightly amused at the frothy bum fluff moustache that now adorned Peter's top lip. "A, erm B, and two Cs, as if you didn't know already. Not enough for any of the Unis I've applied for."

"I wouldn't worry too much, you'll defo get some offers through clearing easy."

"Yeah, I know, I've already thought about that, but I don't know whether I want to end up doing some useless degree in a shithole of a city that nobody else wants to go to. Besides which, I've started applying for a few jobs. I've got an interview with Harpers for a trainee manager's position."

Peter raised his eyebrows, impressed with his friend's eagerness to take control of his life, until he found out later that the manager of the store was a golfing buddy of his old man. It was all set up bet

ween the two of them, requiring no effort from James whatsoever.

"Well, if you do end up getting a job there, do you reckon you could get some staff discount? It'd be handy if I could get some essentials for uni at a knockdown price." Peter scanned his watch for the time as he said it. "I'd have thought the others would be here by now." It was still early but there was a general agreement that on results day they would all meet up down at the Baker's Arms for a few bevvies to celebrate and commiserate the end of a chapter in their lives. "Money bags will be here soon enough, not that he's got anything to celebrate. Any excuse for a drink."

James's face lit up for a second. "Oh yeah! Talking of Jack, I've got a bit of gossip. Not so much of the Mister money bags anymore."

Peter raised his eyebrows. "I shudder to think. What shit has he got mixed up in this time?" Peter's voice carried mirth in its timbre as he contemplated yet another sticky situation Jack's impulsiveness had managed to land him into.

James leaned in closer to Peter and lowered his voice, as if it were a secret to be kept between the two of them. "Well, you know Mrs Thompson, right? Well, he was working round hers with his boss doing some stuff to the heating system. Anyway, to cut a long story short he didn't tighten up one of the pipes on the radiator in the bedroom. They disappear and half an hour later water starts pouring through the light fitting in the kitchen."

They both erupted into choked-back laughter, the type that is more noticeable as a physical emanation of the body bobbing up and down than the stifled giggle from the mouth.

"Fuck sake, has he been sacked?"

"Well, according to my mum, Mrs Thompson was fuming. Barry, Jack's boss, has offered to pay for a new carpet and re-decorating the kitchen ceiling, but a little bird told me that he'll be taking the whole amount out of Jack's wages, and on what apprentices earn, he won't have a bean to his name for the next two months."

Peter's eyes flashed over James's shoulder with a knowing, slightly alarmed expression. "Whatcha Jack." Peter's welcome was the prompt for James to kill the conversation.

"Alright tossers," was all Jack could muster in response.

Peter gave a sly wink to James. "You're just in time Jack to get the next round in."

"Yeah about that, just before I got here I realised I'd left my wallet at home. You're gunna have to sub me tonight boys."

Peter pressed on. "Oh right, got any other news you want to share with us? How's the plumbing trade treating you?"

"Nothing, fucking boring, why?"

Peter and James eyed each other knowingly with the hint of a smile. James changed the subject. "Any idea what Dick and Mick are going to do?"

"Mick's an odd one. He's doing something to do with computers and IT. Reckons that's where the futures going, but he'd be far better off going into politics or some shit like that if you ask me. You know what he's like, always on some debating committee or just any chance for an argument come to think of it."

"Mick's just really good at convincing people he's right. Am I right in thinking that Dick's going up to Edinburgh Uni?"

Jack then offered his two-penny worth. "Might of known it. He's going back home with the rest of the ginger brigade."

James cut in ruefully. "I'll miss that big lump. I can see him ending up joining Green Peace on some mission to save the planet. I don't suppose we'll see much of him if he's all the way up there. If only it were the witch going there instead."

"Wendy's not that bad these days, Tibbsy. She's mellowed, honestly."

With Peter's defensive declaration James snorted into his drink. It's something he had a habit of doing. Luckily the lager he was drinking didn't have a head of froth and only a few speckles of lager splashed onto his face, which he wiped away easily with the back of his hand. "And that's why she still insisted on calling me Tiberius the whole time I was round yours the other day is it?"

Dick and Mick arrived together and casually ambled up to the bar. "What you having, boys?" Mick offered as he gestured to Stan to put his order in.

They all mumbled out their requests, Jack insisting on a snake bite. "And while you're at it ask Stan for a couple of sets of darts." At which they all took up a table next to the dart board on the wall at the far end of the pub, adjacent to a table where four leather-clad bikers had assumed residence.

Jack recognised them; his elder brother had them down as trouble, and the only advice he could offer was to stay away. Jack hesitated before taking a seat. He looked across at them. They were absorbed in their own conversation, completely disinterested in anything else going on around them, so he went ahead and sat down with the rest of the lads.

After a couple more rounds of drinks the banter was flowing and James decided to get a bit more competitive. "Ok then Jack, I've got a proposition for you. Double or quits on that frozen Mars bar I owe you."

The table erupted into laughter, as they always did at the long-standing joke about that frozen Mars bar Jack insisted James owed him ever since the first day they met. Then eerily the table fell silent when Jack took up the challenge and they began to throw darts. The tension lay thick in the air. This is the moment when a long-standing feud that ironically served to bond their friendships may be brought to an abrupt end.

Mick decided to umpire. "Ok then boys, let's make this a proper match. Best of three." Jack took the first round but James rallied and took the second. It was all down to the final third round. James kicked off with a full house.

"One hundred and eighty," Mick chipped in with his best dart's scorer impersonation.

James was so elated with his triumphant start that he threw his arms up and jumped back. Except he didn't just jump back anywhere, he jumped back into Ozzy, one of the bikers returning back to his table with a full pint of lager. Well, he was until James backed into him. Now it was only half full. The rest was on Ozzy's t-shirt and jeans and the floor.

The eerie silence didn't just fall over their table. The whole pub fell silent as everybody watched events unfold with eager anticipation. "You gonna say sorry, wanker?"

James didn't need time to assess the situation. "Soz mate."

Ozzy shouldered past him and sat down, much to James's relief. Mick took control and beckoned the boys into a muted tone. "I'm going to have to declare this game null and void. I think you two would be better off sat down for a while until this blows over properly."

The rest of the pub resumed to a low drone of incoherent conversation. When the bikers finally upped and left Mick felt it safe to release one more morsel of wit. "You do know Tibbsy that you'd have been well within your right to have replied, sorry wanker." They all erupted into laughter, only to be silenced when Stan rang the bell for last orders.

Peter and James headed up to the bar to get the last round in. Once Stan had given him the necessary eye contact to make his order, Peter held back a little, then instead of making his order he asked him a question. "Stan. I've got a bit of a confession to make. When we first started coming here to drink we were all underage. Did you know that?"

Stan laughed to himself "Of course you were, you little fuckers. I remember you sending that big ginger lump over. Can I have five pints of beer please? It took you lot ten minutes to decide between lager and bitter."

"So why did you serve us then?"

"Got to keep the wolf from the door ain I? In the week, there's more life in a morgue than this place, now let me guess, three lagers, a bitter, and a snakebite?"

Several weeks later James started his job at Harpers, Jack continued working as a Plumber's apprentice, finally earning some money, and the rest went off to university.

Chapter Three
Jess

Wednesday 10th February 1993

James was messing about with the display racks which housed various kinds of toasters on the outer edge of the electrical department. It had become a ritual he would follow, but he wasn't focusing on that. He was more intent on scanning across the shop floor to the children's department directly opposite, and there she was, the raven-haired beauty that had captivated his imagination for the past couple weeks. He was mesmerised by the way she swished her hair back over her shoulder as she attended to the racks of tiny outfits.

"She's pretty, isn't she?" The voice from behind was deep and silky.

James quickly picked up a toaster and set it back down again on exactly the same spot.

Roger, his boss, was about ten years his senior and watched James with amusement as he coloured up with embarrassment. "Just say the word and I can get you transferred back over there." Roger was winding him up and this time enjoyed watching James's face crease in disgust. "I'm kidding. I don't think I could last more than five minutes with mad Martha myself either."

"I'm sorry Roger, but I'd rather have my balls removed than work with that mad bitch again."

"Have you spoken to her yet?"

"Who, mad Martha, are you kidding?"

"No, you dumb ass. Jess!"

"No, of course I haven't. Is that her name? Jess."

"I interviewed her so I guess I should know, right. She's good looking in a demure kind of way, but there's a real woman over there." Roger diverted his attention to a busty blonde girl rearranging some hairdryers. She caught his eye as he shifted to glance at her and smiled back before readdressing the hairdryers.

"Cassy, yeah she's a page-three stunner alright. Even her name says page three." James admired her voluptuous figure often, but she was early thirties compared to his twenty-two years—she wouldn't settle for anything less than a real man—and her make-up, although well done, usually by Tina on the beauty counter who she worked with before Roger prised her away to his own department, was a bit of a put off for James. Jess wore make up but it enhanced her natural beauty. It wasn't a mask.

Roger looked at James as his eyes gravitated back to Jess. "Look, I'll pull some strings. I've had a whole batch of new stock arrive. I'll get Cassy to help me check it all in and I'll get Jess over to help you start readying up a clearance counter. It's win win. I get to work my charms on Cassy and you get to chat up Jess."

This was new territory for James. His idea of chatting someone up involved copious amounts of alcohol and then talking complete garbage until the girl he's talking to makes an excuse to move away and leg it. James protested but Roger ignored him; within half an hour Jess sauntered over to electrical goods to search out Roger for her next set of instructions.

"Hi, Roger's just sent me over to you. Something about setting up a clearance counter. Oh, I'm Jess by the way."

James listened for an accent, but as with his it was difficult to pin down. "Err James. Sorry, I didn't pick up an accent. Where are you from?"

"Oh, you wouldn't know it. Overwood, it's about fifteen miles east of Oxford. What about you?"

"Snap, except I'm from a place called Little Piddley about fifteen miles west of Oxford. It's near a small town called Middle Hardwick."

She laughed at the name of the village. "I take it there are a lot of pubs there, and yes, I've seen a few road signs for Middle Hardwick. Never been there though. Any good?" The conversation continued in a banal fashion. She was easy to talk to, always prompting James with more questions. By the end of the day he had established that she was going to the University of London taking a course in fashion and design, and was holding down a part time job at Harpers to help finance her course and understand the retail side of the industry she was hoping to enter.

Roger called James over to see him ten minutes before the end of his shift. "I've been watching you, I think you're in."

"I dunno Roger, I think she's just a chatty person. You know the type that makes everybody feel like they're your best friend."

"Nonsense. Get back in there and ask her out." James's body language said it all. He planted his hands in his pockets and stared at the floor, refusing to make eye contact, his shoulders hunched over. "Look. If you let this spill over like this then you'll be in the friend zone forever, and trust me that'll be the end of it and you don't want that. She'll dump all of her boyfriend shit on you and frustrate the hell out of you with all this, if only they were more like you crap."

James reluctantly mooched back over to the display counter they had both created. Jess was standing back to admire her work. "Looks good, Jess, you're a natural at this stuff. Look, I don't know how serious you were earlier, but I'd be happy to introduce you to the delights of Middle Hardwick."

"I'd love that, when were you thinking?"

"What about Saturday?"

"Ah sorry, I'm going to have to give this weekend a miss. Mikey's coming over, I can't wait, I've got it all planned out. The rest of the girls in the dorm are all going to make themselves scarce so that I can rustle up our very own romantic candle lit meal in the communal kitchen. Any other time and I'd be right there with you."

"Ah, it's ok. Middle Hardwick doesn't have that much to offer compared to London."

"Nonsense. Meet me next Wednesday for lunch and we'll organise something. I usually work Saturdays as well but I can't do this Saturday for obvious reasons. It's valentine's day on Sunday." She flashed her eyes upwards and swayed her head from side to side as she said it.

"How come you get to work here Wednesdays, then?" James quizzed her. He genuinely did want to know.

"Ah well, clever clogs here has managed to wrangle this as part of a study for my course and I get paid for it to boot. Not bad, eh!"

James enjoyed watching her eyes dance and the flash of a smile as she spoke, revealing unnaturally straight teeth. He caught a reflection of them both in one of the display cabinets, and even though she had already told him she had a boyfriend, the image before him rein-forced his own insecurities as he took in the view of a gangly youthful-looking young man standing next to a beautiful young lady. At least he could relax in this knowledge and accept this blossoming friendship to fill some of the void his friends have left behind, apart from Jack, of course.

As Jess drifted back to both the children's department and mad Martha, Roger scooted back over to him. "Well, how did it go?"

"Err, to put it simply I bombed out. It turns out that she's already spoken for. I'm meeting her for lunch though."

"You complete dickhead, didn't you have the wherewithal to check that out first. Now youre stuck in the friend zone. Jees, you young'ns have got a lot to learn. Anyway, forget about that and take a gander at this little beauty." Roger pulled out a mobile phone from his jacket pocket and flipped the mouthpiece open.

"Looks like one of those walkie-talkie things off of Star Trek if you ask me."

Roger flipped it open again and japed 'Phasers on stun' and 'beam me up Scotty'. "Good one James, I'll remember that. If you must know it's the latest Motorola MicroTac. The store has given me one to use as a demonstrator. Trust me the yuppies are going to go mad for it. I was going to try and wrangle you one as well but Bernard tells me he's moving you over to the menswear department next week."

Chapter Four
Heartache

4th November 1993

Friday morning, and Jess's first lecture wasn't till ten, so she could afford to relax and enjoy her breakfast. She pulled on her thick towelling dressing gown to stave off the chill in the stairwell as she headed to the pigeon hole lockers to retrieve her post. She lazily scanned through them, the usual bank statements, some internal mail from the university, and the only one she was interested in. The hand writing was unmistakably Rachel's. Her best friend from Overwood. The envelope felt padded out with several sheets of paper and Jess relished the next quiet hour reading through it over her toast and marmalade.

> Dear Jess,
> I have to admit that I so wanted you to hate being there. Every time I opened your letters I wished that you would hate it and come back to Overwood, but that's just me being selfish. And now I'm plain jealous, it's so boring here and from what you've told me everything is so exciting there.

Jess chided herself for not inviting her friend to stay over for a weekend and read on.

> That's why no matter what you're about to read you must stay there. You must be true to yourself. You must be strong.

Jess's brow furrowed at the ominous prediction of the words. It had the smell of death about it, but she had spoken to her parents just a few hours ago the night before. 'Was it Willow? Were Mum and Dad too upset to tell me? Had the arthritis beaten her? She was such a regal looking dog with her shiny black coat of fur and now her tired eyes and grey muzzle struggle to maintain that dignity as she hobbles between the kitchen and lounge.' Her mind's eye had drifted off into a day dream.

I hope I'm not too late, I wanted you to hear this from me first, not somebody else's vindictive gossip. You see it's to do with Mikey. It's totally out of character, I know he loves you more than anything in the world. He was drunk, so drunk at the Halloween party at the local community centre. Then Chrissie Blackwood turned up with a bottle of Bacardi. I'm sure you don't need reminding that she's the Overwood bike. She's such a slag. She was hanging around Mikey like a fly hangs around . . . well you know what I mean. Anyway, the next day she was bragging about how her mum was away and that she had shagged Mikey on the kitchen table. I confronted Mikey about it as soon as I heard but he tells me he can't remember anything. I don't know what to say Jess, I want to believe him. I'm sorry, but I wanted you to hear it from me first. Call me please. I'm here for you.

Jess's stomach knotted as she read the letter. A wave of nausea replaced the hunger she was feeling moments earlier. Her body took control as she scuttled to the sink to vomit and she wretched uncontrollably as her body tried to physically expel the bad news that her mind couldn't, and then she was numb. She rallied herself to some kind of normality and continued her day to the routine she had become accustomed to, but it was a pretence, and try as she might she could not ignore the news she had just been given. Her mind snowballed from one scenario to another. She tried to reconcile with the devastation, but just as a computer will freeze due to a computational overload, she did too. She spent the rest of the day as if she were in a bubble. The rest of the world was out there but somehow Jess had become insulated from it and all the time her mind was stuck in an impossible computational loop.

Jess made her way back to her halls. Her emotions were drained and she didn't even notice her friend and neighbour, Millie who was sat on one of the benches in the gardened courtyard near the entrance to the dorms talking animatedly on her very own new fangled mobile phone. As Jess entered into the foyer she approached the payphone that was vacant. She took a twenty pence piece out of her purse. It would be all that she needed. She composed herself and as soon as his mother gave him the phone Mikey heard Jess's monotonic voice. "I know about you and Chrissie Blackwood. It's over." And the line went dead.

She made her way back to her room, closed the curtains, lay on her bed, and finally she wept.

After a few hours there was a knock at the door. She ignored it. And then another rap followed by the voice of her neighbour and friend, Millie. "Jess, are you in? I was just wandering what outfit you were going to wear to Astoria tonight?"

Jess did not reply.

She heard muffled voices behind the door. "Claire, have you seen Jess today?"

"No. Hasn't she gone back home to see Mikey?"

"That's just it, we were only chatting last night about having a night out tonight."

"Yeah I know, but you know how loved up those two are. He's only got to say the word and she'd be over there like a shot."

Millie scanned Claire's face whilst she digested the logic. On the face of it, it made perfect sense, but to Millie it made no sense at all. Millie shrugged her shoulders and sighed. "Oh well, it's her loss I guess, but from the way she was talking last night she wouldn't have missed this for the world." Claire sauntered away to get ready, but Millie held back a little bit longer and once Claire was out of sight she crouched down on her hands and knees to peer under Jess's door, looking for some light or any sign that Jess was actually there and had maybe fallen asleep or something. She saw and heard nothing, and gave up to go back to her room, scanning the floor as she did so for a note that Jess may have hurridly written and pushed under the door before leaving for Overwood, but nothing.

After just a few hours' sleep, Jess reacted to the alarm as usual by hitting the snooze button and wrestling herself to wakefulness on the second buzzer. She looked and felt dreadful, but the sense of duty spurred her onto make the commute to the department store. She composed herself as best she could and entered the store.

James was neither sombre nor happy, indifferent to the prospect of a busy day bordering on manic by mid-afternoon. He didn't relish the day's shift due to short staffing. He was having to cover men's casual and the suit department. By two pm he was just able to cope. It was a particularly busy Saturday and he knew things were set to get worse when the after-lunchers made their final round of last minute shopping. He knew there was a surge coming and radioed over the tannoy for assistance.

Ladies underwear was quiet and well under control, so Jess, who had been assigned there for the day and was sorting and matching bras and knickers, was jettisoned to the men's department. She approached James and asked, "Where do you want me?"

What he wanted to say and what political correctness would force him to say were completely different things. "I just need an extra pair of hands on the tills in men's casual." He was too busy to notice the drained look on her face. However, he could be forgiven for this as the blusher and make-up did well to hide it.

It wasn't long before James knew something was wrong. She was normally faultless on the tills, but today she was making repeated errors and James needed to maintain extra vigilance out of the corner of his eye. By 4.30 pm the crisis had been averted. Despite the mistakes, James was thankful for having Jess, and Jess was relieved to be so busy. For a short while her mind was focused on something other than betrayal.

By 5.30 pm it was all quiet apart from the meanderings of a few chaps looking for a shirt or a pair of jeans to wear out later that night.

"Is Mikey coming over tonight?" James asked innocently.

Just the mere utterance of Mikey's name was enough to crush her. She wanted to say something but couldn't, as she knew her emotional control would be broken. She stood silently in a state of flux, her emotions starting to break out, eyelids flickering, a quiver in her bottom lip; she wanted to run but resorted to turning and walking swiftly away instead. The nearest hiding place she could find was a small alcove in the changing area. Feeling overwhelmed, her emotions exploded and she sobbed her heart out yet again.

James caught up with her. "Jess, are you ok? Was it the way I spoke to you at the tills earlier? I was stressed out, I didn't mean to snap."

Finally, she was able to say something. "It's not you, it's Mikey. I've broken up with him." She fell against James's shoulder and James embraced her, allowing her tears and make-up to stain his still crisply pressed white shirt. After a minute or so, anger took over. She beat James's chest and slumped to the ground below. James sat patiently next to her, not saying anything, and soon Jess fell silent too. As they sat in silence, a uniformed figure appeared in the entrance to the alcove, disappeared, then reappeared again in an instant. "I thought I saw something. You're going to have to leave, I'm about to lock up the store."

"Oh right, yeah, sorry Sid. Lost track of time. Come on Jess." Jess looked at him as if half in a trance.

"She ok? You do know that you very nearly got locked in the store. Wouldn't be the first time." Sid smiled to himself at the thought of it.

"Yeah, she's fine. Just had a bit of bad news, that's all." James offered the statement as he helped Jess get up off the floor. He escorted her back to her Halls of Residence and would not leave until he knew she was in safe hands. Fortunately, Millie happened upon them and immediately recognised Jess's distress. James was transfixed with her eyes for a second or two, they glistened and portrayed a happy soul.

"I knew something was wrong. What is it hun? Is it Mikey?" She was already wrapping a protective arm around Jess as she said it and led her away to her room. James had to move quickly now, to make the last train back to Middle Hardwick.

The following Wednesday it was still evident to James that Jess's emotional scars were still raw, open and exposed. She was still terribly upset by Mikey's misgivings. However, she mustered the energy from her inner-resolve to regain her composure. James wasn't fooled. He'd witnessed her vulnerability first-hand and felt a duty to escort her home on this particular evening.

"Really James, trust me, I'm fine. I'm a big girl, I can look after myself."

"Too late, I've made my mind up. Look, its late, and God only knows what dodgy characters hang around the tube stations at this time of night. Anyway, I want to do this so its futile trying to resist, so there." He pulled a goonish face as he finished which made her laugh, and in a similar way it forced her to relent.

"But you'll miss your train."

"No, I've checked it out. There's a 10.15, it'll be empty, give me a chance to catch up with my thoughts."

"Oh God, if you insist, but I think you're mad!"

Jess let herself in through the door that led into a communal area with four private rooms leading off from it. As James stood in the doorway, he could see through a partially open door into the kitchen beyond.

"Jess, I'm parched, is there any chance I can grab a cuppa before I go?"

"I don't drink the stuff myself, but Millie drinks it by the bucket load, go through and I'll see if I can cadge a tea bag and some milk for you."

Jess rapped on her neighbour's door calling out her name. "Millie, Millie are you there?"

A muffled voice could be heard through the door which sounded like, "Hold on a mo!" The door finally opened and Millie appeared.

"Sorry if it looked like I was ignoring you, I just needed to get a sentence finished on that essay I'm writing about globalisation."

"That's ok, I get like that too. I don't mean to bother you but James insisted on escorting me home, he's thirsty and just asked me for a cup of tea."

"Oh, I see, you sure it's just a cup of tea he's after?"

"God yes, what are you trying to say?" Both voices were close to a whisper to ensure James remained out of earshot. Millie couldn't help herself and, with a smirk and raised eyebrows, she flounced past Jess and spun round to face her, the smirk still etched on her face as she swanned passed to the kitchen.

"I need a break from that horrid essay, I'll make us both one." She had an air of mischief about her as she continued to walk past the door and into the kitchen. She flashed James a warm welcoming smile and he was mesmerised once more by the pale-blue sapphire of her eyes and the warm invisible aura that surrounded her.

He stood up from his seat with an involuntary urgency, his movements exaggerated by the plastic chair that tumbled over behind him. He wiped his hand on his trouser leg before extending it out to meet Millie's. It was a subconscious action he succumbed to when nerves got the better of him, usually reserved for meeting visiting dignitaries from the uppermost echelons of management. His face reddened with the embarrassment of his clumsiness.

"Hello James, I'm Millie. We didn't get a chance to be introduced the other day did we, because of the drama queen here." She flashed her eyes at Jess who, by this time, was standing next to her in the doorway. Before Jess could say anything in her defence, Millie interrupted her. "I'm just messing with you." She wrapped her arms around Jess and hugged her.

James welcomed the small interlude, it gave him a chance to regain his composure which, for a brief moment, completely evaded him.

Jess retorted back. "Yes, well in case you haven't noticed, that kettle won't boil itself and James has a train to catch."

"That's it. That's the Jess I know and love. Self-confident and assertive."

James was impressed in the way Millie dealt with Jess's recovery. He was far too sympathetic, allowing her to wallow in her own misery.

Jess stifled a yawn. "I hope you don't mind but I'm just about dead on my feet. I need my bed."

James was the first to reply. "No, please, don't mind me. As soon as I've downed my tea I'll have to leave to catch that last train."

"Kettle's on. One Millie special coming right up. We're fine Jess, off you go."

She was direct with her manner, but rather than take offence Jess found her no-nonsense manner refreshing. Millie moved around the kitchen with aplomb. Her casual attire being furry slippers and a baggy grey tracksuit. Hardly sexy, but very cute in James's eyes.

Millie placed a mug of tea on the table in front of James. She sat herself down in the chair on the other side of the table, facing James, and immediately cut to the chase. "So, what's going on between you and Jess?" Her demeanour was accusatory as her cool blue eyes burned into his.

James was in a state of consternation, he couldn't tell whether she was joking, winding him up or deadly serious. James's reaction to the absurdity of the statement resulted in an acute exhalation of air from his lungs, snorting tea from the mug that he had just offered up to his lips. The freshly made boiling hot tea sprayed back over his face and onto the table top in front of him, narrowly missing Millie.

Millie's face contorted as if she had just witnessed a gruesome scene from a horror movie, however it immediately turned to one of concern as she took in the sight of James's tea-splattered face and shirt.

There was a moment of silence before James's nerves broke through the only way they knew how and he burst out laughing, spilling more tea in the process. His laughter was uncontrollable and so infectious that Millie burst out laughing too. Neither of them knew exactly why they were laughing. Was it at the absurdity of the question, his reaction to the question, or Millie's reaction to his reaction, or plain simple nerves? But they ended up laughing together uncontrollably either way.

She got up and searched the kitchen for a tea towel. Tears streamed from her eyes by this time, making the search for the towel more difficult and even more amusing, forcing more laughter until they were barely able to breathe. She reached out with the towel to wipe the table and, as she did, James extended his hand out to take the towel, believing she was handing it to him, and their hands touched in the confusion.

At that moment something strange happened: the laughter stopped just as quickly as it had started, and their eyes locked together and there was a connection between them—not just in the physical touch. An energy passed between them and they were momentarily paralysed. It was as if they already knew each other and they were reconnecting on a spiritual level.

Millie was the first to break the trance-like state and began to mop the spilt tea and atomised specks that surrounded it.

James finally spoke. "Seriously, have you seen Jess? She's way out of my league. I'm a sucker for anyone that's fallen on hard times, honestly, you've got to believe me. I'm simply reaching out to help. I can only hope that somebody would do the same for me."

Millie believed him, she sensed it when she first met him, but first impressions can't always be trusted.

James glanced at his watch. "I'm sorry, I've got to go or I'll miss my train."

"You shouldn't be so modest about yourself. I think Jess would struggle to find better." James was left speechless for a moment and gave her a quizzical look. He stood up and made his excuses to leave.

James hadn't realised the gravity of the statement he'd given to Jess earlier that evening when he told her that the late train journey would give him a chance to catch up with his thoughts. He stared out the window, trying to come to terms with what exactly had just happened.

An energy still coursed within him, but he couldn't fathom it out or even pretend to understand it. It was as if his life was about to head out into the unknown and it scared and excited him in equal measure and, in some way, he surmised that Millie must be at the centre of it all. Of course, he had no clue as to Millie's feelings or intentions regarding him, only that they were in sync, their souls bonded for a brief moment in time.

The train decelerated as it approached Middle Hardwick, which was enough to break his train of thought. The Hoddingsworth stop had passed him by, completely unnoticed. A shiver ran through him as he tried to shrug off the whole episode. By the time he had reached his front door he'd managed to convince himself that it was all whimsical poppycock.

Over the next few weeks James continued to convince himself that the events of that short spell of time was just one of those things and he elected to dismiss it as just that, a weird and wonderful one off. Equally so he and Jess grew closer. He insisted on taking her to his lunchtime haunts, as much as anything to ensure that she took in some proper sustenance for the rest of the day. It's true that she had lost her appetite and was looking a little gaunt.

He had searched out a few locations just a few minutes' walk from the store. His location of choice depended on the weather first and his mood thereafter. If the weather was good and his mood pleasant he would find his way to a bench on a tow path next to a canal. It could smell a bit, especially in high summer, but it was a very tranquil place, a small haven in the middle of a mad thriving city. There were a couple of small parks, and if the weather was bad he could always go to the mall and people watch. To focus on other people's lives gave him a brief escape from his own, and so it was that Jess became a part of this routine.

It was on one foul day that they ended up in the mall and a large billboard for the latest Oasis tour caught James's eye. They were due to play London in just a few weeks' time. He wanted to go but explained to Jess that his friends back home were into Blur and the experience wouldn't be the same on his own.

Jess jumped straight in. "I'll go with you"

"But you can't stand Oasis. Didn't you say they were all testosterone and no talent?"

"Please James, let me do this one thing. I owe you so badly right now, besides I love the atmosphere at concerts. Come on, it'll be fun. If we don't get in quick they'll be sold out." James was right, she wasn't a fan of Oasis, but she wasn't lying when she said that she loved the atmosphere of concerts.

James relented as if he were the one reluctant to go, when in actual fact it should have been the other way around. They picked up the tickets from the box office in the mall and it was agreed that James would stay over at the Halls of Residence, due to the late finish of the concert. As the date of the concert approached, time was beginning to heal Jess's emotional scars and she allowed herself to enjoy life again. She had made an inner vow never to let herself get hurt like that again, and with the healing process she clad herself with an emotional armour.

24th March 1994
The concert at the '100 club' was all they could have wished for, they were buzzing and, if that wasn't good enough, there was an impromptu party in full swing at the Halls as they returned. Jess went off in search of drinks while James stood in a room full of people he didn't know.

He felt a tap on his shoulder. He turned around and was once again transfixed with those eyes.

"Hello James."

His stomach clenched, overtaken with butterflies, and he wrestled to relax the spasm that took control of his solar plexus to enable him to take a breath and let him speak back.

"Cat got your tongue? Still, at least you haven't got a drink in your hand, we don't want an episode like last time, do we?"

Finally, James was able to speak. "Sorry Millie, you took me by surprise that's all, Jess has gone into the kitchen to get us one." Millie looked confused. James realised that his reply wasn't clear. "A drink, Jess has gone to get us a drink."

"Are you kidding me? You do realise that Jess is like a Queen Bee around here? Once she gets in that kitchen she'll be surrounded by adoring minions all desperate to find out what's going on in Jess world. Come on." She beckoned him to follow her to her room and pulled a half-drunk bottle of vodka from down the side of her bed and handed it to James, then found a glass tumbler from her en suite and a mug from her desk. "There's just one last important ingredient." She extracted a small bottle of coke from her gym bag. "The cap's still sealed, I promise. You won't find any sweaty back-spit in it."

"You really didn't need to tell me that, sometimes there can be too much information." As Millie poured out two large vodka and cokes something crossed James's mind. "Sorry Millie, are you here with friends? Am I hogging your attention? Oh God, please tell me you're not here playing the sympathy chip because muggins here was standing all alone in the lobby?"

"Loosely speaking, I suppose you can call them friends, acquaintances would be a more accurate appraisal. Sorry if that sounds old fashioned, but let's be honest, how many people can you truly call a friend?"

"You're right. I can count mine on one hand, but I'm lucky, where my friends are concerned we've known each other since we were knee high to a grass hopper. There isn't much that we wouldn't do for each other. Anyway, I don't get it, everything about you screams Queen Bee to me, not Jess."

"Oh God, trust me, I don't have the slightest inclination nor the energy to warrant the attention of anybody else wasting their time on whatever I do or say, besides which, Gerald should have been here this weekend and I'm more than a little pissed off right now."

"Gerald, your boyfriend?" James metaphorically kicked himself. How could he be so naïve as to believe that Millie was young, free, and single?

"He's such a shit. I've barely seen or heard from him since we visited my parents a few weeks back. I mean, I know my mother can be difficult, but this really takes the biscuit."

"Seriously, are you trying to tell me that your mother may have scared him off?"

"I don't know what I'm trying to say. Let's just say things were a little awkward and ever since he's been aloof. I'm probably over analysing it all. He reckons there's a family crisis back home and that's why he couldn't make it this weekend. I wouldn't mind so much, but he chose to tell me this an hour before I was expecting to meet him at the station. If I'd known I'd have dropped everything to be with him. He's promised faithfully that he'll see me next weekend. Anyway, that's enough about him, I don't want to talk about it anymore, let's just get shitfaced instead."

Judging by the language, James presumed she was already halfway there. The revelation that Millie was already spoken for shouldn't have come as a shock to him, but the bubble of anticipation had been burst and it did indeed leave him somewhat deflated. On the up side, however, the fact that she was unavailable relaxed him; it allowed James to be James. "Hear hear to that!" He held out his empty tumbler and allowed Millie to fill it up.

They continued to chat about their mutual concern over Jess, and in the meantime Jess was getting locked into conversations about the concert with various friends.

James hadn't noticed her absence and his conversation with Millie was now all-consuming; before he knew it an hour had lapsed in what seemed like a small moment in time, as if a hole had been torn out of the space-time continuum itself.

When Jess did return to the room she was met with a sense of dread. It was nearly a fait accompli. Millie had confided in Jess over her own troubled relationship with Gerald and that she was contending with her own vulnerabilities. Jess watched them together, there was a harmony in the way they moved and expressed themselves. She couldn't hear what they were saying, but she could see they were absorbed in each other as if nothing else existed around them.

Jess's plight wasn't one of jealousy, it was pure unadulterated selfishness and fear. She was hanging onto Millie and James to carry her through her break up with Mikey. She needed them as separate entities. If James and Millie ended up as an item, she would effectively lose her two best friends to each other and she would be left in the wilderness to fend for herself. She bided her time and waited for an opportunity to get between them, and soon enough Millie took herself away for a comfort break. Jess reacted instinctively and bounded up to James, wrapped her arms around his neck and kissed him passionately.

James responded—he was giddy with alcohol and a massive rush of endorphins. They were lost in a passionate clinch.

Millie returned to the room and a pang came over her, she felt weak as if something had struck her to the core; she felt as if life was turning a corner for her, just as James had felt on his train journey home, as if she were on the verge of a new exciting journey. Life was teasing her. It cruelly snatched her hopes and dreams away, but the strong and analytical part of her brain searched for a logical way of making sense of the whole situation, and she resolved that it was in Jess's best interest for her to move on with her life.

Millie let out a small sigh to herself. The vodka bottle was empty so she headed to the kitchen to mingle and search out another drink. Jess led James back to her room and he ended up sleeping next to her after a passionate end to the night.

Jess woke early. She had a clear head, she had barely allowed any alcohol to pass her lips, she didn't need it last night, she was heady with life itself. She sat in the chair at the end of her bed, staring at James's motionless body, listening to the deep rhythmical sound of his breathing as he remained in a deep sleep. Her mind pondered over scenario upon scenario which all revolved around the man currently sleeping in her bed. He wasn't Mikey, she doubted that he could ever make her feel how Mikey did, but he could never hurt her like that either. She didn't want to have to go through that torture again, her life expectations, everything torn to shreds in the blink of an eye.

This wouldn't be so bad, he's funny and caring and he is lovely. 'I just wished that I love you,' she said quietly to herself. The timbre of her voice reflected the inner turmoil of her emotions. He's somebody you could easily spend the rest of your life with. She convinced herself that she could grow to love him beyond the friendship they currently held together.

James awoke blissfully unaware of the fact that for the last hour or so Jess had been wrestling with her emotions. Apart from the splitting headache that he became painfully aware of, as he opened his eyes he was a fatalist. He had allowed himself to drift along with the ebb and flow of life in his short-lived time as an adult, allowing it to carry him wherever that might be.

This was no different, Jess isn't Millie and he truly wished that it was Millie sitting at the end of the bed, but her heart belonged to another. Fate had dealt its cards and this is how things ended up. It had to be right, fate had dictated that it should be this way. He had no clue that Jess had meddled with it. Had she cheated fate or is this how it all should have played out? Only time will tell. For now, their fate was sealed and James accepted himself as the rebound guy.

Chapter Five
Dumb Luck and Infidelity

Saturday 17th December 1994

"So I guess you'll be taking Jess to the Christmas party tonight. Fell on your feet with that one. You can thank me later."

"Get stuffed, Roger. As I recall, according to you I was doomed to the friend zone forever."

"I still haven't figured out how you managed to wriggle off that hook, but well done mate, I take my hat off to you."

"What about you? You're taking Pam, aren't you?"

"Errrrrr, yes. What's it to you anyway?"

"Well, what about Cassy, I assume you're, you know. Still playing away from home."

"Ah yes, alas I think that little dalliance is on the wane. She's met some semi-pro footballer. She'll be taking him to the Christmas party, but I'm still hopeful for one last blow out." With that Roger looked wistfully toward the far end of the store covered with mirrored glazing hiding the store manager's office behind. The whole shop floor could be viewed from behind that two-way mirror.

James always found it easy to converse with Roger. It was almost always banter, but a breath of fresh air after the formal chit-chat he makes with the other managers. Whilst James chatted to Roger with ease about his extra-marital affair, in private, it rubbed against every grain in his body. Why risk a lifetime of contentment for a few thrill-filled moments?

James sidled over to the children's department. Mad Martha was issuing some instructions to Jess so he held back until she disappeared out of sight. "Jess, you did say that you were going to come to the Christmas party with me, didn't you?"

"Oh God, not this again. I really don't know." She messed with some hangers agitatedly. "You know how I feel about these things—cooped up with a bunch of people that I wouldn't normally pass the time of day with."

"Yeah but it's different for me Jess. I'm on the managers' programme. I can't just not go. Bernard would be fuming." James faced her with pleading eyes.

"Look, you know I'll go for you, there's no need for the puppy dog eyes, but at the soonest opportunity we're out of there." James was compliant. "Of course, Jess, anything you say. Err Jess?"

"What is it now?"

James jiffled around pulling at some of the hangers. "Where do see us going?"

Jess stopped what she was doing and took a step back. The truth was she hadn't considered a long-term future with James. Happy to live in the moment. Suddenly her world stood still. "Can't we just enjoy the moment? Christ James, I'm still at uni and you're earning a pittance as Trainee Manager. How in God's name would we be able to survive on that? You've got to be realistic about this."

"So, what you're saying is that if we had the means to save a deposit and buy a house together, you'd be up for it?" James had unwittingly backed her into a corner.

"Well, if you put it that way. Yes, that's exactly what I'm saying."

No matter how futile it sounded, James took the news positively and remained resolute; he'd even began to accumulate a little nest egg from his meagre earnings whilst living at home. He wasn't far off from promotion to assistant manager, but the pay increase wasn't significant. He took it as a positive nonetheless and discreetly shuffled away as Mad Martha registered on his radar.

A crackle echoed through the store as the tannoy sprang to life and Roger's voice bounced around it. "OK everyone, the shift's over dim the lights. It's party time! Bubblies on ice in the cafeteria. Be there or be square." It had become store tradition that a few bottles of bubbly would be downed in the store as a kind of party prequel to the main Christmas party later that evening at a nearby hotel. Even Bernard, the store manager would avail himself to a couple of glasses. In the past he enjoyed this moment, but lately he was plagued with doubt in the fear of company policy and contravention of insurance terms, fire regulations, and God knows what else if the inevitable should ever happen. Still, next year this would be somebody else's problem.

James stood alone for a moment or two, nursing a champagne flute half-filled with cava that wasn't any longer able to give up any bubbles. He was in people-watching mode. Jess was making small talk with Mad Martha, and her head bobbed back and forth with as much exaggeration as her hand movements. Roger had commandeered a bottle of bubbly to himself, gripping it by its neck and somehow it danced with the movement of his arm without spilling a drop. He was of course fawning over Cassy and refilling her glass at every opportunity.

Cassy allowed Roger to top up her glass. Her Essex accent was probably the least endearing thing about her. "Like, I really like 'im Rog, I think he's the one, like, and that's why we can't do this anymore, Rog."

"Ok, I get it. You really like him. So from tomorrow everything goes back to normal. No funny stuff, agreed?"

"Fanks Rog, for understanding like."

"But we've still got tonight, haven't we? What about it, lets go out with a bang." Roger pulled some keys from his pocket and shook them in front of her.

"Nah Rog, I ain't doin it in the store cupboard again, remember that bottle of tippex? Ruined me skirt that did."

A small smile creased from his lips as he remembered the moment. He grabbed her hand and looked her in the eye intently. "Trust me," he said and lead her away.

Monday 19th December 8AM
Bernard approached his desk and sat down in preparation for planning his week ahead. Bernard's 65th birthday was in eight weeks' time.

'Just two more months,' he thought to himself, 'and freedom.'

Soon he would be counting down the weeks and days. Roger was destined to take over from Bernard. Granted, there would be a formal interview process, but there was an unwritten understanding that this would be the case. All Roger had to do was keep his nose clean and the job was his.

As Bernard dragged his chair in farther toward the desk, he felt something soft roll under his left foot. He reached down and pulled out a pair of lacy black knickers. He sat and pondered for a while and concluded that there could only be one reason for this, and by deduction it must have happened on Saturday evening during the Christmas Party prequel.

He looked over his left shoulder and eyed the CCTV camera in the far corner. 'I wonder,' he mused to himself. For the first time in a long while Bernard found some welcome energy to distract him from his normal routine.

He suspected an act of gross misconduct had been committed and revelled in the challenge of unravelling the mystery that surrounded it. He pushed the knickers into his trouser pocket and headed straight to the security office. "Sid, I need to see the CCTV footage for the store on Saturday from six pm onwards."

Access to the manager's office was via the corridor for the toilets, and once the alcohol had taken its toll it ensured the toilets were regularly visited by all staff and was quite a hive of activity. The lights had been dimmed and turned off in most of the store, so it was only possible to make out silhouettes of people.

"What have you got for the camera in my office, Sid?"

He scrolled through and initially the shadows of two people could be seen on the floor, but not the individuals themselves, they were out of shot. They watched the shadows move in the direction of the desk. Suddenly, a ladys stilettoed foot and stockinged ankle appeared on camera. It dangled and danced for seventy-eight seconds, according to the CCTV equipment, then disappeared. Suddenly a man's backside made an appearance and, after a second or two, disappeared again.

"What's that, Sid?"

Sid looked slightly confused. "It's a bloke's bum, Bernard."

"Yes, I know, but what's that on his backside?"

Sure enough, there was some kind of smudge on the bottom in question. Sid zoomed in and, although the image was quite grainy, they could make out that it was the image of a single cherry. Sid copied off the image and Bernard disappeared back to his office. Bernard could have dropped it, but the shear audacity of two of his own members of staff performing the act at his desk was too much for him; he would have to get to the bottom of this!

At seventeen, Roger and a few of his friends were kicking about during their summer break from sixth form. On a whim, they went into the travel agents and enquired about any last-minute flights to any sunny resort. For the princely sum of £35 each, four return flights were booked for the Island of Majorca, due to leave the following day. The next day, ruck-sacks on their backs, they went in search of an apartment and found one in Magaluf, which they secured for the week. Every night they lived a life of debauchery and every day they basked in the sun whilst recovering from their hangovers.

By the third night, Roger hit the jackpot—he finally hooked up with a Dutch girl who he could actually converse with, as her English was excellent. They finished the night in Roger's bed with glorious drunken sex. Particularly glorious for Roger, as this was his first time—he had lost his cherry. The Dutch girl, whose name he could not remember, let herself out in the morning, never to be seen again. The next drunken evening Roger felt the need to symbolise the moment and had a single cherry tattooed on his buttock.

Sid was conducting his ritual of walking the whole store, as much to stave off his boredom more than any other reason. On this occasion, he had a wry smile on his face giving particular scrutiny to the staff rather than the customers. As Sid wondered through Roger's department, Roger couldn't help noticing the smirk on Sid's face; it was the same kind of look Roger would have if he had a particularly good night between the sheets the night before.

"Get some last night, Sid?"

"No, but somebody did the other night." Sid was sworn to secrecy, but he couldn't help himself.

"What do you mean?" Roger asked innocently.

"Oh, I can't say, it's a security issue," Sid replied.

"Come on, you've started now, you can't leave me hanging."

Roger began to work on him and eventually teased out everything he needed to know. It was time to cover his tracks.

He found Cassey and explained that all she needed to do was to say that she went to the toilets as she felt ill during the time of the incident, which should help with the timings and the CCTV footage available. His next task was a little more difficult.

"James, I need a favour. Are you up for it?"

"That depends on what you want."

"Listen, you know that I'm up for store manager in a couple of months? Well, if you help me out with this I'll guarantee your promotion to head my department."

James's interest was piqued. Jess was approaching her finals and James had been saving hard for a house deposit. The extra pay and responsibility was just the tonic needed to prove how serious he was with Jess. All James needed to do now was let Roger draw an exact copy of his cherry onto James's backside. In order to do this Roger had to get a photograph of his cherry. Roger stepped into the passport booth whilst James stood guard outside. Roger knelt on the stool and made the necessary adjustments to ensure his arse was smack bang in the middle of the cross hairs on the screen. He reached behind himself and pushed his money into the slot—which was a feat in itself—before pressing the button.

Five minutes later a strip of four identical photographs of Roger's backside slipped out of the machine. They made their way to the stationery room, where upon Roger, who was one of the very few key holders, locked the door behind them, leaving the key in the door so that nobody else could enter. He raided the felt tip boxes and proceeded to draw an exact copy of the cherry onto James's buttock.

All he had to do now was make sure that when they were called into the managers office 'for a chat' that James went in before him. Roger convinced James that if all went to plan, as a senior manager he would plead James's case on the basis of his young age and stupidity. James was to profess that Jess had put him up to it but to plead with Bernard not to press her for any information because she was so embarrassed and blamed it on the alcohol. There was no need for any more shenanigans.

James got the call first. "You wanted to see me, Bernard?"

"Yes, come in James. Did you enjoy the party?"

"Yes, I had a great time, but I must confess that the champagne went straight to my head earlier on in the store."

"Ahh yes, is there anything you want to tell me on that score James?"

"Errr, to be honest I can't remember, as I ended up drinking so much."

"Now listen James, I'm going to ask you a question which I've already asked the other male members of staff that I've seen. I don't want to offend you, but I'm going to have to ask you to drop your trousers to expose the tops of your buttocks."

James acted suitably offended and put up a sufficient amount of resistance to be convincing. After some coercing, James relented and revealed the recently dried felt tip cherry. As soon as the cherry was revealed, Bernard knew he had his man, but what to do now?

"Right James, I've seen all I need to see, whether you're aware of it or not you've committed an act of misconduct. I'm going to have to consult with other senior team members before I make my decision on how to move forward with this."

"But sir, what is it I'm supposed to have done?"

"Never you mind. I have the evidence should it become necessary. Now off you go back to the shop floor. I'll call for you once I've made my decision."

Bernard sat at his desk deep in thought. The paperwork in front of him was a delivery roster, but he paid no attention to it. His mind was focused on the misdeeds that were carried out at his desk and what to do with the culprit. A rap at the door broke his concentration and it opened before he could say anything. Roger's head popped round from behind it.

"You wanted to see me, Bernard?"

"Yes, come in Roger." Roger sat in the chair facing Bernard and waited patiently for him to say something.

Bernard was renowned for his pensive silences. The jury was out as to whether it was just in his nature or whether it was some kind of management ploy to extract information that wouldn't usually be voluntarily given.

Roger believed in the latter and had determined to freeze him out no matter how uncomfortable it made him feel, but on this occasion his impatience got the better of him. "Well, what did you want to see me about, Bernard? Sales are good, the best quarter we've had in the history of the store, if I'm not mistaken."

Bernard had never had to question Roger about his sales performance. He was a natural. Roger had been his deputy for some years and Bernard knew it was in safe hands whenever he had to relinquish control for holiday cover or come what may. "Come on, Roger, I know full well how good sales have been, especially from your department, I haven't called you in to go through that stuff."

"Well, what have you called me for then?"

"It's our young trainee, James Simpson." Bernard fell silent again. The shear audacity of the event stole his words.

"What about him? I've met him, he's a good lad by all accounts and doing a good job from what I hear."

"Yes, well, he's committed a lewd act on my desk."

Roger laughed. "What?"

"I'm serious, Roger. We have evidence of him conducting a sexual act with a female on my desk. I mean the nerve of it all. I ask you!"

"Come on Bernard, you were young once, weren't you? Once those hormones start dancing with alcohol they take over and you become a passenger. I mean, seriously, if this happened anywhere else in the store would you be taking it all this seriously?"

"I'm not sure what to think anymore. That's why I've called you here, I need some impartial advice."

"Well, let's look at the facts, Bernard. There's strict company policy about the consumption of alcohol on the premises and that's one big black mark against us, not forgetting the improper use of the facilities after closing. God knows where we would have stood with the insurance companies if there had been an incident of some kind. Use your head, Bernard, you're not thinking straight. Take any kind of formal action against him and, with the right representation, he'll tear us apart."

"I know you're right but . . ."

"Look Bernard, let me stop you there. You can still make him suffer without having to make a formal kafuffle about all this. Look, I know for a fact that he hates the children's department. He nearly jacked his job in a couple of years ago. If you remember, we had to reassign him over to me in electrical then back to men's casual. Put him back in the children's department, surely that'll be punishment enough, won't it? Do you really want to jeopardise your retirement with this? In a couple of months' time, you won't give a flying toss about this place."

Bernard sat silently once more, his eyes actually starting to glaze over as if he were in a hypnotic state.

Roger couldn't take the silence any longer. He took his opportunity to drive his argument home. "Listen Bernard, what hormonally charged young man do you know could resist a bit of hanky-panky with an attractive girl in a tight dress and stockings?"

"Stockings . . ." Bernard suddenly came back to life.

"What of it?"

"Stockings, you said stockings."

"Yes, I know, what of it?"

"I never mentioned anything about stockings." Roger pinched himself; he'd allowed his guard to drop and yet again. Bernard's confounded pensive silence had contrived to extract information from his esteemed colleague across the table that would not otherwise have been forthcoming.

Roger rallied himself and casually played the comment down. "Oh, I don't know, I just assumed that a sexy dress demands something a bit more exciting than dreary old tights. Just my dirty old-man mind working overtime. She was probably wearing hold ups. I don't think young ladies wear stockings and suspenders anymore, do they?"

"Look, we're digressing here, Roger. How the hell did the conversation move on to what kind of underwear young ladies are wearing these days?"

"Oh, God knows. All I know is that if it were up to me I'd be giving him an unofficial proverbial slap on the wrist."

"Yes, I know, you're right. I just needed to hear it from somebody else. I think we're done here for now. Send the boy back in will you."

"Of course. Will you be needing me to sit in to give it more of a formal feel, intimidate him a little?"

"No, no we're not the Gestapo. All I'm going to do is reassign him to the children's department as you've already suggested. There's no need for any official stuff now."

James was minding his own business, sorting out jeans into various styles and sizes, when Roger crept up on him from behind and gave him a harsh slap on the back, launching him into a pile of skinny jeans. "You're safe and dry mate. I've just had a chat with Bernard to determine your fate. I don't think I've ever seen him this pissed off about anything, but don't worry bud, good old Uncle Roger's sorted it all out for you."

"And why do I still feel like I'm going to regret this. Jesus Roger, you never cease to amaze me. You're the one who can't keep his cock in his trousers and I'm the one having to take the fall for it, I still can't believe you've managed to spin this one."

"Look, I've managed to convince him to reassign you to the children's department."

James put his head in his hands in exasperation. "No no no, how could you? For fuck sake Roger, of all the places. As if the kids weren't bad enough, I'm going to have to work with mad Martha again. I can't do it, I'm going to tell him the truth, you're on your own mate. Sorry, but that's just the way it is."

"Don't be stupid, you're in this up to your neck now whether you like it or not. That inks indelible. You're past the point of no return, all you'll succeed in doing is convince him that you're trying to cover your tracks. God only knows what other shitty duty he'll drop on you just for refusing to toe the line. Think about it, in just a few more weeks you'll be heading up your own department and a nice little pay rise to boot. Now off you go. Bernard wants to see you now to dish out your penance. Don't fuck it up! Just get in there, act suitably ashamed, and be repentant. At the end of the day it's win win. I get my promotion to manage the store and you get to manage your own department."

Roger was an expert at convincing people to do what he wanted; he was an excellent manipulator.

James knocked on Bernard's door and waited patiently to be called in.

"James, you have committed a grossly indecent act and before you try to say anything I must inform you that we have all the evidence we need to prove it, so please don't make this any worse for yourself than it already is." As he was speaking to James he moved his head in a deliberate movement to face the camera in the top corner of the room and then flashed a knowing glance at James. "Now, I've decided not to take any formal action, but clearly you must make amends for your error in judgement, so I'm reassigning you to the children's department."

"But Sir, surely . . . ?"

"No James, my decision's final."

James truly did hate the children's department, or more to the point, Mad Martha. Roger kept drumming it into him that all he had to do now was hold station for a few more weeks and he would be out of there. Eight weeks later Roger accepted his promotion and assumed his position as Store Manager and, much to the surprise of the rest of the staff, James was duly appointed Manager of Electrical Goods.

Chapter Six
Redundancy

Monday 27th October 2014

It was seven in the morning and, on the platform in Middle Hardwick with the extra light following the clocks going back, came a well-received warmth in the air, not enough to unbutton a coat but welcome all the same. James assumed his position twenty yards to the right of the platform entry adjacent to some solid fencing which provided good protection from the north–by–north—easterly breeze. The usual faces could be seen scattered around the platform, all in their favourite little hotspots. Anybody who was new to the platform would think they had just ended up where they were randomly, but over time, and mankind's uncanny ability to create order, everybody could be identified everyday with pinpoint accuracy.

James' position wasn't the best, but he could normally guarantee a good seat on the last carriage heading to the capital. He mused to himself that if he were to divide the platform into a battleship grid, it would be easy to sink everybody; he even attached points to each location: the three seasoned commuters that held polite conversation and small talk everyday but knew nothing about each other (he could only imagine their horror if any one of them tried to push the friendship into the weekend); the two professional ladies that religiously clutch a Costa 'to go', assumed to be lattes as that's what is trending right now (of course, in the summer the choice of drink will switch to a smoothie of some kind); the students that have chosen to stay at home and commute rather than blow their loan on accommodation and getting wasted four nights a week (never quite dressed appropriately); and the girls especially happy to expose their midriff at little over zero degrees.

Once on the train, forty-five minutes passed, then another stop and James was in the capital; two tube stops and a five-minute walk and it was work as usual. The journey had weaved itself into the fabric of James's existence year in, year out. He witnessed the exponential demand for rail travel for nigh on twenty years, and for the past five years had resorted to taking a man bag with him. It never contained anything of importance, a book or magazine at most. He found a perfectly good coffee shop that had a fantastic variety of sandwiches which he would escape to at lunch time. So, no need to carry his lunch with him. Rarely did the book or magazine exit the bag, his iPhone was enough to consume his time. The bag was merely a ruse to ensure that the seat next to his couldn't be occupied by others. Of course, this didn't work every time, sometimes he would be lucky to find a spare seat at all, and on other occasions his bluff would be called; it's all part of the commuting game James had become an expert in.

There were few places that spiked his interest on the commute, but one place always managed to draw a glance: Hoddingsworth stop. A small garage next door to the station housed six or seven classic and exotic cars, and James allowed his mind's eye to wander for a while, daydreaming of taking the E-type or the big Healey for a jaunt through country lanes to the coast—a picnic on the cliff tops looking out onto a calm sunlit sea whilst watching the yachts, making good use of the sea breezes, or turning up at a top-end hotel and throwing the keys for the Maserati

Quattroporte to the valet while being welcomed by the doorman as if he were their favourite customer.

James's occupation as the store manager for a large department store was probably the safest job in the city five years ago, but not anymore. The fast-paced world of the internet and online shopping had eroded the cost effectiveness of maintaining high street stores. Rumours were rife throughout the store with regards to the future. There hadn't been any investment in upgrades and the store was beginning to look tired and dated. The time bomb finally detonated and James took the call from head office. It was very matter-of-fact. Although it was expected, James struggled to reconcile himself with what he was about to hear.

"Hello James."

"How are you, Roger?"

Roger was always destined for a position of power and authority in senior management. With it came the responsibility of controlling the destiny of several hundred employees. In this instance, it wasn't easy for Roger. None of the staff had actually done anything wrong—there was no misconduct. James and the rest of the staff had to be released for the better good of the retail chain.

"Look, it's not just your store, ten are being closed nationally, and if we don't close them with immediate effect the whole chain will collapse. There's a good redundancy package for you, I've made sure of it." Roger explained it all with an air of sympathy in his voice.

That evening on the train back home, following Roger's call, one thing consumed James's mind: Jess. Should he ring and tell her now to give her time to process the information, or wait for a suitable moment and tell her then? He would have to pick a moment when Olly, their son, would be out of earshot. Seven pm would be the ideal time as he would be locked away in his room doing homework or playing some kind of mass-murder game on his PS4, talking to his mates on his headset, completely oblivious to the real world around him. For that moment in time he would be locked into an alternate dimension. What an amazing world it is when you can be killed, your guts splattered all over the place, and twenty seconds later you're back up fighting, trying, once again, to outwit your opponents while communicating with your friends that are also playing the game in that same alternate dimension. The difference between Olly's games and the computer games James had become accustomed to is that James played against a computer-generated enemy. Olly, on the other hand, was playing against other real people in a computer-generated arena.

The moment James had dreaded was finally here. Olly was in his room and he and Jess were clearing the table and filling the dishwasher.

"I had a call from Roger at head office today."

"Oh, really? You haven't heard from him for a while. What did he want?"

"That's just it. They're streamlining the business due to competition from the internet. They're closing the store down."

"Why ever would they want to close down their flagship store? In London of all the places!"

"They want to stay tight in the north where they originated and, besides which, the figures don't stack up as well for the southern stores err. . . according to Roger."

"Surely they can place you somewhere? Call Roger tomorrow, he owes you James and don't let him forget it!"

"Oh, come on Jess, that was ages ago and he's more than made up for it over the years, you know he's always looked after me."

"I really don't care James. Sometimes you've got to grow a set of balls, man up and stand up for yourself."

She was right. Roger would be forever indebted to James, and if James decided to play the blackmail card, Roger would be helpless. It went against every moral fibre of James's being, but the rest of his life was at stake.

Tuesday 28th October
"Hi Roger, it's James."

"Oh, hello James. Look, I'm sorry I had to drop that bombshell on you yesterday."

"Yes, about that . . . Oh, how is Pammy by the way?"

"She's fine, why do you ask?"

This was the answer James was looking for, as for all he knew they could have been separated or divorced by now in which case digging up any old dirt about Roger's past dalliances would be pointless. "Oh, nothing really. Look, Jess and I were talking last night and surely there has to be somewhere in the company with a suitable position for me?"

"It's like I told you yesterday, James, we're streamlining. We're cutting jobs, not making them."

"That's a shame, give my regards to Pammy. It would be nice to catch up. I'm sure she would love to have a chat and catch up on what went on in the good old days . . . If you know what I mean? Jess has her as a friend on Facebook."

"Oh, Jesus James, has it really come to this? Stop beating around the bush, I know what you're up to. I'm guessing you're desperate or something, look, just give me a couple of days and I will see what I can do."

James was desperate, but even though he had hinted at blackmail there's no way he would see it through. Anyhow, a couple of days later Roger was true to his word and James received a call.

"Hi James, look I've done some digging and I think there'll be an opening for a management position in the lady's underwear section at our Manchester store. We've got a couple of legal loop holes to jump through but it's yours if you want it?"

"The head of hosiery in Manchester, are you kidding?"

"It's all we've got James—honest to God."

"Okay, I'll speak to Jess and give it some thought."

It transpired that an unusual amount of size twelve underwear, namely basques, stockings and suspenders were going missing from the hosiery department in question. Senior management had suspected that it was an inside job and store security had been heightened in that department for the last few months. No evidence of organised shoplifting activity could be identified. The store manager took it upon himself to discreetly position a CCTV camera in the warehouse, focused on the bays holding ladies wear. Bingo, the hosiery manageress was caught red-handed nabbing eight basques, various silky/lacy knickers, and several pairs of stockings.

When confronted she confessed, and it turned out that she's a member of a burlesque dance troupe supplying the necessary attire buckshee. The legal loopholes revolved around the unofficial camera that had been installed and as to whether its contents could be used for evidence, or if it would be considered as entrapment. The lawyers thought there was a strong enough case given the ready confession from the lady in question.

James and Jess argued about the offer, though. James was adamant that he wasn't going to take the position, they had some savings, and besides which they could easily survive on Jess's salary as she earnt way more than him. The only difference being that the nice cars and family holidays wouldn't be quite as nice or as fancy for a while. Jess, on the other hand, was adamant that James should go to ensure they kept the life they had become accustomed to. This was only partially true, as for some time, Jess had felt that they had grown distant from each other and most conversations were ending in arguments. She felt they were searching for different things in life. James was a settler and Jess had always driven to achieve better and more. Jess wanted space to think and this was the perfect opportunity. James couldn't bring himself to do it; he had never strayed far from his beloved 'Little Piddley' and wasn't about to now. He rang Roger and thanked him for the offer but refused it and went on to ensure him that this would be an end to the matter.

James and the rest of his staff were set to close down the store using the time of their notice for the closing down sale. Over this time some of the staff found alternative jobs and could move on freely. On the last day, James and two other staff members remained. It's fair to say that the bones had been picked out of the store and barely anything was left. A representative from the local estate agent met up as agreed and James explained the alarm system and locking up procedure. He handed over the keys and that was that.

Chapter Seven
Break Up

Sunday 2nd November 2014

James sat at his computer, completely blank, both he and the computer that is. He had drifted through the last twenty years without ever having to write a CV. He dug out some old books that Jess had bought upon completing her course. 'How to write a CV' and 'Guide to the Perfect CV'. Although a little dated, it was a start, but at least it gave him a framework to follow.

He searched online for a while and then began to type. His qualifications were mediocre at best, but he had lots of in-house training and certificates that he could throw into the pot, making them sound more like national training awards. He revered himself for being the youngest Trainee Manager in the history of the group to gain a position of Department Manager. Although we all now know how tenuous the circumstances were surrounding that promotion. He concocted fictitious hobbies, such as Golf (there was a pitch and put course at the local park that he and Olly frequented), am-drama—complete lie, and classic car enthusiast (well, he did look at them from afar at Hoddingsworth station and dreamt a little). Several hours later it was complete, a mix of facts, half-truths, and lies.

The perfect CV.

He shortlisted all the department stores similar to his own and posted off his CV to their HR departments. All he had to do now was sit and wait for them to write back begging him to work for them. Several days later, the responses began to filter in.

Dear James, thank you for your recent CV. However, regrettably at this moment in time we are not looking to recruit for individuals with your skillset. We will keep your CV on file and be in touch should our circumstances change and a vacancy become available. In the meantime, we wish you every success with your future career.'

All replies, give or take a few grammatical tweaks, were essentially the same. The smug feeling James had harboured had been wiped clean away.

Jess had begun to enquire as to how his job search was going, and James implied that what he was being offered wasn't suitable. Jess would eye him with a suspicion of doubt but that's as far as it went.

"Have you been to the job centre yet?"

A sense of dread coursed through his veins and hairs actually stood up on the back of his neck. "I'm waiting for a couple more replies and if there's no success, I'll go." The outcome was inevitable and James readied himself. He didn't know what he feared, but he feared it all the same.

Tuesday 9th December 2014
James loitered about outside the job centre, sucked in a big gasp of air, and walked inside.

To him it was alien territory; it was a step into the unknown. He wasn't sure what to wear, so he treated it like a party invite to dress smart casual. Does smart casual include jeans? Probably yes, if smartened up with a nice shirt, but he was uncertain all the same. James's attire was shoes, jeans and a smart shirt.

Once he got inside it was blatantly obvious there was no dress code. It really did range from trainers, shell suit and hoodie, to shoes, slacks, shirt and jacket. Inside he was confronted with a ticket machine just like the ones you find at the deli counter while you queue and wait your turn.

After twenty minutes or so James's number came up and he approached a booth with a thick glass screen in front of it. A voice came at him in his right ear from a speaker whilst he watched the ladys mouth move behind the screen. "Have you completed your application form?"

James had it rolled up in his hand like a telescope you'd make when you were a kid. He unrolled it and passed it through the small slot at the bottom of the screen. She straightened it out and carefully scrutinised it like a teacher does when they're looking for mistakes in your class work. James had been through it a couple of times himself and even had Jess give it a once over for good measure.

Finally, she spoke, her eyes remained fixed on the form in front of her. "Name?"

"Sorry?"

"Your name, what is it?"

"Well, isn't it obvious? It's the first thing on the application form that I've just handed to you. Is it really necessary to tell you as well?"

"Just because you've handed me a form with a name on doesn't prove that you are the person represented on the form." James had decided that she was being officious for the sake of it.

"And me telling you my name doesn't prove it's me either, just like your name tag doesn't prove that your name is Brenda Fergusson, does it, Brenda?" The lady behind the screen remained deadpan. She had become an expert at filtering abusive comments and remarks, and as such it gave her moral authority, although in this instance James had got to her, he'd made it personal, he'd dared to use her name. The audacity of it struck a nerve.

"If you've quite finished, I still need you to tell me your name, and if you must know it's our policy. I don't make the rules, I just abide by them."

"Well, if it's that important, I can verify that I am in fact James Simpson, and before you ask, here's my driving licence as proof. Look, it even has my picture on it."

"There's no need to be facetious, sir, and I have to inform you that I'll need your FULL name before I can allow you to progress to the next stage in the process."

James was losing it. 'Next fucking stage? Jees, just how many stages can there be?' His anger spilled out. "I don't understand the point of this stage. Clearly, I'm just wasting my time. I mean, I've just had to complete a form that you might as well have just completed for me."

"No, we don't do that, sir. Unless there are exceptional circumstances."

"Oh, really, and what might they be?"

"Well, judging by the fact that you're not blind and you haven't had your writing hand amputated, and to the best of our knowledge you appear to be literate and are not incapacitated with a mental illness, then I'm afraid you won't fall under the remit of exceptional circumstances. Now, if you don't mind we now only have two minutes left to complete this stage of the process, otherwise you will have to rejoin the queue and start again."

"Oh, I see, we're allotted a time limit too, are we? What is this some kind of weird production line for employment rejects?"

James watched on as her finger hovered over a small button on one side of the desk. "I'm sorry, sir, but not only do I not like your tone, but I must also inform that your allotted time has now expired and I'm going to have to ask you to rejoin the queue."

James's posture changed and he was ready to blow. Brenda watched on as she toyed with her victim on the other side of the screen. She glanced across at the security guard nearby at the door; he was already alert, his attention spiked by James's raised voice.

James was waiting for some kind of condescending comment about not making it any more difficult for himself by making her call security. He didn't say anything, he wasn't about to let her win, and backed off, but she couldn't stop herself. "Perhaps when you return you should be prepared to be more helpful to both us and yourself, sir."

There's no doubt that her intention was to be condescending, but she was beyond recognising it within herself. The years had hardened her, numbed her to the turmoil and angst of society's victims on the other side of the screen. Everybody that approached her screen were there to abuse the system. She'd long since given up trying to segregate the innocent hard worker who had fallen on hard times from the arrogant little shits prepared to squeeze every little penny of their entitlement and give every reason why they're unable to accept any job that's offered to them.

She seemed to have honed a skill for portraying a face of complete disdain. Within the space of a few minutes James had lost whatever sense of pride he thought he had and felt unworthy of being classed as an upright God-fearing British citizen. He was now a bottom feeder, the lowest of the low. Whatever dignity he had before going into that hellhole had now been lost. James left the job centre feeling empty, he held leaflets explaining retraining and adult courses which he clutched in his hand, but had no intention of ever doing anything with them.

He signed up with a couple of recruitment agencies, neither of which had anything suitable, but at least he was on their books should anything arise. Over the following weeks, James settled into a routine and had, somehow, succumbed to morning TV at its worst. He reached a point where he waited with baited breath for the Jeremy Kyle show to start and, before he knew it, he would be absorbed into the life of Wayne and Sharron and as to whether Wayne was or was not the biological father of their latest offspring. Wondering which heathen would walk off stage first, ranting expletives and stabbing their finger at whoever would listen. James had found a pair of joggers that he usually wore for jogging but had now become a far more comfortable attire for sitting to watch morning TV, along with his sweatshirt.

James was in a downward spiral and Jess was at breaking point with him. He didn't notice or recognise the annoyance caused by half-drunk cups of coffee left lying around and crumbs left on the sofa. Jess was on the simmer and about to boil over. James and Jess had unwittingly forged separate lives for themselves over the last eight years or so. They actually did very little together, apart from eat, sleep and drink, and probably not a lot of that, if the truth be known.

Even sex had become a ritual, one of them would realise that they hadn't touched each other in over a month and this would serve as the catalyst for any amorous activity, hardly romantic. Small things were niggling Jess: dirty underwear left on the floor and not in the wash basket, the fact that she was expected to do the washing, things left lying around and not put away. James had been going through life as if there was a housework fairy clearing up behind him. One morning, as Jeremy Kyle was about to start, James reached into the fridge and took out a beer. Alarm bells rang.

'What in God's name am I doing?' he questioned himself.

He put the beer back and took himself off to the recruitment agency. "I will do anything, please just get me a job, I need to work."

"We have got a few openings for zero hours contract work."

"Please, just see what you can do."

The next day James received a call. "We've got an opening for a night watchman, are you interested?"

"Yes please, I'll take anything."

"We've tweaked your CV a little. You now have a black belt in Karate and have studied several of the Martial Arts. I suggest you peruse the internet to enlighten yourself, in case anyone asks any questions. They want to see you first for an interview."

Friday 30th January 2015

James arrived at the warehouse to meet Geoff, the head of security. A large chap, 6'3" with a beer belly that hung over and obscured the waist band of his trousers.

"I was expecting someone with a bit more meat on their bones, suppose you can handle yourself though, with all this Martial Arts malarkey."

James eyed Geoff and thought it safe to assume that, with Geoff's build and his previous comment, that he knew nothing about Karate or Kung Fu, so James allowed himself to go into jackanory mode, telling Geoff that he was the youngest black belt in his club and had to give it up eventually when he broke his opponent's leg and three ribs with one kick. Geoff seemed suitably impressed and led James to the security office.

"This is where you will spend most of your time. There's CCTV cameras scattered around the place and you can view all eight cameras on these two monitors. You'll be expected to walk the site every hour, too."

"Did the last guy retire?" James enquires.

"Nah, he got jumped by gypsies over Christmas. They got in through the chain link fence on the west side. They roughed him up a bit, but the pit bull terrier they had with them tore a lump of flesh right off his leg, left him with septicaemia. Poor bastard nearly died.

"We kept his place open for him, but the injuries he sustained have restricted his mobility. To be honest he's on more money claiming disability benefits than he'd be getting working here. The other lads have been covering off his shifts but they're starting to get pissy about it."

James grew a new respect for the job. 'Note to self, anyone breaks in, run, hide and call the police'. He made a mantra out of it, 'Run, hide, call the police, run, hide, call the police'.

James told Jess he had finally got a job as a night watchman.

"For fucks sake James, are you crazy? Taking on a shitty minimum wage job that any halfwit can do? This is pointless, I need some space. I can't believe what I'm hearing. I'm going to the gym." After a few minutes, Jess had prepped her gym bag and left slamming the front door behind her.

James sat on a stool in the kitchen, dumbstruck. It seemed that whatever he did was wrong in Jess's eyes. Olly popped his head round the door. "In the dog house again, Dad?"

"Guess so. You know how feisty your mum can get. I'm sure she'll be fine once she's thrashed it all out on the treadmill. Come on, what are you wanting for tea, which by the way is what I was about to ask your mother before she stormed off."

"McDonalds?"

James didn't take any time to consider the request. "Get your skates on quick, before I change my mind." Olly had witnessed the tensions rising between his mother and father long before James's recent misfortune in losing his job, but things had escalated to a new level since that moment. Generally, where Olly was concerned, the failing health of James and Jess's relationship remained a moot subject, ignoring the elephant in the room.

Besides Jess's outburst, James took on his new role as a night watchman, and at the very least it gave him a sense of purpose. In the meantime, he used a couple of hours in the afternoon to continue his job search between waking and his household duties, which he would find any excuse to avoid, and finally leaving in the evening for his shift.

Wednesday 11th March 2015
James completed two more job applications and settled down to take in his regular hit of 'Doctor Doctor', a soap about yes, you've guessed it, doctors. As all good soaps do, it drew him in, day in day out, leaving a cliff hanger at the end of every episode. In the previous episode, Dr Aktar had failed to recognise the symptoms of depression in his patient Miss Sombre.

James sat on the edge of his seat as he watched her stand in front of the bathroom mirror clutching a full bottle of pills. She unclasped the lid, lifted the bottle to her mouth and poured it in, knocking back a tumbler of water to ensure they reached their target before a gag reflex took over. In this episode, Miss Sombre's partner returned home unexpectedly to fetch some paperwork he'd forgotten. James watched anxiously as he collected up his papers with no clue that his partner lay unconscious on the floor of the bathroom just a few feet away.

Whether the panic of making himself late for his appointment had caused stress incontinence in his bladder or he just plain and simple needed to urinate, he, at the last minute, rushed back to the bathroom to find Miss Sombre in the nick of time. It was all just a story, but for those few moments in James's imagination, it was real. After a good old stomach pump in hospital she made a full recovery and James was then left with the cliff hanger that the practice was being sued for malpractice and that Dr Aktar faced suspension and the possibility of being struck off the register.

James reacted to the unjust allegations put against Dr Aktar by popping the kettle on for a cup of tea and a biscuit. As he relaxed, the new imposed irregular sleep pattern and his body's natural afternoon biorhythms colluded to drag him into a deep sleep. Olly was home by four and let himself in. Apart from the sound of the TV, there was no sign of any other presence, so to satisfy his own curiosity, he conducted a small search of the house, which didn't take long as after the kitchen the lounge was the next obvious room. He didn't see the need to wake his father, besides which he'd get some quality time on the PlayStation instead of being coerced into completing his homework.

The front door opened again and it was Jess this time. She sauntered down the hallway just as Olly had earlier. She could hear the muted tones of the TV in the lounge beyond the partially open door. As it happens, it was another show that James had become addicted to: 'Wrightey's Right'. This show's title was 'Is my Marriage a Sham?' where couples were being interviewed about why they remained in a marriage without love.

Jess sniffed at the air in the direction of the kitchen. There wasn't an aroma of cooking in the air because nothing was being cooked. She wondered what the excuse would be this time. It was an agreement they had that whilst James was seeking out a 'real' job, he would take on all the usual household chores. Initially, James applied himself to these tasks with much gusto, verve, and enthusiasm, which lasted about a week and gradually tailed off from there and things began to slip.

She pushed the door open farther into the lounge to see James slouched on the sofa, legs stretched out, and his body had slipped down so much that his back was resting on the seat cushion and his head propped up by the back rest. A small wet patch nestled on the chest of his T shirt, catching the drool from his mouth as he slept. Jess scanned the room and counted three empty or half-drunk mugs, two empty glass tumblers, and the open packet of biscuits that rested in his crotch.

She left him there for the time being and headed to Olly's room. Her knock and calls went unheard, so she opened the door to find him sat in front of the TV, a PlayStation controller in his hands and headphones covering his ears.

The light from the door was enough to catch his attention, and he glanced up to see his mother's lips moving. He recognised the consternation on his mother's face and knew better than to ignore it. He paused his game and allowed his headset to slip down around his neck.

"Tell me that he at least made you some tea!"

"Well . . . I didn't want to wake him."

"What, so that you can play this crap? What about your homework?"

"I haven't got any. I did it at school in break."

"Don't expect me to believe that, I'll be checking with your school tomorrow and if you're lying, that thing's going." She flashed her eyes at the game's console. Olly watched his mother's chest lift as she exhaled a sigh of exasperation, and with that she turned and disappeared from the room.

Olly had two choices now: he could sit and eavesdrop on the ensuing argument that was about to erupt between his mother and father, or he could choose to replace his headset and continue with his game and delude himself that if he can't hear anything everything was fine. He chose the latter option. What child wouldn't? It was a coping mechanism he had re-sorted to far too many times lately, but judging by the look on his mother's face this was different.

There was a determination in her manner, a resolve to complete and push home whatever it was that was on her mind, something she had been harbouring for a long time. She had soldiered on burying her inner conflict behind her marriage vows and duty to ensure a good, healthy, balanced family relationship for the sake of Olly, but it was becoming a sham. Olly knew in his heart of hearts that things were awry, which is why he sort sanctuary in his room so much. Whether James and Jess knew it or not, Olly wasn't being fooled for one minute.

James awoke with a start and became acutely aware of the reason for this once the nerve endings in his calf had conveyed the sensation of pain after being kicked with the pointy toe of a kitten-heeled shoe.

"What the hell was that for? Jesus Christ, Jess, that bloody well hurts!" His face contorted into a grimace as he massaged life back into his calf muscle.

Wrightey's voice projected itself from the TV set. "So, when did you realise that your marriage is actually a sham?"

"Ah diddums, was I being spiteful? Well, do you know how spiteful this is, you slobbing around while I'm out working and then expecting me to come home and clear up after you?" As she spoke she retrieved the open packet of biscuits that lay on his crotch and threw them back in his face.

A lady's voice then projected itself from the TV. "Well, for me it was when I realised that Gerry was just looking for a substitute for his mother. I mean, I ask you, I've had my children and the youngest has just left for uni, and here I am still playing mother to this lump of lard!" The words were harsh but the chap did look clinically obese.

"Come on Jess, this is just a one off. Anyway, you know how I've been struggling with things lately."

"Oh, okeydokey then, and what was your excuse three weeks ago, three months ago, three years ago? You're not going to change James, and I'm not going to put up with it anymore."

A male voice emanated from the TV this time. "It doesn't matter what I do, I'll never be good enough for you, will I? It doesn't matter what I do for you, you'll always want more."

"Jesus James, take a good look at yourself, you're pathetic. You've never really grown up. I mean you still insist on putting stupid fucking Mars bars in the sodding freezer! Aaaaagh.!"

Jess yelled out in exasperation. She heaved in a deep breath before releasing the bomb she had been harbouring for so long.

"This is pointless. I want a divorce." The words were in stereo as both the lady on the TV and Jess's words echoed each other. Jess repeated it to herself as if to reaffirm the secret that lay deep down inside, only this time she repeated coolly and calmly. "I want a divorce." For Jess it was an epiphany.

Wrightey's voice emanated from the screen once more. "Well, I think that concludes it, it's the end of the show and it would seem it's also the end of your marriage."

It was an obstacle they had been avoiding for years, but it was exactly that, an obstacle, preventing them from continuing with life and nurturing their souls. It required bravery and strength, and right now Jess had it in droves as she towered over James's slouched body on the sofa. Even Jess's work attire out-gunned James's chocolate-stained joggers and drool-stained t-shirt. He was at his lowest ebb in life, he was worthless, pathetic—he was beaten. Jess took nothing from it, she was numb and wished to remain so.

"I'll go and tell Olly," she spoke softly. "Best get it done with now."

"No! Please allow me this chance to do one thing right for once. Please let me. I've let you both down, I know that. He's my son, it's my duty." His self-esteem was at an all-time low and if he allowed it to slip any further, then just like Miss Sombre, he might well have downed a bottle of pills to end it all. He needed to clutch on to what little self-respect he had left, and that meant manning up to his own son.

James let himself into Olly's room and once again Olly's eyes shifted from the TV screen to his father as he approached him to sit beside him on the bed.

"Scooch up." James gestured for the spare controller as he made his request.

Olly shuffled his bum over and handed the other controller to James. Once more he allowed his headset to slip down and nestle around his neck. "What do you want to play?"

"You know I'm crap at war games and FIFA, so I guess it's got to be a racing game of some type." Olly set up the console for two-player mode and the TV screen split into two halves. They set off racing each other and they were equally matched, albeit that James was far more animated with his controller, leaning into corners and twisting it as if it were a real steering wheel. Olly, on the other hand, conserved his energy and remained stationary, knowing full well that the only influence on his car was from the movement of his fingers on the toggles.

"You know your mum and I haven't been getting along so well lately, don't you?"

"Duh. I think that's the understatement of the century, Dad."

James out-braked himself and ran wide, allowing Olly to cut through on the inside. "Right OK. I didn't realise it was quite so obvious."

"Yeah, well, I guess sometimes it's easier to see these things from the outside looking in. If it's any help, Mum can be pretty harsh when she wants to."

James was taken aback, a little, at the words of wisdom coming from his own son's mouth. "Ah, I know, but that's no excuse for my behaviour. I've been a lazy-arsed, self-engrossed, good-for-nothing so and so."

"True, you haven't made any of my fixtures this season. I bet you don't even know that I was voted Manager's Player this year."

"Really? Why didn't you tell me?"

"If you'd have made it to the awards ceremony, you'd have found out for yourself."

"Believe me, I only wish that I could have, but times were hard at the store, we were going through a rough patch and, well, if I knew what was coming I'd have made it to all your fixtures and the awards ceremony. The trouble is none of us have a crystal ball, kidda."

"So, what are you gonna do now?"

"Well, there's the rub. I don't know how to make this any easier on you, so I'm just going to come right out with it. Your Mum's asking for a divorce. Actually, strictly speaking, she's demanding a divorce. I honestly don't think I can do anything to change it. You know what your Mum's like, once she's made her mind up about something."

"The same thing happened between Ben's Mum and Dad and he reckons things are better now. He gets to see his Dad when he wants to and they don't fight over stupid stuff anymore. Maybe it'll be the same between you and Mum."

"I can assure you that's a dead cert, unlike me beating you in this game. Damn it kidda, how much did you beat me by?"

"Forty seconds. God Dad, you're rubbish at this."

"We'll see, once I've got my own place I'll get the opportunity to practise, and by the next time I see you I'll be whooping your butt. Anyway, I'm not finished, best of three?"

"Nah, Ben's online. He wants me to play him at FIFA."

"Right then, I think I know when I'm not wanted anymore. I think your Mum will have calmed down by now and she'll be desperate to know how this went. Am I OK to tell her everything's fine?"

"Sure Dad. . . . Dad?"

"Yes, what is it?"

"You won't be moving far away, will you?"

"What, move away from Little Piddley? Never."

Olly smiled and that was all the approval James needed. James exited the room, impressed with the resilient demeanour of his son. As he left the room he was met with the aroma of spaghetti bolognese that wafted up the stairwell from the kitchen. He hesitated before entering the kitchen but there was no need. "I'm making spag bol, there's plenty to go around. I'm guessing Olly must be starving."

"That's great, but if you'd have given me a chance I'd have—"

Jess cut him off with her own train of conversation "How did he take it?"

"What?"

"Olly? How did he take being told about us?"

"Surprisingly well . . . err relieved, I think. In fact, I think he saw it coming before we did."

"Oh, thank goodness for that, that's a relief. So, where do we go from here?"

"Well, look, I'll take the spare room for the time being and I'll start looking for a rental locally. I think there's some flats up for rent on Wellington Mews around the corner."

Jess agreed she had no intention of being swayed back from her decision in a moment of weakness by continuing to share her matrimonial bed.

James ended up finding a two-bed semi on a newish estate on the outskirts of Little Piddley at £750 a month. It was a bit pricey, but it was perfect, and more importantly it was still in his beloved village. A fortnight later, James hired a van and, with the help of his best mate Peter, he moved most of his belongings into his new pad. James had most of the stuff covered, but he had bought a sofa, a bed, and some other furniture and, seeing as he had hired a van, he opted to pick up everything and save any delivery charges.

If 'I owe yous' were handed out for favours, James's pile would look paltry in comparison to Peter's. Peter is one of life's natural altruists. He has a natural disposition to help a friend in need. James accepted his help guiltily, but he knew he didn't have a choice; Peter wouldn't allow it. The move had gone well, and by teatime James was in and settled.

"Pete, I've booked a table at 'Razzle's' for eight. You and Kate must get your glad rags on and I'll meet you there. Dinner's on me."

"I'm sorry mate. I'm afraid you're going to have to unbook it. Kate's already rustling up your favourite."

"Christ mate, the only way I'll be able to repay you will be with a kidney at this rate!"

"Yes, well, should that time arise you can be sure I'll hold you to it. You can come as you are, there aren't any airs and graces at our place."

James and Jess made some informal arrangements over Olly's well-being, and it was agreed that as they were only five minutes walk away from each other that Olly could come and go as he pleased, as long as he messaged them as to his whereabouts.

It was as if a great weight had been lifted from Jess's shoulders, her mood was upbeat and she took on a new verve for life that took years off her. James didn't change in that respect, but the past few months had been stressful and now he seemed to have crossed that hurdle and set his life back on track. Not the track that he started on, but another track to a new yet-to-be-discovered destiny.

Chapter Eight
Quiz Night

Wednesday 1st April 2015

James took himself down to The Bakers Arms for quiz night. He and his four best friends met up religiously, without fail, at eight pm every Wednesday evening. The only thing that would ever stop them would have to be a life-threatening illness, or perhaps a woman scorned. They all had an understanding that if 'her indoors' were on the rampage about something, then, if necessary, the quiz night would have to give.

James was first in and strolled up to the bar.

"The usual?" Bill asked. Bill had owned the pub for the last six years. He was personable enough and up to date with the local gossip, yet nobody knew anything about his life outside the pub.

James nodded and Bill proceeded to pour a pint of draught French larger.

The door opened and a voice half bellowed, "Get one in for us, Tibbsy."

James raised his hand above his left shoulder in a vague direction of the door, as a gesture of acknowledgement. He scanned the bar for the guest ale. "Oh, and a pint of Badger's Breath."

Bill nodded, proceeded to finish topping off James's lager, and went on to pull the pint of Badger's Breath. The voice was Peter's. James ushered his way to the far corner table, near the open fire place where they always sat. The pub could get cold in the winter, and Bill wasn't one for wasting money on heating, but you could guarantee that this particular table would be roasty toasty throughout.

Peter was staring at his phone, a little perplexed.

"You ok, Peter?" James enquired.

"Ah, its Wendy's wedding. Apparently the wedding car business she had organised has literally gone up in smoke, some kind of garage fire."

"Oh shame," James replied sarcastically. "How's the witch taking that one?"

"Not good, we've got a fortnight to organise a replacement and everyone we've tried is fully booked. I'm at a loss mate, come on Tibbs, I need some help here. What am I to do?" Peter massaged his temples, trying to conjure up a solution as he swiped through his phone. "Do you know what, Tibbsy, it's not even as if Dad will be travelling in the car with her. I don't know why she doesn't just drop it."

James looked confused. "How so, I mean, why's your old man not escorting her in the car?"

"Ahh well, he won't leave Mum's side, ever since, you know, the stroke, and she's insisting that it wouldn't be right for her to travel in the same car. So, there you have it. Dad's going to take Mum and get her settled in and meet Wendy outside the Church to walk her up the aisle."

James could gauge the kind of conversation he was about to have with his friends simply by the way his nickname was used. Tib was used more as an utterance to get his attention. This version was usually used when one of the boys would get up to buy another round of drinks, accompanied with the shake of an empty glass, and would only require a nod of acceptance. Tibbs would be used when one of them was searching for an opinion on something, another way of saying what do you think? Tibby tended to be used when a favour is asked for. It tended to be drawn out a little in an enquiring manner. Tibbsy would be used to get attention from afar, as Peter did earlier when he entered the pub, or as if you're calling for the ball in a football match, and also used when the lads were being jocular. This is the form of his nickname which was used most and the one James was at ease with.

Peter shuck himself out of his conundrum with a pang of guilt, the break-up of his best friend's marriage was still raw and he should make sure things are ok.

"Shit sorry mate. Here I am dropping my crap at your doorstep when you've got enough of your own to deal with. Are you settled into your new pad? Erm . . . heard anything from Jess lately?"

"Don't worry about me, I'm quite enjoying the freedom and, as far as Jess is concerned, we're getting along fine all things considered."

Peter watched James as he spoke. He knew the traits James's body language would offer up: wiping his hand on his trousers or equally brushing his hand through his hair repeatedly. Neither were on offer, in fact Peter hadn't seen James this composed in a long while.

"And what about the new job?"

"Oh, yes. I've managed to swap Wednesday evenings with one of the other guys that didn't want to do the Sunday shift. I couldn't miss this, it keeps my sanity intact."

Gradually the rest of the gang arrived. Dick first, still a gentle soul, very worldly and protective of its precious resources. Even at the tender age of eleven he would enlighten everybody about the harm aerosol sprays were doing to the ozone layer and the creation of greenhouse gases. He was his own man, he had no sides. He had his own opinions and views, but saw no need to convince anybody else of his way of thinking. James wished there were more people like Dick. He was a truly wonderful person.

Jack came in next, motorcycle helmet under his arm, looking like a cross between a Michelin man and somebody who has just filled their pants. This wasn't a slant at Jack, it's just that, to James, the crotch on bike leathers hung low as though something had been deposited in them. Jack seemed to live in two worlds: the real world, holding down a nine-to-five job, and then his second imaginary 'rebel without a cause' world.

"Alright if I crash round your place tonight, Tibbs?"

"Yeah sure, of course mate."

Jack lived in Middle Hardwick about ten miles away and he fancied a few beers tonight, instead of just the one.

"Good, I've already left my bike on your drive."

James didn't see this as being cheeky, they had all known each other long enough to come and go as they pleased, within reason. James was grateful to have somebody else about the place. Most of Olly's creature comforts were at Jess's, so he didn't see as much of him as he would like. Olly simply couldn't sleep over at James's on the days he was working nights.

Last but not least, Mick turned up, still self-assured, blunt, forthright and clever with it. He wasn't the type of person to get into a debate with because generally speaking he would win hands down. He understood politics and the manipulation of the world through mankind's hands. James unwittingly had a mine of enlightenment at his fingertips. All of them would lay down their knowledge and expertise for each other willingly, but none of them would expect it. This was true, God's honest friendship.

Quiz time was upon them and Sally, one of the barmaids, floated through between the tables, dropping off the game sheets and pens. She was at sixth form earning a small income to ensure that her wardrobe was equipped with up-to-the-minute trends, for driving lessons and whatever else a teenager wants and needs.

They looked forward to seeing her smiley face—she was easy going and happily tolerated the bad taste banter from these men nudging into middle age—laughing with her mates about them back at school.

There were five other quiz teams that night. There was no limit on teams or sizes. Each team would give themselves a name. James's team were called 'The Gang Bangers' and the team on the next table were 'The Gangster Grannies'. They were all Grandmothers, granted, but the eldest was a spritely forty-eight, all very lively with plenty of life in the tank, barely middle aged. On another table, there were two young couples in their mid-twenties with some vomit-wrenching name like duplicity. Next was a group of retired gentlemen calling themselves 'The Old Farts'. The last two teams were 'The Fast & Curious', a couple of chaps assumed to be gay but no one knew for sure, and finally 'Try Hard Too' a play on Die Hard Two, another group of middle-aged men. These are what the lads called 'The Out of Towners'. They had moved out of their poky Georgian terrace city houses into the grandest abodes in the area with money to spare and simply commute into London daily.

Peter was still scanning his phone for prospective wedding cars.

"Still no joy?" James quizzed.

"Nah, we've got the £200 deposit back though."

Jack cut in. "How much is a wedding car these days?"

"About £600's the going rate."

"What do you get for that then?"

"Oh, a cheap bottle of bubbly, three hours and a thirty-mile radius."

"Nice if you can get it," Jack finished.

James and the others listened on intently, whilst each team anted up the £5 fee to take part in the quiz, vying for a £15 bottle of plonk; that's at Bills prices and probably only £6 from the local supermarket. Bill assumed his position at head of house in front of the bar and began the quiz. Sally resigned herself behind the bar and continued to serve as and when required.

The quiz followed the same format, week in, week out. It covered Geography, Science, Art & Literature, Politics and Current Affairs, finishing with General Knowledge. On this particular evening, the lads were neck and neck with 'The Out of Towners' right up to the general knowledge questions. Things were becoming tense and there was a lot of under-the-breath utterances as they debated their answers and equally cursed the other team.

"Okay folks, we're down to the final ten General Knowledge questions and the scores are as follows:

"Fast & Curious eighteen points; Gangster Grannies twenty-three points; Duplicity twenty-eight points; The Old Farts thirty-three points; and it's neck and neck between 'The Gang Bangers' and 'Try Hard Too' on forty-one points each." Cheers rang around the pub for each team, getting louder and louder the higher up the list they went.

The rule of thumb was a pint to every round of questions, so by this time the lads were well-oiled.

"Okay, so on with the general knowledge questions, and the first question is . . . which planet is closest to the earth?"

It was a 50/50 shot between Venus and Mars, Gang Bangers went with Venus and Try Hard Too opted for Mars.

"Question two: when giving a grid reference on a map, which line do you refer to first, latitude or longitude?" Gang Banger went with longitude, Try Hard Too went for latitude.

"Question three: what is the main current that affects the British Isles?" Both teams went with Gulf Stream.

"Question four: a number that is divided by another number is called what?" Gangbangers went with dividend and Try Hard Too, fraction.

"Question number five: what is the synonym for the word talked?"

Mick jumped in on this one. "That would be spoke," and Try Hard Too also went with spoke.

"Question six: what sign would a composer use to create a rest in a piece of music?" Jack's turn this time, he played the guitar and could read some music. "I think that's a small rectangle." Try Hard Too hadn't got a clue and guessed at a couple of dots. At this stage, they were even-stevens and still locked on the same score.

"Only four more questions to go peeps, so let's press on. What is the hollow between two waves known as?" Dick got this one he was good at Geography and Geology and had done some surfing. "Think that's a trough," he said between a sip of beer. Try Hard Too had no clue and guessed at relief. Finally. The Gang Bangers moved ahead.

"Next question is what is the second largest object to orbit the sun in the solar system?" The Gang Bangers deliberated and were split. Dick and Peter were convinced it was Saturn, whereas Mick and Jack said Jupiter. James just didn't know and he chose the only way he could, eeny, meeny, miney, mo and ended up on Saturn. Try Hard Too were correct with Jupiter and both teams were neck and neck yet again.

"Question nine: what is the largest organ of the body?" Both teams answered correctly with skin.

"Last but not least, the final question is what is a group of dolphins called?" Mick debated that they are mammals and their offspring are called calves so wouldn't it be correct to assume that they would be called a herd. It made logical sense, except that last year, James, Jess and Olly had been to Florida and visited Ocean World where they swam with a pod of dolphins. Nobody argued and put pod as the answer. Try Hard Too had used the same logic as Mick and answered incorrectly.

The Gang Bangers had won and erupted with a cheer, slapping James on the back. "Well done Tibbsy, saved the day again," Mick shouted.

After a couple of minutes, The Gang Bangers began to settle down and Mick headed over to the bar to collect their prize. As he was passing The Try Hard Too team, one of them piped up. "It's a shame they can only win by cheating."

Mick stopped in his tracks, he didn't normally swear, his sophistication of language was better than that, but he was more than tipsy and an outright accusation of cheating was too much. "What the fucking hell are you talking about?"

"Your mate over there," singling out Peter, "has been on his phone all evening looking up the answers."

Silence, once again—one of those moments where a noisy environment stops dead. The whole pub zoomed in on the altercation. Peter was incensed to the point where he was speechless. Jack strode over to stand next to Mick to add some intimidation, still half clad in his motorbike leathers. Dick and James sat silently but completely alert. Finally, Peter interjected, "No, no, you've got it wrong. I've been trying to . . ."

"Save the excuses mate," the Try Hard Too member shouted over him.

Bill knew he had to act quickly and with authority. "There will be no trouble in my gaff, if you've got some gripe take it outside and sort it out there. If this goes any further in here you're all barred." He gave Mick their prize, leaned over the bar, grabbed another bottle and handed it to the Try Hard Too team. "Take this if it means that much to you." It meant nothing to the Try Hard Too team, but the last thing any of them wanted was to be barred from the pub.

Mick grabbed the bottle and he and Jack made their way back to the table, eyeing the Try Hard Too team with contempt.

Dick was staring out of the window as they made their way back to sit down. "Chip van's here!"

They all had that hankering for chips soaked in salt and vinegar that a belly full of beer demands. It served as the perfect distraction from the brooding that simmered on after the altercation. They had to move quickly, catching the chip van was a little bit like trying to get to an ice cream van when you hear that unmistakable music whilst you're semi-naked in the back garden, searching for some shorts and a t-shirt and slipping on some flip flops, half running up the driveway frantically trying to attract the driver's attention, or checking if there is a queue in which case you could allow yourself to slow down to a calm walk.

The chip van's main objective was Middle Hardwick, but the driver knew that if he dropped by Little Piddley on quiz night he could pick up some reasonable trade. It would be half an hour before closing, allowing time to get to Middle Hardwick by last orders.

Once the lads had their grub they began to stroll home, Dick and Mick in one direction, James, Peter and Jack in the other.

James roused to the noise of a revving motorbike engine leaving his driveway at speed and realised it was Jack leaving for work. He allowed himself to drop back off to sleep. James had become accustomed to sleeping through till early afternoon as part of his nightshift routine, however, on this occasion, at eleven am, he was awoken again by the sound of his phone ringing.

"Hello," he said groggily.

"Mr Simpson, it's Sarah from Dunwold's, are you still looking for a Store Managers position?"

"Yes I am. Do you have something for me?"

"We have great opportunity for you. It's for a Department Manager's position at a large retail store in London. It's short notice I'm afraid, it's for 2.30 tomorrow afternoon, they had a cancellation from a candidate due to illness."

James didn't hesitate with his reply. "Yes, no problem. I can do that."

"Great, I'll email all the details over to you."

James put the phone down. He was awake now and suddenly acutely aware of his splitting headache. He went to the bathroom, splashed some water on his face to freshen up, and made his way downstairs to the kitchen, switched the kettle on and reached into the cupboard for breakfast cereal. As he poured his cereal into a bowl, he noticed a note Jack had left, written on the back of the previous night's quiz paper. Jack must've stuffed it in his pocket the night before.

Excellent night last night, showed those Out of Town tossers how it's done. Helped myself to breakfast, cheers.

James reached into the fridge and pulled out an empty bottle of milk. Well, not quite empty as there was just enough for a murky brown cuppa.

"Bastard," James uttered in a muted voice.

He pulled a draw open and took out a blister pack of paracetamol, only to find that they had all been popped. He carried on reading the note:

Oh yeah, had a banging head this morning so helped myself to some paracetamol.

"Oh Jack, you bastard." His voice wasn't muted this time. He poured himself a shitty cup of tea to prepare himself for a walk to the local shop. As he strolled to the shop, which also doubled as the post office, James considered that Jack staying last night wasn't a coincidence. They had all visited him in his new abode more often than usual and James had determined they were keeping a watchful eye over him and suspected that it was Jack's turn last night.

Jack was probably, right now, texting the others:

Just left James's place, sleeping like a baby. Made sure he couldn't overdose cos I took the last paracetamol for my banging head lol. Oh yeah, checked his freezer out, no fucking Mars bars . . . Tosser.

The local shop was a godsend for the inhabitants of Little Piddley, as the nearest decent superstore was in Middle Hardwick and that just wasn't the ticket when all you needed was a bottle of red and a bar of chocolate for Saturday night TV. By the time he got back, he had a few hours to kill his headache and make some hot food to settle his queasy stomach to ready himself for the night shift ahead.

Chapter Nine
Wedding Car

Friday 3rd April 2015

James awoke, feeling fresh and alive. It was midday and he had just enough time to shower, breakfast and don his interview suit before his old familiar journey on the train, albeit later in the day. He didn't take his man bag, it wouldn't be necessary for travelling at this time of day.

As usual he glanced into the garage at the next stop to see which cars were on display. A cheeky little red Lotus Elan, a navy-blue Jaguar Mark II with wire wheels, a Rover P5, and a blue Bentley Arnage were all he could see in passing. He lost himself in a daydream behind the wheel of the Lotus Elan, squirreling through a plethora of twists and turns on a country road.

He was jolted out of his dream as the train came to a stop at Kings Cross. He had already had the joy of several interviews for Department Head positions; however, James's knowledge and experience worked against him. It seems that a store manager does not want somebody with equal or possibly more experience occupying a position beneath them, as they perceived this to be a threat to their own indispensability. James expected this interview to go in the same direction: perfectly polite and respectful, but as soon as he was out of the door, a big red cross plastered against his name. James decided to take a different tactic in this interview; he decided that he would imply negligence on his part as to why the store closed and that he couldn't handle the responsibility. He just wanted to be a department head as he was comfortable there.

All through the interview James played himself down, how he was great at taking orders and being given set tasks, but didn't relish giving them out. He made himself out to be a good dependable loyal servant and it seemed to be working, the store manager lapped it up. By the end of the interview James felt certain that he had bagged the job, but at the same time he felt hollow. He didn't feel pleased with himself or excited, after all, it's something he had done all his working life.

'Is this really what I want?' James questioned himself. His mood was dark as he boarded the train back to Middle Hardwick. As he approached the garage at Hoddingsworth, James craned his neck and eyed the Bentley, squinting intently. He was able to make out the price on the screen, £19,500.

'Fuck it,' he thought to himself. He reached for his phone and called Peter. "Peter, have you got that wedding car sorted out yet?"

"Yes and no, I've got a guy that will cancel his other appointment if we stump up £1,200. Daylight robbery if you ask me. Personally, I don't trust him. I haven't told Wendy yet, she'll just tell me to get it whatever it costs."

"Split the difference between the six hundred we spoke about in the pub and his figure, how about a Bentley Arnage for £900, a dead cert, no questions asked?"

"I'd take it hands down but . . ."

James stopped him. "Just trust me, I'll guarantee it. Just promise me you won't go anywhere else."

"Of course, James. I don't know what you are planning but of course I trust you."

"Good, got to go."

James leapt out of his seat, raced to the door, and threw it open just as the train was about to leave the station, much to the annoyance of the guard.

He made his way to the garage to take a closer look at the Bentley. As he peered through the side glass a voice emanated from behind his right shoulder. "She's a beauty, isn't she sir?"

The chap appeared behind him like some kind of apparition. James played the comment down, almost ignored it; he knew sales and he knew how to remain indifferent. "What's the mileage?" James asked coolly.

"85,000 on the clock and I've got the complete service history to back it up, all stamped by Bentley main dealers."

"Any movement on the price?"

"She's already competitively priced, you can save £750 if you don't take up the parts and labour warranty."

James considered himself to be a risk taker but that was gauging himself against his father, who took no risks whatsoever. Risk taking was one thing but this car was fifteen years old and James considered that it would be reckless not to take the warranty with the repair costs this kind of car could command. "Eighteen and a half grand and we've got a deal. I can get the money to you by the weekend."

The salesman laughed. "I'll wait till the weekend, it'll be gone, I guarantee it."

"Come on, work with me here, I've got to take this home and convince the wife I've got a good deal. Surely you can understand that?" James was lying but he needed to get the salesman on side somehow.

"I'll do it at £19,000, but that's it."

"£19,000 and a tank full of fuel." James put his hand out in readiness to seal the deal. The sales man hesitated but eventually caved and shook James's hand.

"I'll need £1,000 deposit now, we'll take credit or debit card." James obliged and arranged to return at the weekend to collect his new prized possession, following the necessary bank transfers.

'There goes most of my redundancy,' he thought to himself. His mood lifted and a new sense of purpose engulfed him as he continued his journey home, desperate to get started on a website for his new business venture.

While James set to his new career, Jess was as equally absorbed in setting her own life back on track. She sat at her computer staring at Mikey's profile picture. It wasn't for the first time. She had done so for several years, wistfully thinking of what might have been, never taking it any further than that. Two years ago, his status changed to separated and twelve months later to divorced. Although inquisitive, Jess stopped herself from contacting Mikey, out of respect for her own marriage. Things were different now she was separated, currently in a state of flux between two life paths. Her finger hovered for a moment over the friendship request icon and then she pressed it. He had become more ruggedly handsome than the devilishly good-looking young man she knew from before. His hairline receding a little, a few craggy lines around his eyes and evidence of a small paunch under his shirt.

Peter and James exited the train at the Hoddingsworth stop. Peter was like a dog with two tails, he was more excited about James's new adventure than James himself. He insisted on travelling with James to pick up the Bentley.

Likewise, James was glad for the company and support. As they both drove back in the Bentley, they revelled in its luxuriousness, cossetted in the cream leather-hide seats and deep pile navy-blue carpets, quiet with just a hint of a rumble from the big V8 engine in front of them.

James had spent the last few days developing his website and hoped to use some photographs from the upcoming wedding to complete it. After the initial euphoria had settled, Peter broached the subject of James's current status with Jess.

"I blew it Peter, I spent . . . we spent too many years taking each other for granted. We barely spent any real time together. I worked it out that if you take sleep out of the equation, we only spent ten hours a week together, and most of that was eating and completing chores. I know it's a cliché, we do love and care for each other, but we don't have that deeper connection of being in love with each other. She chose me as a safe option. After her break up with Mikey, she locked her heart away and I was never truly able to unlock it."

Peter sat quietly listening. He knew there was nothing he could say that would make a difference. Peter was lucky he and Kate loved each other implicitly. They were one of those one in a million couples that married their first true love and lifelong soul mate. "Kate's cooking up one of her chilli specials tonight, you up for it?"

"Since when have I not been?"

"Great, pop round for seven."

Kate's chillies were a challenge, a great meal for helping to sweat toxins from the body and an onslaught to the taste buds, but a fantastic challenge all the same.

After a couple of days, Jess received her reply from Mikey.

God Jess, is that really you? I couldn't help but notice from your profile that you're separated. Are you okay?

Yes, if I'm honest, it was a long time coming. There just wasn't enough glue in the relationship to keep us together any longer. I actually feel liberated right now. What about you with your divorce?

Much the same. I just couldn't give Faye all of me, it was impossible, a part of me was stolen away.

Jess knew exactly what he was inferring and felt the same way—they both had a piece of each other locked in their hearts. Fate had contrived to ensure they were both single at the same time, two decades later. Fate had determined now was the time for them to complete each other and fate had one more trick up its sleeve; Mikey lived just twenty miles away.

James was a little nervous on the run up to his wedding car debut and spent a few hours the day before checking out the church location, the reception venue, and all possible routes and detours, just in case. Besides which he had a devilish plan in mind if that witch even dared to try and push his buttons.

The wedding day was upon them and James rolled up in the gleaming Bentley, forty-five minutes before the church service, knowing full well that he would sit outside Wendy's parents for a quarter of an hour whilst they finished primping the witch, leaving just enough time to get her to church, twenty-five minutes away.

Inside they were chaotically looking for the veil and shoes that they had put in a safe place earlier in the morning, eventually found by accident. A little last minute attack with the blusher and she was ready. James had decided that if she wasn't rude to him he would be the perfect chauffeur and discharge his duties appropriately. Peter hadn't mentioned a word to his sister as to whom the driver was, just that he had secured the services of a fine-looking Bentley.

As Wendy approached, James stepped out and opened the rear door. She was attractive in a school ma'am kind of way. There were stern features that matched the character within. James could have been transporting Victoria Beckham for all he knew—she could easily pass as her double, pouting, never smiling, not a laughter line in sight. James smiled and nodded to her as she approached, but she had no time for anybody else right now, just how she was going to enter the car and sit without ruffling the dress. Once in, James closed the door, stepped in and waited patiently. "What are you doing, you imbecile? What are you waiting for?"

"Do you have a chaperone?" James enquired.

"There isn't one, not that it's any of your business. Now drive on."

He couldn't win . . . or could he? He set off in the direction of the church until out of sight of the house and immediately took a detour.

"Driver, are you a complete idiot? I think you will find the church is in that direction."

"Ah yes, that would be correct, ma'am." James turned around to look at her briefly, so that she could make no mistake as to his real identity.

"Tiberius! Oh my fucking god, are you kidding me?"

"Oh yes, afraid so."

"Now you turn this fucking car around right now."

"Tell you what, let's play a game. For every apology I get, I start to head back towards the church."

"You've got to be joking, stop the car and let me out now."

"Can't do that, I've been paid to do a job and I'm going to see it through, even if you are too late for your own wedding. Why don't we start by apologising for calling me an imbecile earlier?"

By this time, James was as far away as he wanted to be, it was now or never as to whether he turned back to make it on time. He held his nerve but hers broke. "Okay, I bloody well apologise if that makes you feel better?"

"You're sorry?"

"I'm sorry!" she screamed.

James took a turn back towards the church. "Now then, what about all those times you insisted on calling me Tiberius just to get a cheap laugh from anybody that would listen?"

"Oh my god, is this what this is all about?" James started to indicate to head away from the church. "Okay, okay, for fuck sake I'm sorry."

"Good, well let's get you to that church then."

She sat silently, knowing that any slight against James would cause another wrong turn. They arrived a few minutes late but that's a bride's prerogative after all.

Peter and his father rushed down to the car with a deliberate and intense walk. Gerald hooked his arm around Wendy's and off they went. There was barely any time for pleasantries, apart from Gerald gushing about how beautiful his daughter looked as they strode away. Peter held back a little. "That was inspired mate, making her arrival late. The whole place is on tenterhooks and Tim's literally shitting himself."

James gave a wry smile and said, "It's all part of the service mate."

Meanwhile the church service went without a hitch and everybody emerged chattering, smiling and generally waiting patiently as the bride and groom readied themselves to set off to the reception. Wendy's smiles appeared natural but they hardly ever were, unless of course she was mentally torturing somebody.

When James managed to catch her eye, he could see that she had a face as black as thunder. She wanted to dispel James right then and there but she needed that car for the photo-graphs. She needed to be seen being wafted away in the luxury limo, she needed the car for the time being, so it was checkmate to James.

Peter approached. "Looks like you've got me as an extra passenger Tibbsy, something about making sure you don't lose your way to the reception."

"Great, look forward to it," James replied.

James behaved himself from here on in and, once out of the car at the reception, he snapped up some photographs of his own. As soon as he was back, the photos were uploaded and his website was complete. He still had enough time to make his night shift at the warehouse. In the upcoming months, James honed his skills in his new trade and a few orders came in for the rest of the season.

Setting up the business late in the month of May seemed suicidal, but James had his nightshift work and the decision was, after all, opportunistic. It served to ease him into an industry he had no prior knowledge of and there was sufficient work to ensure that the car got a good run every two or three weeks. He even added some of his own touches, like having some extra number plates made up, JU 5T for the back and MA 88 IED for the front. He would blue tack them on at the reception venue for photographs to be taken. It was nice touch and the newly married couples and photographers loved it.

James got to know a few photographers, generally the same repeat faces, and offered to promote their services through his own website as a package. His aim wasn't to profiteer from this. It just gave a bit of leverage if anybody was reluctant to pay their bill. No money, no photographs!

Just as James applied himself to his new business, Jess applied herself to her newly rekindled relationship. Tentatively, at first, a meeting on neutral ground in a popular coffee shop, picnics in the park, the odd evening meal. They initially pitied each other over their failed marriages, but quickly moved on by just wanting to be with each other.

Mikey had become a more grown up Mike and before long they were filtering Olly into their time. He took to Mike straight away. As long as they have the language of football all would be good, and Mike did speak the language very well. They didn't support the same teams, but they did mutually appreciate good players, good teams and managers, and equally analysed the failings of the teams heading for relegation. Mike regularly took Olly to his weekend game when James was on wedding duties.

James had always struggled to commit to Olly's football games, quite often working in the store on a Saturday and relying on Jack, whose son also played in the same team, to do the fetching and carrying. Jack was always ok with it, but it did make for a sizeable round trip on some of the away games. Of course, home games for The Little Piddley Warriors made no difference to him whatsoever. Jack didn't want to like Mike, but he too was sucked in by Mike's grasp of football and his expert commentary.

After a few matches, his brusque demeanour had dissolved and they generally stood next to each other, analysing the game and encouraging the lads to do their best. Olly and Danny both played forward positions: Olly on the right wing and Danny as a centre forward. They had known each other for as long as they could remember and their interplay was instinctive, giving them a formidable advantage over the opposition's defence. The pairing was probably the reason for the team topping their league, even though they were playing against teams with a far more formidable player line up.

Chapter Ten
Fringe Benefits

While Jess's rekindled love life was blossoming, James had spent so much time and energy over recovering his own life and his new business venture that he hadn't even considered the idea of a new relationship. There were no secrets between James and Jess, he knew that Mike was back on the scene and he knew that Jess was settled and content, and James was happy for her.

James's life was settling down too, considering he'd started his business so late in the season. As far as bookings were concerned, he had done well, but more importantly his order books were filling nicely for the following year and he had a healthy bank account full of deposits. James was able to maintain his night watchman work, it gave him an escape, the income he still needed, and a chance for a bit of banter with the other chaps on change over. By this time, James could afford the extra insurance needed for private hire and made the necessary applications to allow him to do luxury airport runs, theatre runs and prom nights that were becoming ever more popular. His availability for evening work and early morning airport runs were awkward, but he'd got to know his other work mates well enough to know which ones were up for the extra hours and, generally, he could arrange cover.

Every now and again James would receive a call where it would transpire that Jess had passed on his number, in recommendation for his services, and James was grateful for this, seeing it as a stamp of approval from Jess and her willingness to support him.

Before long, James found himself taking a booking for Jess's own wedding to Mike. The divorce had already been filed and everything was proceeding as smoothly as these things can. Jess agreed to buy out James's share of the house. She had the means to do this herself and James made no bones about it. The money from the house would allow him to seek out a modest abode for himself, instead of renting, which he perceived to be a waste of money. He always believed that money in property would work for him.

Whilst James had restructured his career path, he had no clue how to remodel his love life; he was a great believer in fate but dating had become so contrived these days with social media sites and the internet. It was something James simply wasn't interested in.

Every now and again his friends, or his friend's partners, would be keen to hone their matchmaking skills with recently separated or divorced friends and acquaintances. James would make up excuses not to go on dates for no other reason than the fear of the unknown. However, every now and again, his excuses would dry up, and the shear persistence of his friend's wives, especially Peter's wife Kate, would prevail. It had become her mission to find James a suitor.

The three ladies she had lined up for him were all attractive, intelligent and financially independent. A chap really couldn't want for more, but the fact that these ladies were so successful just served to unnerve James, rendering him unworthy of their attention—in his mind.

Eventually, he relented. He met with Pauline first, which had to be in the afternoon, due to James's evening shift commitments that week, and ended up as a picnic in the local park. It was fine until three wasps, a swarm of midges and an army of ants decided to join in. The midges served to cause a general itchiness, especially in the hair line. The ants formed a regimental line to the cake and began to dismantle it, removing it, crumb-by-crumb, back to their nest. The wasps conducted air-to-air combat, consisting of fly pasts, causing both James and Pauline to get up and run whilst the wasps would settle onto a glass of wine for refuelling.

James insisted on soldiering on, but Pauline was ready to give up. If only James had taken the hint. It was only a matter of time and, whilst James scratched his scalp with his right hand, he had no other option than to waft at a wasp with his left, holding a glass full of wine, the contents of which discharged itself onto his date, leaving a large red/purple stain on her cotton-white dress. Despite James's rueful apologies, the death knell had been raised, cutting the date short, for Pauline to escape home and freshen up.

Marge invited James round for an evening meal and it was glorious. James didn't need, nor was he allowed, to lift a finger. He was plied with homemade cake to finish, which was divine. For a few months, James would have loved being mothered, but he knew it couldn't last, he knew that after a few months he would start to feel smothered. He knew that living with a smother mother would lead to a slow, unhealthy, monotonous life.

Carla insisted on taking him to the gym for a workout and then a healthy lean meal afterwards. James ached a little during the meal and awoke in the morning barely able to move. He imagined life with Carla as a strictly regimented regime of exercise and diet and, besides the fact that his life would probably be stretched out for another five years, he really didn't relish the thought of six o'clock Sunday morning runs and an hour in the gym afterwards. So, it was a no to Carla too.

James's sex life wasn't quite so arid. It's something that he had never reckoned on, but he did cut out as a handsome figure in his uniform and, from time to time, he was the subject of admiring glances from wedding guests and bridesmaids alike. He actually caught the attention of a lot more women than he noticed. His modest manner didn't allow him to rec-ognise some of the more subtle flirtier behaviour. In fact, if any of them wanted to engage with him further than an admiring glance, they would have to physically present themselves and, from time to time, this did actually happen.

The attention was never expected but a welcome perk of the job. James had no idea when he entered his new profession that anything of this nature would occur. It's something that became a favourite topic of his jealous mates at the quiz nights. James would refer to these encounters as 'fringe benefits' but Jack, of course, being the ever so slightly crass individual that he is, would refer to them as James's 'minge benefits'.

Saturday 25th July 2015
James's first sexual tryst will remain etched in his mind as a short-lived but glorious moment of his life. James had assumed his usual stance, a few yards away from his car, picking a quiet spot away from the gathering guests, and watched on as the photographer did his best to ensure that the photographs would paint a picture of the perfect wedding, be-tween the two love birds, regardless of

whatever the reality was, good or bad. Brides and grooms now seem to organise elaborate stag and hen parties weeks before the big day, however, the temptation of a last-minute stag/hen night alcohol-fuelled binge appears to be irresistible, resulting in a semi-present bride and groom on the big day. Of course, although the bride and groom are loved up, it doesn't necessarily mean that their respective families are equally loved up. Regardless of these issues, the photographer does what he is paid for and produces the picture-perfect wedding every time.

James had observed the bridesmaids and, on this occasion, and as usual, there was one stunningly beautiful, two or three attractive, and one or two fugly girls, or ladies, as the case may be. The fugly girls generally reflected their physical size with their character—larger than life. On this occasion, they were wearing electric-blue body-hugging mermaid dresses, flesh-coloured tights or stockings, he couldn't make out which for sure, but there was a shimmer to them; he surmised that their leg's natural colours would be much paler and they lacked the orangeness of a fake tan. Their hair was pulled back and beautifully set in an up style. All the girl's make up had been applied impeccably and lips caked in glossy poppy red lipstick.

They served as an enjoyable distraction for James as he watched on. He thought he had caught the eye of one of the girls. She had glanced over on more than one occasion, but he dismissed it as mere coincidence—that they happened to be looking in the same direction at the same time and, if he was honest with himself, he was quite taken with her attractiveness and wouldn't have been surprised if he was making her feel uncomfortable with his staring, so he deliberately averted his eyes for the rest of the time. James had invested in a rather fine-looking charcoal-grey chauffeur uniform, complete with a peaked cap. His figure was perfect for his six-foot frame and even Jess would comment on how fine and dandy he looked.

After some time, once he thought it safe to do so, he glanced back across at the group of ladies. The one he had spied earlier had peeled away.

'Must've gone to the powder room,' James thought to himself.

Just at that moment from behind his right shoulder he heard a whisper in his ear. "I'm not wearing any knickers."

James was taken aback. This was the last thing he expected to hear. "I'm not wearing any knickers, either." He was pleased with his quick-witted retort. To all intents and purposes, it could have been a clandestine conversation between two spies.

"Is that your car? What is it?" She was stood next to him, but distant enough not to be identified as conversing with the chauffeur-suited chap next to her.

"Yes, it's mine, and it's a Bentley."

"I've never been taken in the back of a Bentley before."

The manner in which she spoke was flirtive and suggestive, and whatever doubts James had about the train of conversation melted away—the moment was his for the taking. "Would you like me to take you for a ride in my Bentley?"

"That would be lovely, but I won't be able to slip away for an hour, will you wait for me?"

"I'll be here in an hour's time and will wait for ten minutes but no longer. I've got other commitments later this evening."

James disappeared to do some food shopping, to make good use of what could turn out to be wasted time. He wasn't familiar with the area and guessed that he could find a quiet country lane nearby. As the hour passed by, he had convinced himself that it was all a folly and he would be sat outside looking like a complete mug as they all came out to witness his stupidity and down a shot, as part of one of their drinking games.

As he trundled around the supermarket, he bought a pack of condoms all the same. He pulled up in the Bentley precisely one hour later to the side of the hall, away from windows and the main entrance door, and away from prying eyes. Five minutes later, the passenger door opened and the bridesmaid stepped in and sat next to him.

James didn't wait to be asked, he started the engine and moved away. She knew the area and directed him. As the journey progressed through the town, she wasted no time and hitched her dress back up to her waist. James was right about the flesh-coloured tights, hold ups, to be exact. James was a sucker for stockings, he found them extremely sexy and the stirrings within his trousers served as proof of this.

As she finished hitching her dress, she revealed her bare womanhood; she hadn't been lying about the knickers. Her quim had been neatly trimmed and waxed to Brazilian perfection. She reached over and placed her hand into James's lap and gently rubbed at his stiffening cock beneath.

James concentrated on his driving as much as possible, to distract his brain and senses away from such a pleasurable act. She moved away and grabbed his left hand. He could drive easily without it. The car was an automatic and the steering light.

She grabbed his index finger and pushed it between the lips of her fanny onto the small hard nubbin beneath. She closed her eyes, as if in deep concentration, and stroked and teased her clitoris with James's finger. James approached a set of traffic lights; he prayed for them not to turn red, but his prayers weren't answered. He pulled up to a stop.

Most cars don't warrant attention from other motorists, but where Bentley's and other prestigious cars are concerned, people are intrigued to see inside, to see if there is a driver or passenger of any note. This time was no different. An elderly couple pulled alongside.

'Please turn green,' James wished, but they were held on red for what seemed like an eternity. The elderly lady peered in and a look of disgust came over her face. The elderly gentleman, less disgusted and more entertained, looked on in wistful reminiscence. Finally, the lights changed and James was able to liberate himself from the whole embarrassing situation.

The young lady next to him was in full swing by now, ordering James to take the next left and pull up into a field entrance half a mile ahead. Just as he pulled into the field, she thrust his finger into her womanly depths, holding pressure on her clitoris with the side of his hand, she sighed and quivered and he felt her involuntary muscle contractions on his finger as she climaxed. After a few seconds of silence, she reminded James that she still hadn't been taken in the back of a Bentley.

This was James's invitation and he didn't need to be asked twice. She jumped out of the passenger door and straight into the back. James pushed the necessary switch to force the passenger seat to glide as far forward as possible before getting out to join her.

She took James's cap and placed it on her own head, unbuckled his trousers, dropped his flies and carefully peeled away his pants, allowing his cock to spring out, rock hard and pulsing as the blood from his body engorged it to the point of bursting.

She slipped her bright poppy red lips around his organ and teased her tongue around his throbbing tip. James gently pushed her head away—he was losing control. He pulled a condom from his pocket and she took it from him. She tore it open to remove the latex sheath and gently rolled it onto his cock.

James knelt on the carpet and she slid herself down to meet him. He pulled her dress top down to release her bosom, nipples already erect with excitement. He slid himself inside her and she let out a sigh and a stifled squeal as he took her right breast in his mouth and nipped at her nipple.

She started to writhe her hips and James began to thrust, but the excitement was too much. In just a few seconds he had exploded, ejecting himself into the latex sheath with such deep intensity that he could barely remember such an experience happening to him before.

She wasn't offended, she had already had her fun. She took it as a compliment to her sexiness. "Come on, we need to get back before my husband suspects anything. He thinks I'm booby trapping the bride and groom's room."

James dutifully dropped her off, never knowing her name and never to be seen again. He just had enough time to make his shift and spent the rest of the evening with a cheery smirk on his face.

Chapter Eleven
Bunnygate

Wednesday 23rd September 2015

It would be difficult to top that first sexual encounter in his new lease of life. It was totally unexpected, and a very exciting and memorable moment. However, there were a couple of other trysts that year that were as equally exhilarating, but the novelty of that first time would always remain as James's favourite. One such incident caused such mirth with his quiz team that they lost concentration and lost out to the 'Out of Towners'. Jack had made it his mission to ensure that he knew everything about James's sex life and the usual question was asked.

"Had any 'minge benefits,' this week Tibbsy?"

"I don't know whether I can tell you, it's too bizarre, you won't believe me!"

Unlike Jack, they knew that James wasn't one for embellishing the truth. "Come on, I'm up for a good story tonight," Mick interjected.

"I'll go and get a round in, don't start without me," Dick pronounced with glee and so James began to tell his story.

As usual, he was approached as he stood near his car, whilst the photographer did his best. A shapely lady in her early thirties, he guessed, began to ask a few direct questions, enquiring as to his marital status and, in a short space of time, asked James if he would like some fun later. She was pretty and James did indeed fancy some fun and agreed. He didn't have any shift work that evening as he had an eleven o'clock wedding the next day and couldn't handle both, so he had already arranged cover.

He came back at 8.30 pm when it was dusk and full darkness was rapidly approaching. He pulled up at the reception venue and soon after both rear doors opened. The lady from earlier got in and so did a man which he guessed was her husband, or partner. "Look, I'm not into threesomes, especially with another bloke," James explained agitatedly.

"Oh no, he's only come along to watch, trust me, it'll be fine."

"Yeah, just forget I'm even here mate," the man offered in support of his wife.

James agreed begrudgingly, his senses were telling him to get rid of them and run, but he was never any good at listening to his gut. He drove off and regretted it instantly.

Dick offered his opinion, in no uncertain terms. "For fucks sake, are you mad? That could have been another Fred and Rose West moment. If you weren't here now, for all we know, you could be buried under a patio somewhere."

Mick and Peter nodded in agreement.

Jack butted in, in his usual fashion. "Not a problem for me, I would have taken them out before they got anywhere near me."

They all laughed at Jack in disbelief and James carried on with his story.

They directed him out into the countryside and this time, all kinds of life and death scenarios were playing through James's mind. They directed him into a popular dog walker's car park. James relaxed a little when he spied several other cars. A few of them flashed their headlights at him, which seemed odd.

The woman turned to her partner. "Geoff and Gilly are here tonight, look."

"Oh yeah, and Malcolm," the chap replied.

"They'll get a surprise when they see us get out of this car," she said proudly.

James hadn't noticed the bag they had brought with them, which was probably a good job, as he would have definitely freaked out. She pulled out a couple of rabbit masks complete with floppy ears, a couple of belts with a pompom glued on each one and finally a dog mask. She threw a rabbit mask and a belt at him and said, "Here you go, put these on."

'Oh my fucking god, a dogging site,' James thought to himself. He relaxed a little more at the thought of it, but it made him feel silly rather than sexy, and he couldn't be sure that he would be able to perform for the audience in the cars and bushes. The bunny girl's partner had put on his dog mask by this time and disappeared into the bushes.

She led James round to the back of the Bentley and pushed him back until he was half sitting on the boot. She unzipped his flies and teased his soft cock out from behind his underpants. She wanked him until he was turgid and, from this point, continued with her mouth until he was fully hard, her rabbit ears bouncing against his stomach.

After a minute or two she swopped places and draped herself over the boot with her chest against the boot lid, her skirt and panties removed and her arse facing James invitingly, white pompom tail sticking up in the air strapped to her back at waist height.

James pulled out a condom, his last one in fact, and rolled it onto his cock. He stood staring and actually looked like a rabbit caught in headlights.

"Well come on, fuck me then," she shouted into the boot of the car.

James moved forward, slid his cock into her, and began to pump. Her voice was quite loud, as if projecting to an audience, which was exactly what she was doing. "Oh yeah, fuck me Bugsy. Oh yeah, bunny, fuck me."

Meanwhile, James could hear growling noises in the bushes around him and now and again a woof woof. It was so unnerving that he could feel himself losing his erection.

"For fucks sake, you're not going soft on me, are you? They'll tear you apart if you don't finish me off."

James conjured up scenes from his favourite porn movies and tried to ignore everything else. He could feel his erection returning. He thrashed at her in a desperate effort to maintain the necessary stimulation for his erection. She was turned on good and proper. He was bucking like a manic duracel bunny on speed and it worked she was lost in her first climax, squealing with delight.

James continued to buck with all his duracel might, and it was working for him as well, he could feel himself close to the point of no return.

She squealed again with a second climax and the excitement she could sense with James's own impending climax brought on a third as he came inside her. She lay face down on the boot of the Bentley completely frazzled.

James became aware of the human dogs howling now and heard them running over. 'Sod this for a game of soldiers,' was all he could think as he pulled himself out of her, jumped in-to the driver's seat and drove off as fast as he could.

The woman slid off the car and dropped to the ground, still in a blissful daze following her shag fest. James was angry at himself for his naivety. The chap in the dog mask arrived next to his wife as James sped away. "Where the fuck's he going? I was just about to congratulate him on a job well done."

"Tell me about it. Gilly wanted some of that. She's fuming. You ok to stand in?"

"Well, I guess a dog's got to do what a dog's got do."

"Cheers mate, I owe you one."

"And finally, the first production car to be made with a built-in CD player was the Nissan Figaro." The lads were so engrossed in James's story that they had missed two whole banks of questions and answers.

"I haven't finished yet guys," James exclaimed.

They looked on dumbstruck. How could there be more? "Oh no, don't tell me they came after you?" Mick enquired. James was completely unaware that they were actually coming over to congratulate him.

"No, no I managed to get clear of them," James continued with his story. He drove away from the car park realising that for the moment he hadn't got a clue as to his whereabouts. He had sat nav but no time to waste, so just drove away as fast as he could for a good five miles or so. His driving, still erratic, spurred on by a good rush of adrenalin. This hadn't gone unnoticed.

The white car with blue and fluorescent green chequers down the sides watched on from a side road as he charged by. "See that Bentley, it's going a bit quick!"

"Wouldn't expect to see a Bentley being driven like that at this time of night. Doesn't seem right, better check it out." They set off in pursuit.

Luckily, James had settled himself a little by this time, and a bit further down the road pulled up and set his sat nav.

"He's pulling up, just hang back and we'll follow him for a while."

Once the destination had been set and the route calculated, James set off once more. The car behind caught up and once close enough radioed through his registration number to HQ for ID. His driving had settled by now. "He's not driving like he was earlier, do you reckon he's clocked us?"

"Yes, bastard! Look, just keep following him, you never know he might have a dodgy indicator or brake light we can pull him for."

James glanced down into his lap and witnessed his limp cock still protruding from the gap in his flies, still sheathed in the condom, held in place by the laws of gravity alone. He let his window down and threw the condom out, his steering a little erratic, as he focused more on the job in hand than his driving. "He's swerving about again, did you see that? He's just thrown something out of the window."

"He's definitely fucking clocked us, could be getting rid of some drugs."

"Fuck it, let's pull him!" They put on the blues and twos and James eyed the blue flashing lights behind in despair. He pulled over and quickly made sure that his cock was put away and flies done up. He lowered his door glass once more.

The police officer peered in with an odd look on his face. "Off to a fancy dress party, sir?" he quizzed.

James had forgotten that he was still wearing the bunny mask, however, he was relieved that the perfect excuse had been offered to him on a plate. "Err, yes I'm going as the Mad Hatter, in fact." His chauffeur uniform fitted the image perfectly.

"Look, we've been following you for the last few miles and your driving's been a little erratic, have you been drinking or taking any kind of substance?"

"No!" James said honestly.

"You threw something out back there, what was it?"

James looked around for inspiration. He kept a few humbug sweets in the ash tray and suggested it could have been a sweet wrapper from the sweet he had just eaten, and offered a sweet to the officer. The officer eyed him suspiciously, released the sweet from the wrapper and smelt it to check that it wasn't some kind of narcotic, and once satisfied he popped it into his mouth.

In the meantime, his colleague walked back to see if he could find what had been thrown out of the window and strolled back to James's car. "Find anything?"

"No, just a used condom. Local youths, I suspect, don't know how to keep it in their trousers these days."

"Remove the mask and step out of the vehicle please, sir. I have reason to believe you've been driving under the influence of alcohol or an illegal substance. I'll need you to blow into this bag and we'll need to take a swab as well, sir. Oh, and whilst you do that, my colleague is going to inspect your car. Ok, sir?"

Of course the question was rhetorical and James nodded and agreed. Both of the tests were clear.

"Find anything?" the officer asked his colleague.

"No, all clear mate."

"Ok sir, I have to warn you that littering is an offence."

"Yes officer, sorry about that, it won't happen again, better that than half-eaten McDonalds I passed earlier. Probably those pesky teenagers that dropped that condom."

"Yes sir, well never mind about that, that's our job, you just ensure that you conduct your own affairs lawfully."

"Yes, of course officer."

"On your way, sir." James drove away carefully.

"Oh no…… for fucksake Tibbsy, the 'Out of Town' wankers have just beaten us because of you," Jack exclaimed, clenching his fists and rolling his eyes as he said it. Dick, Peter and Mick pulled a face of indifference—they were still in awe of James's story. The 'Out of Towners' leered across a few times, slowly and deliberately opening their prized bottle of wine and sipping at their glasses in an effort to draw attention, which normally worked to rub it in, but tonight it wasn't forthcoming, as James's friends continued to digest the whole story that James had laid out before them.

Chapter Twelve
Foiled

Monday 8th February 2016

A few months passed by following 'Bunnygate', the nick name his friends had given to the incident involving his escapade at the dogging site. Nothing of any interest had happened to any of them. In fact, it was just life as usual.

The phone rang and James answered it.

"Hi, is that James?"

"Speaking."

"Hi, yes, you don't know me but an acquaintance of mine has given me your number. I'm enquiring about hiring a wedding car." The man's voice was quite plummy and posh, but there was no telling for sure. From time to time James would be fooled by the airs and graces given over the phone and end up picking up from a traveller's site or some notorious urban black spot.

"Oh yes, when are you looking for?"

"Ah yes, it's a bit short notice I'm afraid, we've had a bit of a mix up, but to cut a long story short we need it for the 19th March, in about six weeks time."

"I'll check the diary but it would be a miracle if I'm available. What time of day are you looking for?"

"It's a late one, three o'clock, we've got visitors travelling you see."

"That might work in your favour, let's see now. I've got an eleven o'clock, its touch and go, where will it be held?"

"It's in Monksford."

"Never heard of it, where's that?"

"Yes, it's about thirty miles to the north of Oxford."

James reckoned that to be about an hour from his place and an hour and a half from his other venue. His hire of three hours would make it logistically impossible, but quite often he's done in two hours, which would make it doable. "Let me have a look to see what I can do, I'm not promising anything but I need to make a call first. Oh, and by the way, who was it that gave you my number?"

"I don't know her myself, it's an old friend of my sister's. I think she said it was someone called Jess?"

"Oh ok, I'll come back to you."

'No pressure then,' James thought to himself.

James needed to check who the photographer was for the wedding on that day. He made a couple of calls explaining that he'd like to talk to the photographer first, to make sure that he can get the best possible shots of the car. James was in luck, it turned out to be Johnno, one of his regulars.

"Hi Johnno, it's James. Now listen, you've got a wedding to do on the 10th of July, right?"

"Well my diary's full so I guess I must have."

"I've been in touch with the party that booked you and I'm doing the Limo. I need a favour, if you can do it please?"

"Of course mate, I'll try if I can."

"I've got someone who needs me for a three o'clock but I've got to be away by one o'clock. Is there any chance you can do the car photographs first, so that I can slip away a bit earlier?"

"Sure, sure, no problem at all. Leave it with me." Johnno was an affable chap and James didn't think it would be an issue, but there was no sense in assuming that this would be the case.

"Great, I owe you one, bye, and I'll see you then if I don't see you before." Without any hesitation, James picked up the phone and rang the man with the posh voice back.

"Hi, it's James. Sorry, I didn't get your name earlier."

"It's Johnathan Rossford."

"Look Johnathan, I can do it, but it's outside my operating radius, so I'll need to charge a little extra, it'll be £900."

Judging by the plummy voice on the other end of the phone and the fact that they were probably desperate, he didn't think this would be an issue, and he was right.

"Ok that's fine, book us in please."

"All sorted, I'll need a deposit straight away if you don't mind. I'll email over my bank details and I will look forward to seeing you on the big day."

James put the phone down and wondered to himself who Jess knew in that neck of the woods. Nothing came to mind straight away and he dropped the thought as quickly as it came.

James was struggling to balance his hectic schedule. He was financially solvent and was considering dropping his night watchman job, but needed it for the time being to give him eligibility for a mortgage application for his impending house hunt. Without this, he would have to wait until he had three years' worth of accounts.

He soldiered on, but was becoming increasingly weary. He was knee-deep in prom night runs and was finding himself partaking of the odd cat nap here and there whilst carrying out his night watchman duties. He had become accustomed to absolutely nothing happening at the warehouse, night after night after night. The truth is, although he kidded himself these were just cat naps, they were, in reality, deep slumber naps, and he had resolved himself to taking an alarm clock in with him.

It was only a matter of time; during one of James's deep slumber naps the chain link fence was breached. Two hooded figures wearing ski masks expertly snipped their way through with ease. Even if James were wide awake, he wouldn't have seen them—they had obviously done a bit of research and identified a blind spot between the security cameras. This wasn't to be a quick snatch and grab, this was to be a full-on heist. A consignment of five hundred flat screen smart TVs had come in earlier in the day, to be dispatched the following day, about £250,000 worth to be exact, and would fill four good-sized Luton vans.

They hunkered down and ran across to the toilet block area on the far side of the warehouse, using whatever cover they could find—a pile of pallets here, lorry trailers and lorry tractor units there. One of them hobbled as if he were carrying some kind of leg injury. Every now and again they would be caught on a camera and disappear just as quickly. They un-bolted the welded bars in front of the windows and smashed one of the panes of glass out. A bit of noise now was less risky than setting off the alarm by jemmying open the window and breaking the alarm connection on the frame.

They were in!

The plan now was to find the night watchman, overpower him, disable the alarm, and open up the gates and loading bay doors. From here on in, all they needed to do was load the booty in the four box vans outside. It was a slick operation and there must have been some kind of inside knowledge involved. They found their way to the night watchman's office, ready to beat the living daylights out of him. Luckily for James, all they found was a skinny bloke sleeping like a baby. They didn't take any chances and tied James's hands behind the back of the office chair, strapped his feet to two of the base prongs that the castors nestled in and used a rope to strap his body to the backrest of the chair.

One of them disappeared into the warehouse, the other stayed with James and disabled the alarm system. He flicked the button on the tannoy and spoke into the microphone on the desk in front of him. "Ok boys, get them in and let's get loaded." His voice bounced around the inside of the warehouse.

James's slumber wasn't disturbed by this and he remained completely unaware of what was going on around him.

It would take about an hour to load up; one of the lads just had to keep guard on the night watchman, which was easy in this case. After a quarter of an hour, the initial adrenaline rush had worn off and boredom started to kick in. He found a black marker pen, used for marking up various boxes and crates, and began to doodle on James's face: Firstly, a pair of Michael Caine-style spectacles, then a couple of large black sideburns. His fun didn't end there. He untied James's hands and wheeled him in front of a CCTV camera to pose with him, holding James's hand up as though he were waving at the camera and holding his other arm around his assailant's shoulder. After approximately twenty-five minutes, his inquisitiveness got the better of him and he left the office to see how the loading was going.

"We're about half done, what the fuck are you doing out here?"

"It's ok, he's sleeping like a baby." At that very moment James's alarm went off, just inches away from the tannoy. The alarm sound rebounded around the warehouse. "Fucking hell mate, I thought you'd disabled the alarm?"

"I did, they must've fitted a backup system."

"Shit, stop loading and get out of here with whatever we've got! Come on. Hurry, hurry."

James woke to the alarm and tried to get up to turn it off and couldn't understand, to begin with, why he couldn't get up, resisted every time by the rope and his taped-up feet.

Suddenly, his assailant hobbled in and punched him in the side of the face. "How did you get the alarm to go off? You fucker." The accent in his voice was Scottish and harsh. Probably Glaswegian.

Another figure entered. "Come on, let's go or we'll leave you here."

"Fucking bastard." He hit James again and then hobbled off as they made their getaway.

James, by now, was in no doubt that the warehouse was being robbed. 'Run, hide, call the police' kept playing over in his mind, but he could neither run nor hide. His phone, however, was in his trouser pocket. Fortunately, his hands were still untied, so he grabbed his mobile from his pocket and dialled 999. He dragged himself over to his alarm clock, switched it off, and concealed it in the back of one of his desk drawers.

The police arrived in minutes. Two officers burst in through James's door. "It's ok, sir, we're the police."

'Obviously,' James thought to himself while looking at the two uniformed figures in front of him.

"Just give us a minute sir and we'll get you out of that chair. Looks like they roughed you up and had some fun at your expense!" the officer exclaimed as they unshackled him.

James struggled to understand what he meant; he knew that he had sustained some bruising, but what else?

"Someone's been doodling on your face, best check it out in the mirror. See if it will wash off, hey! Before we let you freshen up, though, is there anything you can tell us?"

James thought for a while "No, not really, they must've snuck up on me and knocked me out cold, I remember waking up strapped to the chair, but for some reason my hands were free."

The head of security, Geoff turned up. "Geez, you ok James?"

"Yeah, a bit shook up but other than that, I'm fine."

"Bastards weren't just satisfied in roughing you up, hey!"

"I guessed the alarms had been disabled, but, because my hands were free I managed to drag myself to the tannoy on the desk and use the alarm tone from my mobile phone . . . it sounded like a real alarm." James was thinking quickly and did a great job of embellishing his story.

"Must've stopped them taking about a hundred grand's worth of TVs. Well done, mate!" Geoff was chuffed he'd be able to report back that his team had headed his advice and saved them a fortune.

"Did you get a look at any of them, sir? Can you tell us how many there were?"

"Not a lot. The one that roughed me up was wearing a ski mask. He had some kind of leg injury and was hobbling when he disappeared out of the door. Hold on a minute, he had a strong Scottish accent as well."

While James was speaking, Geoff brought up the CCTV footage. "Four Luton box vans, one driver in each and two others, no reg numbers I'm afraid. Hold on a minute, nothing really, just got some footage of the fucker hobbling around, dragging you about in the chair and waving at the cameras. He's pulled your arm around his shoulder and lifted the other one up to the camera, like you're waving at it. Little fucker, well the joke's on you now mate!"

Geoff's phone started to ring. "Hi darling, no not too bad, could've been worse. James managed to spook them . . . I'm just helping the police with their enquiries, I'll have to report back the boss as well, he's on his way out here now . . . No, I'll stay and see my shift out now, no point in coming home for the sake of an hour . . . Only clue we've got is that one of them was Scottish and hobbled when he walked, got some kind of leg injury . . . Shit, why didn't I think of that? I'll let the police know . . . I know, I know, ok listen, I'll see you later . . . Yeah, love you too." Geoff ended the call.

"The wife, Gilly," Geoff explained to both the officers and James. "Look, while I was on the phone to the missus she reminded me about the bloke we bought you into replace: Bill McCarthy. Remember, I told you a dog tore a lump of flesh from his leg? Worth checking out," he remonstrated to the officers. "I'll get his details for you."

Both officers' walkie-talkies sprang into life with a message from HQ. It transpired that they had already managed to trace two vans, one full of TVs, the other one empty, both stolen with fake number plates. "Ok sir, we're done with you for now, we'll take your details and then you can go. Strange, I thought I recognised you from somewhere, can't think . . . Never mind sir, you get yourself home, clean yourself up and take it easy for the rest of the day."

James looked back at him innocently blank, but just as he said it, it dawned on him that this was one of the officers that pulled him over during 'Bunnygate'. It was probably a good job that his face had been doodled over, otherwise he would have been recognised and they may have put two and two together and made five. James had another thought . . . 'Geoff and Gilly – 'Bunnygate'. Surely not?'

James made his way from the room, desperate to return home to nurse his bruised eye and ego and catch up on his sleep, but just as the door closed behind him it opened again.

"Jim, look I know you just want to get home but I've got something important to ask you."

"Look, Geoff, don't take this the wrong way but I'm fucking frazzled mate. Can't it wait?"

"Yeah, sure, of course. Look, come in early tomorrow, we'll need a bit more of a debrief on this, but more importantly I've got something I want to put by you. It'll be worth it, I promise you."

James was too tired to join in with the anticipation of what Geoff wanted to discuss with him. James begrudgingly agreed, still desperate to find his home and bed.

"I'll make sure you get paid the extra hour, don't you worry about that." Geoff expressed it as if he was doing James a favour, but James didn't care either way and made his way home with one eye open and one eye closed.

As James looked in the mirror, he took in the full extent of the graffiti on his face. It was indelible ink and no amount of washing and scrubbing was going to get this off, and a black eye to boot. James tried to look on the bright side: They could have drawn on a cock and balls, with the tip of the cock finishing at the corner of his mouth. He then imagined the police officer's interrogation, littered with innuendo— "Now come on sir, spit it out, and don't be giving us any cock and balls story."

There was only one thing for it, he had to allow his sideburns to grow to mask the ink beneath and duly sent Peter out to buy some large sunglasses that would hide both his black eye and the Michael Caine spectacles.

Peter tried to be sympathetic, but found James's face too comical.

James placed the new sunglasses on his face. "How do I look?"

"Oh-huh-huh," Peter replied in his best attempt at an Elvis impression. "I'm sorry mate, you look like a very bad Elvis impersonator, which is great because ironically the worse your Elvis impersonation is, the better it is, if you get what I mean."

And so, it was that for the next few weeks—James was marmite man. Some wedding guests loved it and thought that a premium had been paid for the Elvis impersonator, and others watched on in disgust, as if he were making a mockery of the big day. For the next few weeks he received emails complimenting him and berating him in equal amounts.

Chapter Thirteen
House Hunt

Tuesday 9th February 2016

In the meantime, James left for work an hour early as agreed to meet with Geoff. Geoff had his own little office as head of security, which was about the same size as a cleaner's cupboard and probably was once a cleaner's cupboard. It was big enough for a desk and a chair, but add an extra chair and human being and it was positively claustrophobic.

James knocked at the door and Geoff appeared at it in an instant. Geoff winced and pursed his lips as he took in the grape-coloured bruising around James's eye. "Come on in Jim, there's no need for formalities here, not for the hero of the day at any rate." He ushered James through, but in order to do this he had to extricate himself from the room as there just simply wasn't enough room to squeeze another person past himself, the door, and the desk. "Thanks for coming in early, Jim. Sit down mate, take a load off. Good news by the way, they've found the other vans and all the TV sets. What a result, eh? And that's all down to your quick thinking mate, and that's why I've called you in."

"Oh, and what about the debrief? I thought you wanted to go through everything that happened last night?"

"Well, that was part of it, but seeing as everything's been recovered, I think what we got from you before will suffice; besides, I've got something much more important to talk to you about." Geoff fell silent relishing the thought of it.

"Well, what is it Geoff?"

Geoff glanced over his shoulder to check that there wasn't anybody within earshot and lifted himself from his chair to close the door which although pushed too wasn't fixed on the latch.

"Crickey Geoff, if I didn't know any better, I'd swear that you were planning a bank job or something."

"Nah, but I have foiled plenty, which gets me back to why I've called you in. Listen, before I started doing this Mickey Mouse stuff, I served as an officer with Scotland Yard, put twenty-five years in and took my pension, this shit's just pin money till I get sick of working."

James had gotten him wrong. He thought that he was just a slovenly layabout looking for an easy passage through life.

"Anyway, there's a big prestigious event going to take place soon in the city, London and me old mucker George from the Yard has asked me to drum up some trustworthy security guards to make up the numbers. I've already shortlisted a few, but after what you did last night, well, I want you on my crew. Now I know what you're thinking, what's in it for me? Let me put your mind at ease. It's a grand each and an extra grand for the set up and rehearsal for two days before the main event. So, what do you say?"

"I'm interested, of course. I mean, who wouldn't take a grand for an easy day's work? But I need a date. If it clashes with a prior appointment with the limo then my hands are tied, erm, if you'll excuse the pun after what happened last night."

"Sugar! I hadn't factored that in. The trouble is that if I give you the date you'll be able to work out what the venue is and I've been sworn to secrecy until seventy-two hours before the event. They don't want any breaches of security."

"Okaaaaay, so will you be needing me to schedule in any overtime in the near future?" James gave Geoff a knowing stare and Geoff acknowledged it with the tilt of his head and a raised eyebrow. "Well now, let's see." As he spoke he opened the diary in front of him, fingered through the pages, stopped, and rested his finger on a day and date in his diary. "It's very probable we'll be needing you . . . err . . . for some overtime for then."

"Right, oh, I'll check that out and get back to you."

"Jim, don't take this the wrong way, but I need to know soon."

"No problem mate, I'm good for it. The diary's in my phone. I've just checked it and I'm clear."

"Fantastic, good to have you on board, and remember." Geoff tapped the side of his nose.

"Yeah sure, Mum's the word. Anyway, I'd better get going, my shift's about to start." James lifted himself from his seat and waited patiently whilst Geoff removed himself from the room to allow James to escape.

James and Jess were moving along with their divorce without any hiccups, and before long the solicitors had done their work and Jess had officially bought out James's half of the house, she increased her mortgage and duly deposited £150,000 into James's bank account. Finally, he could start searching for a house for himself. He had been looking around for some time and had a shortlist to hand.

He made his respective appointments to view five properties, all in Little Piddley, ranging from an immaculate two-bedroom flat to a rundown three-bedroom detached house. He valued Jess's opinion above all others, nobody knew him better than Jess, and so it was that she and Olly accompanied James on his viewings.

Thursday 3rd March 2016

James was won over by the two-bed modern swanky flat with small balcony, bistro table and chairs, and modern fitted kitchen. "Well, what do think? There's plenty of space for me, and Olly when he chooses to visit. The balcony is south facing, great for a glass of wine and topping up the tan."

Jess on the other hand was less convinced. "Oh, and what about the parking? There's only allocated parking for two cars? And, in case you haven't noticed, you already have two cars, and the nearest safe spot to park around here is about half a mile up the road. What about visitors? Are you expecting them to park half a mile away and walk here?"

James was slightly exasperated as he watched Jess morph into Kirsty Allsoppy, a TV presenter from a property programme on the telly. "Well, actually, I did think about that and I was hoping to park the Bentley around yours."

"No no no no nooo! Time for you to man up and be responsible, besides, Mike's moving in and we need space for our stuff."

'Damn you Kirsty Allsoppy'. James was regretting sitting on the sofa watching those damned programmes with Jess.

Olly sidled up to his Dad's side as Jess made a beeline for the door. "Never mind, Dad. If it's any consolation, I like the place." Both James's and Olly's initial thoughts were sod the visitors, but there were other properties to look at and he tried to keep an open mind.

A tired old cottage came next, no heating apart from a fire in the front room, a 1950s kitchen and a slightly more modern 1970s avocado bathroom suite. A stale damp smell exuded the walls and floors, the driveway could accommodate a couple of cars and the roadway was clear if visitors needed to park. Last but not least, if you cleared the dust and mildew from the back window and peered through the overgrown wisteria hanging over the window, a small overgrown garden could be observed. The place had fantastic potential for a builder or someone of that ilk, but for James it was a step too far and a money pit to boot.

James looked at Jess. "Too much work?"

Her body language said it all, she cringed as she entered every room, deftly avoiding the cobwebs. "I just want to get out of this shithole."

"Good enough for me, let's go." Two more two-bed terrace properties came next, which were ok but both only had downstairs bathrooms and James couldn't bring himself to live with that. Nor did he want to go down the route of having a costly disruptive extension built.

Even Jess was beginning to doubt herself. She began to think that she had been a bit presumptuous about the flashy flat, but there was still one more property to view; got to try and keep the faith.

The final property was a tired three-bed semi in need of redecorating throughout and new carpets. The kitchen and bathroom were both functional, but in need of replacement. On the plus side the windows and doors had been recently replaced and the property boasted a one and a half-size garage big enough for the Bentley and off-road parking for two more cars. James didn't relish the amount of work involved, but knew it made good financial sense.

Jess worked on him. "Wow! I think this is the one James."

"Really? I'm not convinced. It needs a lot of work and money spending on it. Kitchens and bathrooms don't come cheap these days."

"Think about it. You've got the garage you need for the Bentley, which will mean less cleaning and cheaper insurance. This also has a freehold and no ground rent to cover, which, if I'm not mistaken, will save you around about £1500 per year."

The property had been on the market for a good while and was ripe for a cheeky offer. James rang the estate agent and negotiated a little bargain for himself and all being well would be stepping over the thresh-old in about eight weeks' time.

Chapter Fourteen
Posh Vamp

Saturday 19th March 2016

James readied himself for the day ahead: two weddings and a tight schedule. The first wedding was going to plan, with a bit of luck as a shower took hold just after the photographs were completed.

James proceeded to make his way to the second venue, on time, and allowed himself to relax, revelling in the prospect of netting something in the region of £1,500 for a weekend's work. His best yet! He arrived at a large country house—not quite a stately home, more of a mansion.

He sensed that there was old money here as he drove along the long gravel driveway. Halfway down he was joined by a couple of hounds, and some more followed up behind with a couple of horses, mounted with immaculate red tunic riders.

'Must be returning from a hunt,' James mused. He exercised extreme care as the hounds circled his car inquisitively as to the occupant inside.

As he pulled up at the base of the stone steps leading up to the main doors of the house, a few stable hands appeared and took control of the hounds and the horses as the riders dis-mounted.

James sat outside confused. 'Why on earth would they want my sixteen-year-old Bentley for such an austere occasion?'

A gentleman in black tails knocked on the door glass and James duly lowered it. "I'll need you to reverse up to the stable block, sir. I'll see you back."

James obliged and followed the immaculately clad doorman back to the stable block entrance. As he sat there, two beautiful vintage black and tan Rolls Royce's pulled up at the base of the stone steps. James felt out of his depth.

Why did they need his mediocre wedding car as well as the two beautiful cars ahead of him, one of which was obviously destined to carry the bride? Had he been double booked by mistake? The doorman didn't seem to think so.

James kicked himself for not quizzing the doorman before he left and resigned himself to watch on as four identically clad ladies teetered down the steps in their high heels and entered the first Rolls Royce.

One of them stopped and turned to head in his direction and was quickly gathered up by another of the maids. They were some distance off but he could make out the movement of the others mouth as something like, "We haven't got enough time, we're already running late." She had hold of her hand and pulled her back to the car.

The actions served as a distraction for him, but before he could surmise or draw any conclusions for the odd actions he'd just witnessed, the rear door opened on James's car and a young man entered dressed as a page boy carrying a well-groomed Yorkshire Terrier complete with diamond clustered collar and a silver bow tied to a tiny tuft of fur on its head. James was no longer confused about the reason for him being summoned there. The pieces of the jigsaw finally fell into place. His car wasn't meant for the bride, it was for the Bride's pet dog.

"Don't ask mate," the chap exclaimed, referring to his garb.

James assumed he was a stable hand feeling very uncomfortable in his new attire.

"Drew the short straw?" James offered.

"Something like that. When the first Rolls pulls off, follow it and stay close, her Ladyship insists that 'Princess' arrives at the same time as the bridesmaids."

James pulled up outside the church behind the Rolls as instructed. He expected something grand, but it was twee and quaint, like any country church. "Expected something a bit more awe-inspiring than this." He gestured to his passenger.

"It's all about tradition mate, goes back to the fifteenth century." Both he and the dog exited the car.

James had a little time to think again. Who in God's name does Jess know that mixes in these circles? He came to the conclusion that there wasn't just old money here, there was nobility too, especially with this prestigious occasion. He didn't expect that they would be including his car in any of the photographs, so he sat back and enjoyed the prospect of the easiest money he would ever earn.

James completed his duties ferrying the bride's precious 'Princess' back to the mansion where a large marquee had been erected in the grounds for the reception to take place.

"Better wait here mate for a while, just in case they want some photos of 'Princess' with the car."

James sat tight, pulled out a paper and started to do the crossword. It had to be a tabloid as his intellect couldn't stretch to a broadsheet crossword, let alone the fact that a broadsheet would prove to be a handful in the driver's seat of any car, no matter the size. Every now and again he would look up and see the photographer capturing guests arriving, so he resigned himself to giving it another half an hour before finding somebody to make his excuses to leave. He didn't need to do this, his three-hour time limit had run out and he would be well within his rights to up and go.

James was struggling with three final clues and was essentially beaten. He stared out of the window for inspiration only to see a glamorous lady and the groom walking towards the car. The lady looked to be in her forties and the groom in his thirties. They stopped outside and James could just hear their muffled conversation. "Please stay a little longer, Mother."

"Listen Johnathan, I've had a lovely time, but without your father here I'm nothing but a fish out of water, besides which, that bore of a man insists on talking to me. Look, the meal was lovely, the speeches are over and the formalities are done with. I've done my duty, which is more than I can say for your father." She opened the rear door of the car. "I'll need you to take me home driver."

"I'm sorry, but I'm off the clock, I was just about to leave for home myself."

"Of course you are, don't worry I'll make sure you are paid handsomely." She blanked the pleas of the groom from the other side of the door.

"Where might that be?" James enquired. She gave the address of Commerton Hall. James entered it into his sat nav and it came up with a range of sixty miles and one and half hours' travel time. "I'll need £400 by the time I've got you home and made my way back to my own base. I'm sure it would work out a lot cheaper if you ordered a taxi."

"£400 it is, and if you're good I'll ensure there is a good tip for you."

"Well ok. If you're sure!" James envisaged a nice tip.

"I'm sure. Drive on, driver."

As they pulled away her phone rang. "Really Missy, I'm fine. If your father were there I'd have stayed, out of duty to him, but he's not and I'm not . . . Yes, yes, I'm in safe hands." She stopped to lift her head to look at James with a quizzical expression. "I am in safe hands, aren't I?" she offered the comment to James, which was rhetorical. "Yes, of course I am." She continued, "Look, I'll see you tomorrow and you can tell me all about it. I'm sure it will be wonderful . . . Now don't you worry about me, you just enjoy yourself. That lovely young man Joshua seems very taken with you . . . Ok I'll stop interfering . . . Yes, of course I will, love you too, bye darling."

Missy by this time was stood at the bottom of the steps able to relax from a gruelling schedule of photographs, the meal, and speeches. She scanned the driveway in the hope of seeing something she had spied earlier, but sadly it wasn't there. She put her phone back into her clutch bag and headed back to the marquee.

James looked back at the lady in his rear-view mirror to see if he could identify any signs of her real age, which he estimated to be mid to late fifties. The immaculate make up helped with the disguise, but even so, she could easily compete with the youngest of the 'Gangster Grannies' back at The Bakers Arms.

She caught his eye in the mirror. "What's your name, driver?"

"James, ma'am," he replied.

"I think we can drop the formalities now. You can call me Veronica."

James felt a little uncomfortable, preferring the formality that his occupation demands, but she was the customer, after all. "Veronica it is then."

"Do you enjoy your job, James?"

"I do very much ma—Veronica."

"Are you married, James?"

"The divorce will be through in a few weeks' time."

"Is it amicable?"

"Yes, Jess even helped me with my house hunt, we're still good friends. In fact, I think we've always been friends rather than lovers. I'm relieved I've got a chance to find real love."

"I admire your naivety, but I fear you are chasing the elusive golden egg, my dear boy. At least you're not tied down by the shackles of duty for your country, I envy you that."

She pulled her phone from her handbag to make a call. "Hello Mary, I'll be back shortly, I won't need your services for the rest of the evening, go home and have some extra time with your family . . . I know it's not, but I want some time to myself tonight, thank you Mary." She eyed James once more in the rear-view mirror and said, "Lovely lady, but wants to Mother me all the time."

James turned down a gravel drive to be met by a large set of wrought iron gates, framed within a lodge. "Be a dear and enter in 1965 followed by the hash key on the pad." James did as he was asked and the gates opened to welcome them in. He drove through to the stately home several hundred yards behind. "You've had a long day, James. Will you partake of a night cap with me before your journey back?"

"No, I won't drink and drive, thank you."

"Oh, come now, a cup of tea at least. Besides, I have your money inside and you wouldn't want me to have to come back out into the cold to bring it to you, would you?"

James just wanted to get home, dress down, open a beer and chill in front of the TV. He assumed that she was lonely and stalling for time.

"Ok, a cup of tea, then I really must get back." He followed her to a side door that lead through the service quarters to the kitchen.

"Let me take your jacket and hat for you."

He would have been happy to sit as he was, but allowed etiquette to prevail. She disappeared into a boot room to hang his jacket and hat up, he assumed. She was gone for a few minutes and James started to become restless, eyeing his watch. She returned into the kitchen wearing a pair of riding boots, James's jacket and hat, and perhaps underwear, but James couldn't tell. She had a hip flask in her hand, reached into a cupboard and pulled out a couple of tumblers. She emptied the contents of the flask into both glasses.

"Look I'm tired, I just—"

"Yes, I know dear boy, that's why I have to insist that you stay in one of the guest rooms for the night, now come along, drink up and, besides, if you want this back—" referring to his jacket and cap "—and this—" as she lifted a roll of £20 notes from his breast pocket "—you'll have to come and take them from me." The penny finally dropped, the Lady was looking for a bit of rough.

A moral nerve twinged in James. "What about your husband?"

"Oh, I'm sure George doesn't want to join in," she joked. James didn't laugh. "He's sorting out some kind of diplomatic emergency in the far east. Poor, deluded man, put his country before his own son's wedding, besides which he hasn't been able to get it up for the last ten years. On a good day with the help of a little blue pill, maybe—speaking of which, I took the liberty of pepping up your drink." She glanced down to see the growing bulge in James's trousers.

The whiskey had relaxed him, and ordinarily he would have no hesitation in taking the beautiful sexy temptress before him, but he was wary of his surroundings. This wasn't neutral ground; she had lured him to her lair and everything was on her terms.

She sauntered over to him, passed one arm around his waist, the other clasping the nape of his neck, and kissed him passionately, allowing her navel to press against his bulging trousers. She pulled her lips away and eased them to his ear.

"I gave my drink a little pep, too," she whispered through exhilarated breathing. "Are you hungry, James? There's some cherries, strawberries and cream in the fridge, bring them over to the table."

He did as instructed. He couldn't imagine anyone disobeying her orders. As he turned to approach the table, she was laying on it, jacket unbuttoned and draped by her side, allowing her naked body to be exposed. Her smooth silky skin belied her true age.

"I am your plate, James."

James was a little dumbstruck and froze for a second or two. "Right then," he pronounced in a pragmatic way and proceeded to dollop out some cream onto her nipples and navel. The ice-cold cream made her flinch as it encountered her nipples, which became quickly erect as her skin contracted to the cold. He placed a cherry on each breast and a strawberry over her cream-filled navel.

He feasted on the cream and cherries, giving a gentle nip on the erect nipples beneath, finally wrapping his mouth around each breast and caressing them with his tongue until the cream had been completely consumed. As he lost himself in the act, which he was enjoying on so many levels, she reached into the cherry bowl, pulled out a single cherry by its stem, reached down between her legs and pressed it passed her engorged moist lips.

As soon as he had eaten the strawberry and cleared the small well of cream from her navel, she clasped his head. "Take my cherry, James." She opened her legs and guided his head.

He pulled on the stem of the cherry to release it, glazed with her own sweet juices. She pulled his head back into her with both hands this time.

He thrust his tongue between her lips in search of her very own cherry beneath and gently caressed it. Luckily for James, she was highly aroused, her carnal senses magnified by the intensity of blood flow brought on by the little blue pill. Her hips started to buck.

He restrained her, which turned out to be the catalyst she needed to throw her over the edge and out of control. She tried to buck three or four more times and finally gave into the waves of an intense orgasm that consumed her for several seconds.

Once the waves had finally subsided she sat up. "Oh, you poor dear boy," she exclaimed as she unbuttoned his trousers and flies to release his hard throbbing cock. As it had done with Lady Veronica, the little blue pill had magnified its intensity with him also.

She removed a strawberry flavoured condom from James's jacket and gently rolled it onto his cock. James hadn't noticed that it was flavoured and the irony was lost on him. She jumped off the table, pulling a riding crop from inside one of her riding boots, and gave it to James. "I want you to see me over the finishing line with this." She stood, bent over, resting her hands in front of her, and presented her buttocks to him.

James approached her and let the tip of his penis touch the entrance of her hot, wet womanly depths. He held still for a few seconds, as if to savour the moment, and then allowed himself to glide inside.

She let out a small gasp, her eyes widened and rolled back slightly and, once more, she was close to the edge.

James worked his magic, holding the curve of her waist in his left hand and spanking her buttock and thigh with the riding crop. Her head was bowed in concentration and she re-leased a whimper as she approached her goal. James moved his left hand, bending over her to search for her cherry once more with his finger, spanking her faster and harder with the crop. This had to work—he was beyond the point of no return himself.

It did.

They both became momentarily paralysed as a crescendo of nerve endings sent a wave of orgasm through their bodies. James cradled his head on her back as they both recovered from the moment.

"You can remove yourself now, my dear boy."

"Yes, yes, of course, sorry." He pulled himself away, removed the condom, tied a knot in it and tucked his still hard cock back into his trousers.

"You'll need to take that with you, the staff guest room is down that corridor, second door on the left." She pointed in the direction of the opposite end of the kitchen. "You'll need to be gone by 5.30, I really don't need the distraction of tongues wagging amongst the staff." She took off his cap, slipped out of his jacket, dropped them both on the table and walked away naked, all bar the riding boots which still adorned her feet. "I told you there would be a tip in it for you if you were good." She spoke without looking back as she disappeared from the kitchen.

He enjoyed a small guilty secret as he viewed the red spank marks on her right buttock and thigh.

James set the alarm on his phone and immediately fell into a deep sleep with no interruption until his alarm awoke him, which seemed as if it were five minutes later. However, the true time addressed itself with birdsong and bright sunlight forcing its way through the curtains. He strained to peel his eyelids open with a dry gritty feeling on his eyeballs.

The bed was so comfortable, adorned with crisp clean sheets. He wanted so badly to close his eyes and sleep some more. It took monumental effort to throw the sheets back and sit up, only to be welcomed by his pill-induced morning glory.

For a second, he was reminded of the good time he had just a few hours earlier, which brought on another cheery smirk. There was an en-suite shower room which he used to rinse his face and relieve his full bladder. He guessed that he shouldn't leave any evidence of his lodging, so decided against using the shower and remade the bed. He left via the same side door they used to enter the building and the electric gates opened automatically for him to leave the grounds.

Chapter Fifteen
Mike, Quiz Night!?

Wednesday 23rd March 2016

The 'Gangbangers' had been struggling of late. They had lost the last three meetings against the 'Try Hard Toos'. Most of the lads didn't care too much, but Jack was competitive and determined, so on this Wednesday evening he brought out his secret weapon—Mike. During their conversations at various football matches, not only did he have a good in depth knowledge of sport, he also prattled on about politics, current affairs and worked in the music industry, and so it was that Jack summoned him to their quiz night.

James strolled into the pub and glanced across to his table to check that all the lads had drinks, which they did and he immediately noticed Mike sat next to Jack. "What the fuck's he doing here?" his inner thoughts vocalised out loud to himself. He regained his composure and proceeded to the bar.

"Usual?" Bill uttered.

"Yes please, mate," James uttered back. He leant on the bar as his pint was being pulled and looked back at Mike quizzically, wondering why he was with the team.

No sooner had he approached the table and Jack piped up, "Now listen Tibbs, we haven't been performing well lately, partly because of your distracting stories, so I've asked Mike to come along and help out." James felt no ill will towards Mike and was sure he was a nice enough chap, but he had already made the ultimate sacrifice of relinquishing his marriage for him and even providing the services of his car for their upcoming wedding, and yet now here he was sat at their sacred table as part of his quiz team. James didn't know whether he could reconcile himself with the whole situation.

Mike stood up. "Look, I'm sorry. I've been a bit of a prat, I didn't know what I was thinking to even come here, I'll go." He turned to leave.

"Hold on a minute, sit down," James insisted. "It's not your fault, it's this tool here." He motioned to Jack. "You must have worked out by now that he is completely socially inept."

Sally popped out from nowhere and was the perfect distraction from the awkwardness that engulfed the table. Especially tonight as she bent over to place their answer sheet on the table, dressed in skin tight jeans and a tight white crop top. Raised eyebrows circled the table as they absorbed every detail of Sally's nubile body.

Jack couldn't help himself. "Cor, Sally, if only I were twenty years younger." The rest watched on silently embarrassed by Jacks uncouth statement.

"In your dreams, old timer!" she retorted, turned and bounced away with an air of self-assurance.

"You will be tonight," he shouted back.

"And I rest my case," James pronounced. They all broke into a laugh, half at the quip and half at the relief of the cloud of angst that had been lifted from the table.

The first three rounds went well and Mike's knowledge was invaluable. He was wining them at least one or two extra answers per round and, as a result, they were leading. They broke for a comfort break and a chance to get some drinks in. Dick and Jack disappeared to get the drinks, Mick and Peter went to the toilet. "Look James, I feel really uncomfortable about this. Jack said he had cleared it with you, I had no idea."

"No, it's okay. Jack's Jack, it's the way he works, he's an ignoramus, but his heart's in the right place and it would be a boring old world if we were all the same. Forget it. Anyway, if it weren't for you we wouldn't be wining tonight, and those 'Out of Towners' need to be taught a lesson or two."

"Steady on, we haven't won yet," Mike replied in a more relaxed fashion. He was enjoying himself this evening, it was addictive, and he secretly hoped that he would be able to attend as a regular member of the team.

Jack and Dick returned with the drinks. "Sorry Mike, I couldn't bring myself to order a Bacardi and coke so I got you a lager instead." Dick just rolled his eyes behind Jack's back and shook his head.

Mike accepted it out of courtesy but really couldn't stomach lager and sipped at it slowly and deliberately. Peter and Mick returned to the table deep in conversation about the latest political trauma and how the economy was going down the pan, yet again.

"Minge benefits, Tibbsy," Jack requested. Peter couldn't believe his ears, none of them could.

"Jesus Jack, do you ever let up? Not only do you not recognise the awkwardness of bringing the man that's about to marry Tibbsy's ex-wife to the quiz team, you sexually discriminate the barmaid and now you're asking Tibby here to divulge his sex life to, yet again, the man who is about to marry his ex-wife—un-fucking believable."

"Don't see anything wrong with it myself," Jack replied.

"Oh, come on Jack!" they all bellowed.

"Well, as it happens I do, but I need Mike here to promise not to say a word to Jess. She probably wouldn't believe you anyway, you couldn't write this stuff."

Jack agreed. "Un-fucking believable mate, next football match I'll tell you about 'Bunnygate'."

The next quiz round was about to start. "I'll tell you later after the quiz, suffice to say that it involves a Lady and a stately home." Like Pavlov's dogs they all metaphorically salivated at the thought of it.

The quiz continued and the 'Try Hard Toos' rallied themselves to win the next round convincingly. It was all down to the last round. Mike's general knowledge certainly did win through as he snaffled up an extra three answers that had flummoxed his teammates and, as it would turn out, the 'Try Hard Toos' as well.

Bill secretly had a soft spot for 'The Gangbangers' and was only too pleased to announce them as winners. Over the last eight meetings the 'Try Hard Toos' had won four of them, and the 'Gangster Grannies' had picked up a couple, as had the 'Old Farts'.

Peter went up to pick up their bottle of plonk and James settled down to tell them the story of Lady Rossford and his pudding at Commerton Hall.

"You lucky fucking dog," Jack exclaimed. No surprise there, but Jack had been divorced for the last three years and his own love life was non-existent. Ever since the lads could re-member Jack had over-embellished his life to compensate for his own insecurities and his harboured fear of the opposite sex. In essence, he overcompensates to mask his inferiority complex. One thing is certain, though, and that is his loyalty for all of them is unquestionable, and if anyone of them had a practical issue, he was their go to man. Car broken down—call Jack, toilet not flushing—call Jack, bought a dodgy car—call Jack, lawn mower not working—call Jack. His practical knowledge was invaluable.

One of the 'Gangster Grannies' had taken a shine to him. Jack wasn't a wine drinker and had originally given his glass of wine to Donna, one of the divorced 'Gangster Grannies'. At the time, she took it as a lovely gesture, he just wanted to get rid of his drink. She was curvy and vivacious, matching her own amplified character. It had now become a kind of tradition that if the 'Gang Bangers' won Donna would come over to claim her glass of wine from Jack.

"Aye aye Jack, she's on her way over," Peter said in an amused matter of fact way.

She planted herself on his lap. "Hello Jack, have you got something for me?"

"Here ya go, sweetheart." Where upon he handed his glass to her.

"See you later, lover boy." She jumped off his lap and sauntered back to her teammates.

Mick stared at Jack. "You waiting for a written invitation or something?" He couldn't restrain himself, he had to say something.

"She's just using me for the wine, that's how women operate," Jack replied. Jack knew that he would be a gibbering wreck on his own with a lady like her. His alter ego only seems to appear when he's in the company of others, where he can summon his act of bravado.

The chip van turned up bang on 10.30, so they downed their drinks and left the pub. James wasn't hungry and didn't want to bother queueing and neither, it seemed, was Mike.

James made his excuses. "See you Sunday," he reminded Peter. Peter and Kate had invited him over for Sunday lunch and if Peter and James were lucky enough, Kate would let them disappear to the pub for an hour to down a couple pints.

James and Mike strolled off. "Great bunch of friends you have there. That Jack's a right character."

"Yep, known them all since man and boy, there's nothing I won't do for them, and as far as Jack's concerned, peel off the layers and there's a frightened little boy inside, just like the rest of us."

"I'm still embarrassed about gate crashing your quiz team. You've got to believe me when I tell you that I insisted that Jack clear it with you first."

"I do, I know Jack—act first and suffer the consequences later. The trouble is, he was right, you were on fire tonight, we couldn't have beaten the 'Out of Towners' without your help."

"No problem, believe me I enjoyed it."

"Changing the subject, how's Olly getting on with his football?"

"Star in the making there, mate, both he and Jack's son are a force to be reckoned with. Got a couple of friendly's coming up and possibly a tournament, if you can make it. I'll text you over the dates."

"Thanks, I'd like that, if I don't have a clash in my diary I'll be there. Look, I'm off this way, so see you next Wednesday if you're up for it?" James handed Mike the olive branch and Mike took it.

"Try and stop me," he replied. "Oh, and one other thing, what's with the nickname?"

"Had it ever since school, I'm sure Jack will fill you in at the next football match."

Chapter Sixteen
Jess & Mikes Wedding

Saturday 16th April 2016

Jess and her bridesmaids were in chaos. The bridesmaids being Kate—Peter's wife, Jenny—Dick's wife, Sarah—Mick's wife, and Samantha—Jack's ex-wife. Kate had volunteered her house for Mike to slope off to, to get ready for the big day. He had made arrangements for his best friend Donald to act as his best man who was travelling down that morning.

James was both driver and guest today and was feeling a little apprehensive, just as he did on his first few wedding day duties. Although he took the deposit, he had no intention of charging anymore, this was to be his wedding gift to Jess and Mike. In truth, he knew he had nothing to worry about, she only lived a five-minute drive away from the church and the reception was no more than twenty minutes on from there. He wanted Jess's day to be perfect and would never forgive himself if he caused even the smallest ripple in the pond of perfection that was welling up around them.

As usual, he ensured that he turned up fifteen minutes early. He had no need to walk up the drive to announce his arrival, a mature lady and gentleman opened the front door and approached his car. It was Margo and Philip, Jess's mother and father.

"James, how are you dear boy?"

"Very well, thank you, and how are you keeping? It's been a while, but I must say you both look very dapper."

"Very good of you to do this James, ahem er, given the circumstances."

"I wouldn't have it any other way. I'd have been disappointed if she hadn't used my services."

"Yes, of course dear boy. Well, look, I insist you come and sit with us for a while, after the formalities have been dispensed with, of course."

"I will Philip, lovely to see you both again."

"Yes well, we really must get the bride out here or she'll be late for her own wedding."

Margo was always reserved where James was concerned. He guessed that a shop manager, regardless of the size or prestige of the store, just didn't cut the mustard. He wasn't the company executive or the director she had wished for as a son-in-law. Mike fitted the bill much better as a respected music executive, mixing with celebrities in London on a regular basis.

James thought she may lighten up on him once her daughter became betrothed to a more appropriate suitor, but any kind of conversation with her would continue to be cold and frosty. Philip was naturally gregarious. He was a chameleon, as comfortable in a top-end restaurant as he was in a spit and sawdust pub. He had an incredible ability to see the good aspects of people he met and filter out their bad traits. When he offered for James to sit at the head table he meant it.

Finally, the front door opened and four pink ladies emerged, teetering down the path in their pink high heels to Peter's car. He owned a nice silver Mercedes which served as a perfect form of transport for the bridesmaids. James had a vision for a moment of Mike turning up to the church dressed as a leather-clad Danny Zuko from the movie Grease.

Distracted by his thoughts, he didn't see Jess until she was halfway down the drive heading towards his car. She had an athletic figure and wore an elegant off-the-shoulder fitted dress with a fish tail—she looked stunning. James could only imagine she must have been a dressmaker's dream come true with barely any alterations need, a perfect hanger for a perfect dress.

She floated up to the car with her father on one side and Olly on the other. James had been so busy with work that he hadn't seen either of them for a good week or two. "Hi Jess, words fail me, you look absolutely stunning, lovely dress."

"You're looking quite dapper yourself, if you don't mind me saying so?" she replied. It was true, in both cases they were reborn, in a sense, allowing themselves to be who they really are instead of trying to be who they thought they should be. The perception of this was felt by others around them as a new life force coursed through them both.

Outside the church, after the bride and bridesmaids were duly delivered, James allowed himself some time to stroll over to Peter. "How's the groom doing?"

"Cool as a cucumber when I left him and his mate, a famous music producer. Lost on me I'm afraid, but I'm sure Olly will make a beeline to him for an autograph or something later." As Peter spoke James looked a little distracted, staring past him over his shoulder. Peter turned to see what had taken his eye. "Might have known you'd have your radar switched on, couldn't help noticing her myself, she is stunning. Looks like a movie star or something, very glamorous."

'Must be on Mike's side,' James thought to himself. She wore a sky-blue chiffon dress hugging her slim body with matching kitten-heel shoes and hat. She was not only physically beautiful, but there was an air of beauty about her, graceful in the way she carried herself. James was used to seeing many beautiful ladies dolled up to the nines, but for her it seemed effortless. There was something else though, something that registered within him, as if he knew her from somewhere. He dismissed it. He assumed that he had seen her at another wedding he had chauffeured for. They both watched her disappear into the church.

Mick, Dick and Jack ambled up to them. Dick's sense of style was interesting, looking more like Dr Who with his eclectic choice of clothing. Dick refused to invest in a new suit because he would only be wearing it on once-in-a-lifetime occasions and couldn't reconcile the necessary consumption of the earth's resources in its making. Mick wore suits daily and accessorised for the occasion with a new shirt, tie and cufflinks. Jack's suit was very flash, as would be expected, but a few years out of date, not cutting the mustard now, but he felt good in it anyway.

"Jess is heading in," Mick piped up. They all walked quickly and planted themselves on a rear pew to their right with barely a minute to spare before Jess and her father entered the church. They both walked down the aisle slowly and deliberately, Mike looking back, his initial apprehension now waning, giving way to relief and allowing him to take in the full beauty of his wife to be.

Everybody was transfixed on the father and bride as they gracefully floated along the aisle, but three quarters of the way down James's eyes were temporarily distracted, caught on the profile of the lady in the blue dress further down in the pews ahead of him.

'On the bride's side,' he thought with a little consternation.

The rest of the service was as expected, a slightly eccentric vicar, a couple of popular hymns that nobody really knew how to sing, and a request from the vicar not to throw rice and confetti in the courtyard which everybody ignored. The new bride and groom left the church and everybody followed soon after.

James hadn't really considered this part, this is when they are greeted outside the church and James wrestled with himself trying to find the words he would need to say. This was awkward, this was his ex-wife after all. It couldn't be just a bland congratulations, he needed to convey his true happiness for her and his approval, as her ex-husband. He was kicking himself, he should have anticipated this moment and found the words well before now. It was too late, he approached her and the words were spontaneous. "Jess, I'm so sorry I stole you away, this should have been yours years ago, please forgive me."

"No James, we stole each other away, there's nothing to forgive, I've found my way and now it's time for you to find yours. We are both guilty, but I don't regret a minute of it."

James was holding up the queue, backing them up into the church. He looked back at the restless people behind him. "I'd better get the car ready."

She smiled and kissed his cheek. "Thank you, James," she whispered as she moved away to let him go. A wave of guilt that had been harbouring inside each of them had now ebbed away and their spirits lifted some more.

James quickly shook Mike's hand. "Well done mate, I hope you know what you're letting yourself in for!" he quipped.

"I think so," Mike replied.

James moved away and stood a little while with Peter until his mother, father and Olly appeared, where upon he went over to them. Olly had accepted his new fate with Mike as his stepdad, he liked him. However, he wished he could spend more time with James, but was acutely aware of James's new work commitments and how the unsocial hours worked against them. James's feelings were mutual and he knew that unless he could cut back his night watchman work to just a few days a week he would have to ditch it completely.

James's mother and father, Giles and Mary, feigned their happiness for Jess and Mike, but inside they were sad. They were old school, the sanctity of marriage was like one of the ten commandments, it was set in stone and, if it wasn't working, then you bloody well made it work. Besides which they liked Jess a lot, she was the perfect daughter-in-law material: pretty, pleasant, respectful and polite. She would be a hard act to follow in their eyes. James knew this and dreaded the moment when he would have to introduce them to the new girl in his life, but for now there wasn't one, so there was no point in worrying.

Unusually for James, on this day he was required to be in front of the camera. Ordinarily he would find some discreet vantage point and people watch, something that always amused him, but not today, today he was in the thick of it, unaware that the lady in the blue dress was watching him intently.

It was back to work momentarily whilst the photographer fired off his last few photographs of them entering James's Bentley to leave for the reception venue—a large hotel set in idyllic open grounds approximately ten miles away.

As James drove them to the reception, an air of awkwardness enveloped them as ex-wife, ex-husband and new husband were unnaturally forced together in the close confines of the car. Jess and Mike's joy and excitement were muted as if not to want to rub James's proverbial nose in it.

In typical British style, James broke the silence. "The weather held out, there were a couple of showers in the morning. I don't think Aunt Edie's hairdo would have stood for it." James and Jess laughed.

Aunt Edie had a tendency to go into meltdown if the slightest thing were out of place. The conversation continued and whatever awkwardness there was before had cleared.

Chapter Seventeen
Wedding Reception

Finally, James could dispense with his official duties, relax and enjoy the rest of the celebrations. He parked up the car and left his jacket and cap on the backseat, loosened his tie and headed back to the guests to claim his glass of champagne and seek out his friends. He spied Dick first, his dress sense standing out like a belisha beacon, and began to move to-wards them, but as he turned to head in their direction he heard his name being called over his left shoulder. He stopped and turned again to be met by the lady in the blue dress, now just a few feet away from him.

"How are you, James?" she asked.

He recognised the voice now and her facial features were unmistakable nearly two decades later. His solar plexus clenched, and he was left breathless for a moment, unable to speak. At last, apart from the sound of his heart pounding in his ears he was able to muster a reply. "Oh my god, Millie, how are you?"

"Talk about déjà vu!"

James looked confused and Millie enlightened him. "Cat got your tongue? Remember."

"God! You remember that?"

"Like it was yesterday, I don't think I've laughed so hard since. I still have the picture of your tea-splattered face and shirt etched in my memory." She put her hand to her mouth and began to giggle at the thought of it.

"You don't know the half of it. I spent the next two days walking around with a bright red face. Everybody thought that I'd sat in the sun too long and then quickly realised it was the middle of winter." As Millie's giggle began to fade it was erupted once more by James's new confession. "Anyway, you kept throwing curve balls at me."

"I don't know whatever do you mean?" The laughter stopped as she eyed him with a mischievous look.

"Do I need to remind you of the time when you launched that offensive against me with regards to my intentions towards Jess."

"Oh, let's see, and where did that end up?" She was teasing him.

"Anyway, I thought that Jess had lost contact with you after uni?"

"Yes, I know. We did, but social media can be a wonderful tool for catching up with old friends."

Whilst James understood this, he himself didn't buy into rekindling old friendships through social media. The train of conversation settled into a rhythm following some staccato awkward silences as they negotiated the conversation around Jess and the breakup of the marriage. Their conversation didn't go unnoticed. He glanced over to his friends, only to see Jack thrusting his right index finger into the hole he had made with his left index finger and thumb. Mick and Dick giving an impressed nod of the head, tipped slightly to one side, similar to the way you might appreciate a fine wine, and Peter gazed on in awe.

There was something about James's life that left Peter wanting. James, it seemed, was riding a rollercoaster right now; at one moment he would be speeding headlong towards the ground only to be swept back up to a pinnacle point of euphoria for a brief moment in time. "At least you know you're alive," he muttered to himself. In comparison,

Peter felt like his life was flat lining, no highs or lows, just continuous mediocrity. Little did he know that James would swap lives with him in a heartbeat.

There was one other interested party—Jess. This was no coincidence, she needed to make amends with karma, she needed to remove the guilt and restore the destiny of fate between two people that she had wrenched apart for her own selfish ends. Only time would tell now, as to whether their destinies were to entwine. Fate needed to complete its job. She had tried once before to contrive in their meeting, but for reasons she will never know it wasn't meant to be. At least here she had control. She wanted them to meet naturally, but was prepared to throw them together if she had to. No need now. Her job was done, from here on in it was up to fate to take over.

Before they knew it, everybody was being summoned into the dining hall. Jess didn't take any chances, she had ensured that although Millie and her plus one were on a different table, it was adjacent to James's and they were to be sat back-to-back no more than three feet apart.

In the meantime, while they were still in the bar, Millie's plus one came and stood next to her. "Here sis, managed to wrestle the last two glasses away." She handed a fresh glass of champagne to Millie.

"Sorry, I'm Vanessa, Millie's little sister." Reaffirming what James had already gathered. There were too many similarities in their appearance to think otherwise.

"James," he replied.

"Aren't you the chauffeur?" she quizzed.

"And a guest on this occasion, it's a bit of a long story and besides risking the chance of boring you to death, we really should be heading into the dining hall. If we don't hurry they will be waiting for us to be seated."

"Well, you really must share your story with us after the meal, James." He sensed she was bored with the events of the day, which essentially revolved around wasting time waiting for things to happen and hankered after some conversation to make the evening pass a little quicker; here out of duty to her sister. She was attractive, but lacked Millie's grace and beauty. While he would be happy to converse with her, for Millie's sake, he actually only wanted to spend time with Millie.

There was so much they needed to talk about, so much to catch up on. To do this he would need to unleash his secret weapon, the only weapon he could draw up from his arsenal—Jack . . . Good old uncouth Jack.

It didn't take long, as soon as they sat down Jack was leaning across to James. "Tibbsy, you lucky fucking dog, how the hell do you do it? Her mate's not bad. What are my chances?"

James thought about a thousand to one on a good day. "Her sister, you mean? Yes, of course mate, we'll scope them out later once the formalities are over. When the entertainment starts would be a good time."

"That figures. Can't wait." Jack was acting like a little boy that had been handed a big bag of sweets. The others looked on astonished.

Peter turned to James. "You got some kind of death wish or something?" He offered the words secretly in a low barely audible voice, his mouth hidden by his napkin.

"I know it's risky, but I need to get Millie away from her sister, she's stuck to her side like glue, and well Jack . . ."

"Shit, yes of course, he's the only distraction you've got."

"We just need to hold out until the disco gets started," replied James.

"If I can I'll act as Jack's wingman to round off some of his rough edges." Peter sensed that James was back on that rollercoaster and was bracing himself ready for the next plunge.

A chinking of a glass caught everybody's attention and, as tradition demands, Philip rose from his chair to give his speech. As James expected it was flawless, switching between humorous anecdote to grave seriousness, balanced and careful not to offend, ending on a funny note. He referred to Jess as a metaphorical relay baton, how they were proud and glad to hand the baton on to James's safe hands in the first instance, trusting that he would employ the utmost care in carrying the baton and fearing that he may drop it before the finishing line has now happily passed it on to Mike to finish the race. He gushed about James's bravery and grace in the manner that it was done and how sure they were that Mike would continue to treasure their precious gift.

Donald rose next and was nowhere near as composed as Philip, but he executed his task as best he could. Granted, he had the support of some of his and Mike's friends, kindred spirits, but his speech was a little uninspiring compared to Philip's.

Mike gave a well-rehearsed speech, thanking those closest to him and presenting flowers to the bridesmaids as tradition requires and, of course, spoke lovingly about his beautiful wife, but none of that mattered as he explained that he would have still married her even if she walked down the aisle wearing a bin liner.

Finally, the food was served and everybody tucked in. James was distracted, almost irritable. On a few occasions in his life he had looked back at his first meeting with Millie and knew there was something different, a deeper connection. Yes, she was beautiful in physical form, but if all that were stripped away it would expose the essence of a beautiful soul, too.

Here she was, just a few feet away, and he was helpless. He turned several times to catch her in conversation with others at her table. He loved the way she moved, gracefully attentive to all in her company, oblivious to James's admiring gaze. James couldn't wait for the meal to end. His chair was like a prison cell. He was locked into it until the formalities were complete.

Peter leaned into James. "You ok, mate? Unlike you to be so quiet." Peter looked over at Jess at the head table and presumed that this moment of closure between her and James was finally sinking in. He kicked himself for asking such a dumb question. "Sorry mate, look, you know if you ever need to get anything off your chest Kate and I are always there for you, our door's always open."

"No, it's fine, I guess I'm just over-analysing stuff. Oh, by the way, I didn't get to say how beautiful Kate looks today."

"Yes, she does, I'm a very lucky man."

'You certainly are,' James thought to himself. Not because of her physical beauty, but because of her inner beauty, they complimented each other so well. Finally, the meal was over and the guests were asked to leave the room while it was prepared for the disco and evening entertainment.

As James rose from his chair and pushed it back, it clashed with Millie's as she stood at the same time. They both apologised to each other in unison, laughing as they used the exact same words at the exact same time. There it was, the smile behind her deep blue eyes, he was transfixed for a moment, taken back to that very first meeting at the Halls all those years ago.

Then they were wrenched apart again, Millie's sister ordering her to accompany her to the ladies room and Philip barking over to James. "James, sorry, with everything going on I forgot to invite you up to our table."

"Not a problem, this is your family day, not mine, but thank you for the thought, it means a lot to me."

"He's got a hard act to follow, my boy."

"Trust me, I've seen them together, they are made for each other. You have nothing to worry about. Sorry, I must go as I promised Kate and Peter a ride in the car."

"Yes of course, off you go my boy, fine looking car by the way."

James turned and left. He had lied about Kate and Peter having a ride in the car, but he couldn't allow Millie to slip from his grasp again.

James headed over to the bar where he knew the lads would be. The timing was impeccable, as he approached the door to the bar Millie and Vanessa arrived from the other direction. "We really should stop meeting like this," Millie said in jest.

"I know, it's uncanny. Let me get you both a drink." He opened the door to the bar and gestured for them to pass through. The lads were at the bar as expected. "Here he is, got you some of that shit lager you like," Jack shouted.

Mick piped up. "Are you going to introduce us to your new acquaintances, Tibbsy?"

"Ok, give us a chance, this is Millie and her sister, Vanessa, and this lot of rabble and retrogrades are Jack, Peter, Mick and Dick." Each one lifted a hand or smiled and nodded as their name was called.

"Now then, what can I get you girls to drink?" James asked. Vanessa ordered Vodka and Red Bull and the lads cheered in an impressed manner.

"Now we're talking," Jack said, "get us one in as a chaser mate."

"Ok, calm your horses a minute I'm sorting the ladies first. What would you like Millie?"

She was slightly embarrassed. "Cinzano and lemonade, please."

There was no cheer this time, just quizzical glances from the lads with the odd giggle. "How old are you? That's a drink my mother would order," Mick cut in.

"I know, but I like it, what can I say?"

James was impressed she was unwavered by their remarks. "A Cinzano and lemonade it is," James acknowledged.

No sooner had James handed Vanessa her drink, she downed it in one. Another cheer from the lads and Jack leapt straight in. "Let me get you another."

"She's a live wire," James leant in and whispered to Millie.

"Tell me about it, I'll be playing mother later," she whispered back.

Music started to pulse through from beyond the bar room doors.

"Disco's started, shall we go through," Dick announced. Jack gave a freshly filled glass to Vanessa. This is where Jack would come into his own. Only a few people knew his little secret. Jack was a trained dancer, competing in ballroom up until the age of sixteen, winning many competitions, but he couldn't find it within himself to resolve his inner conflict wishing to be seen as a man's man and having to mince and ponce around on the dance floor. It gained him the nickname of Cinderella at school. Taunts of "going to the ball this weekend Cinders" were commonplace.

Anybody with stronger resolve would have ignored it, but Jack just couldn't, his ego was too fragile. There is one thing that is certain, he was a prodigy. His parents and trainer were beside themselves when he announced he no longer wished to dance, but to no avail, his mind was made up.

Tonight, it would be time to unleash his dormant talent, and what better way than with the Bee Gee's song, 'You Should be Dancing'. Jack pulled Vanessa onto the dancefloor next to two other ladies that were already up and dancing. Suddenly time evaporated and he was once more that teenage lad strutting his stuff. Vanessa had also clearly had some dance training and, to all intents and purposes, they looked like professional dancers hired as entertainment for the evening. A circle of onlookers formed around them. They were actually unaware of the awe and admiration that surrounded them as they focused on synchronising their unrehearsed dance moves. They both came off breathless, and the onlooking crowd engulfed the dancefloor immediately behind them. Peter and James had no need to fret. Vanessa was loving the attention from her caveman who dragged her away to the bar for refuelling.

Millie turned to James. "I don't know about you, but I could do with some air after watching that."

James agreed and they stepped out into the now freshening air as twilight began to take hold. Millie wrapped her arms around herself. James watched her shudder a little as she tried to ward off the chill of the evening. "My car's just over there and my jacket's in it, if you would like."

"Please, it's cooler than I expected." James opened the rear door and she stepped in. "Can we sit here for a minute, whilst I warm up?" She picked up his jacket and cap and shuffled over to let James in. She slipped on his jacket and couldn't resist putting on his cap.

'What is it about that damned cap?' James pondered to himself, releasing the merest hint of a smirk as he recalled past events. He watched on as Millie craned to catch a glimpse of herself in the rear-view mirror, his smirk turning to a full-blown smile. "Yes, you do look lovely and cute," James said, affirming her thoughts.

She sat herself back down, their bodies touching side by side. This was the closest they'd ever been together. There was a frisson between them now, an air of excitement and anticipation. She turned to James and he to face her. "Not as lovely as you looked in it earlier today," she said whimsically, their eyes locked onto each other and triggered some kind of vortex that drew them closer and they kissed. For a short while the physical world around them disappeared as their souls locked together and transferred to an alternate dimension.

A scream in the car park nearby summoned enough external stimulus to break their passionate clinch. They watched on voyeuristically as a man chased a girl across the car park with a balloon full of water. A few of their friends gathered around, unable to contain themselves for the inevitable outcome. They ended up circling around one car. The man threw the balloon, but his aim was poor and it hit the windscreen, not bursting but bouncing off right towards the girl who caught it, however her immaculately manicured nails were too much for the taught skin of the balloon and it gave way, showering her with water.

A cheer ensued. "Oh my goodness, that poor girl. Her dress is ruined." As if Millie's pleas of unjustness had been heard, three burly lads grabbed the man and dragged him over to the hotel fountain, which adorned the central courtyard and tumbled him into it, immediately followed by another cheer.

As the crowd drifted back to the hotel and the entertainment over, Millie broke the silence in the car. "Come on, I still need to take in some fresh air." Millie squeezed past James, opened the door, grabbed his hand and pulled him out.

James wanted to stay in the car, cocooned away from the rest of the world for a little while, but was happy to leave the car as long as he didn't have to share her with anybody else.

As they strolled, holding hands, Millie quizzed James about how difficult it must have been to see his lifelong partner led away in the arms of another man. James put her straight. He had never felt more alive than right now. It was as if order had been restored in his life. His life before that was out of order.

She loved the analogy.

James didn't care to talk about himself. He was only interested in Millie's life journey. "What about you, Millie? Ever married, or any men in the closet I should be worried about? I don't know anything about you!"

"It's complicated. I'm not snow white, of course, there have been men in my life, but none of them last more than a few months. Maybe I'm too demanding. I don't know."

"Pish, I'd put my life on the line if someone really mattered to me, I don't get it." James was confused.

"Think about it, James, what do you really know about me? We met over twenty years ago, and here we are now having spent barely two hours together."

"Yes, but didn't you ever look back at that time and wonder what if?" That brief encounter had haunted James. He knew it was a pivotal moment in his life.

Millie's answer, right now, was far more important to him than anything. "Yes James, I've always thought back to that evening. My heart did sink a little when Jess snatched you away from me, but she was hurting with a broken heart and you were the cure, you were the antidote she needed."

James loved her more than ever now. The fact that she was willing to make such an altruistic sacrifice for her friend impressed him immensely. "But weren't you seeing somebody anyway . . . Gerald, wasn't it?"

"I don't think I ever saw him again. He kept making up pathetic excuses not to see me and the whole thing just petered out. I don't think we actually broke off the relationship, it just never progressed anywhere."

The unmistakable start of the 'Macarena' echoed out into the car park. "I love this, come on James."

He followed her into the dance and stood on the side, watching on as she joined the line of bridesmaids dutifully carrying out the set moves the dance required. As the night drew to an end, the tempo changed for the slow dance and James approached his now slightly breathless companion, where she slumped herself into him, nestling her head into his upper chest as they gently swayed to the music.

James didn't want to let go. A bump from behind briefly caught his attention as Jack also cossetted his prize. James was pleased for Jack and surprised that he hadn't done or said something stupid to scare her away. If she could spend just a little more time with him she would find out that there was actually a kind and sensitive person hidden inside the protective social armour he had clad himself with.

The music stopped but James and Millie clung onto each other. The lights came on as if to reaffirm that the celebrations were now at an end. They walked arm-in-arm to stand in the crisp air once more, but their time together was brought to an abrupt end.

Vanessa charged over. "Come on Millie, our taxi's here." She grabbed Millie's hand and began to lead her away. They were sharing with a couple of other people already sat patiently waiting inside, the windows misting up. Vanessa dragged her into the car, James following helplessly behind.

A sudden realisation came to him. He knocked on the glass to catch her attention. "Your number!" he shouted, making a telephone sign with his hand against his ear. She wrote it in the condensation in the glass. James had no pen and paper with him, after all, why should he? He grabbed his phone and took a photograph as the car began to move away.

"James, come on, the minibus is here." Peter's voice became louder as he approached his friend. "Come on James, he won't wait any longer." His voice was calm and collected now. James turned and followed Peter as he led him away.

As they sat in the minibus, James scrutinised his phone for the picture, thankfully he could see the number clearly enhanced by the flash of his camera, albeit in reverse, but then was lost for a moment looking at the beautiful girl behind the window.

Peter leaned in "Jesus, you've got it bad mate."

"I know, but I don't think it's just me." He gestured towards Jack who sat quietly staring out of his window. James was right, Jack would normally be drumming up some kind of gross rugby song or bragging about his exploits earlier in the evening, but not on this occasion, instead he just sat quietly and reflective, almost dumb struck.

Chapter Eighteen
Home

Sunday 17th April 2016

James awoke at 12.30 in the afternoon, a time he had become accustomed to. He felt fresh as he had hardly drunk anything the night before and could quite possibly have driven him-self home, but no point in taking risks, not in this day and age. He reached out for his phone on the bedside table.

There was a message from Peter:

I've got my car back let me know if you need a lift to pick up yours.

Great thanks, in an hour, ok? James texted back.

He received a message back in what seemed like a nano-second later:

Ok see you soon.

He pulled up the camera on his phone and stared at the photograph he had taken the night before. He smiled to himself as he took in the beauty of the girl behind the misted window. It spurred him on to get up, find a pen and paper, and decipher the reversed telephone number.

He was peckish and had enough time to rustle up some beans on toast before Peter was due to arrive. He thumbed in Millie's number and searched within himself for the words he wanted to say. He decided to text rather than call.

In the cold light of day, she may have decided that last night should remain as just that. A text would test the water and a positive response would give the green light. He tapped in a text.

Great night last night, thanks for the company, James.

He kept the text low key so as not to sound too pushy or needy. He did it more to ensure that Millie would have his number as much as any other reason. Once sent, he saved her in his phone as Millie.

Peter's face appeared at the window. He knocked and waved to catch James's attention. James made his way to the front door to let him in, picking up his post that still lay on his doormat from the day before as he opened the door.

"Got time for a cup of tea first mate?" he asked.

"Yeah sure," Peter replied. James popped the kettle on and opened his post. Mainly bills, but James was only interested in the one franked by his solicitor. He read it through carefully, ignoring Peter for a moment, almost forgetting he was there.

"Everything ok, Tibbs?" Peter enquired.

"Oh yeah, sure, the contracts have now been exchanged and we complete a week on Friday."

"That's fantastic news. Do you need me to take the day off?"

"Any help would be gratefully appreciated."

"Of course, no problem mate. Things have been quiet at work so they won't miss me for the day I shouldn't think."

James felt a little guilty, Peter seemed to be giving so much of himself lately, yet he had done nothing in return. He determined that he needed to make a gesture.

Peter dropped James off behind his car and duly shot off. "Got to go, I promised to take Kate shopping."

"No worries, cheers mate, see you later," James responded.

Once back at home he booked two theatre tickets for Pete and Kate, and decided that he would be their chauffeur for the evening too. He texted Peter to make sure they were both free for that evening, feigning that he wanted to invite them round to his new house to cook for them.

His phone pinged; it was the message he had been waiting for from Millie.

Sorry, only just picked up your message, I didn't hear it come through in my bag. I'm at a Polo match, what are you up to?

James texted: Just got my car back and heard from my Solicitor that I get the keys to my new house in a week on Friday.

That's so exciting!

Yeah, fantastic news, although it needs a shed load of work doing to it.

The phone began to ring, and it was Millie. "Hi James, it's Millie. Seemed silly to keep texting. Please let me come and help on Friday."

"I'll take any help I can get right now, but it will involve handling some heavy stuff."

"Come James, don't get all male chauvinist pig on me."

"Shit, I didn't mean for it to come across that way."

"I'll be home later this evening, give me a call then and you can let me know where I need to be. I've got to go now as my mother is calling me over, speak later . . . bye."

The ice between James and Millie had been truly broken and melted away and they conversed regularly up until Friday, which they both looked forward to with anticipation. For James, it wasn't getting the keys to his new house that he was getting excited about. It was to get to see Millie again.

Friday 29th April 2016
James returned to his rented abode in the early hours of the morning for one last time. He wouldn't get any shut eye that morning. He threw the McDonald's breakfast he had picked up on the way back onto the kitchen work top next to a box full of kitchen utensils he had already packed the night before. He found a kitchen stool from the lounge, placed himself on it and calmly consumed the energy he would need to see him through the day.

There were just a few more items to box up, strip the bed, and carry out a final clean ready for inspection by the agent to ensure the return of his deposit. He was told to expect to pick up his keys to his new home by 10.30am, but expected that it wouldn't be until after twelve pm. He didn't know whether it was true or not, but somebody had once told him that if the solicitors could hold onto the funds until midday they could ensure an extra day's interest into their accounts.

At nine am Peter turned up and parked the hired Luton box van outside. James watched him stride down the path leading to his door with a hint of a swagger in his step. Peter had never driven a vehicle this big before, it was a kind of low order bucket list thing for him, the only thing that was missing was a Yorkie bar. "Which boxes are we shifting first mate?" Peter was keen to get to work.

James was not so enthusiastic. "Steady on mate, the kettle has just boiled and I need to use up my last two tea bags."

"Are you sure?"

"Yep, we've got plenty of time. We've only got my stuff to pack, hardly anything there. It's all boxed ready. Anyway, what's new with you?" James enquired as he poured out two cups of tea.

"Apparently Jack's off to Vanessa's this weekend. To look at them you would think they were chalk and cheese, but there's definitely something more there between them."

"Good for him, I'm rooting for him," James replied.

"What about you and her sister . . . Millie, isn't it?"

"Yep, hopefully you will see her later as she wants to help with the move."

"Wow, that's commitment for you."

"I know its early doors yet, but something feels right about this."

"I hope so. In the meantime, these boxes need to get shifted." Peter sprang from his chair, tea still only half drunk, he couldn't contain himself any longer and started to sift through the boxes. "Come on James, which ones do you want loaded first?"

James lifted his half full cup of tea, sipping at it whilst he searched through the boxes that filled his lounge. As James suspected, by eleven am the van was loaded, ready to go, leaving the house feeling eerily empty. All that remained now was the final spruce up of the place before the agent arrived for the inspection. It was passable as it was, but they had time on their hands so gave it a last little tickle.

"You going to give the solicitor's a call?" Peter enquired.

"They'll ring when they're ready," was James's response.

"Are you kidding mate? You have got to push them, you know what they're like."

James thought this was worse than being married, but also knew that he did have a point. He gave them a call only to find out that there was an issue. They rang back to advise him that a signature was required on a piece of documentation. From this moment on it would be a waiting game.

The phone rang again and it was Millie this time enquiring as to whether she should go to his old or new address? She arrived about half an hour later, drawing up in a metallic red Mazda MX5, top down, enjoying some of the late summer sun.

James went out to meet her with Peter a few steps behind, both impressed with her choice of transport. She immediately apologised for having such an impractical car. James apologised himself for the fact that at the moment there was nothing to do but wait and suggested that they make their way to The Bakers Arms and sit it out there and maybe get a lunchtime snack.

By 2.30 pm doubts started to creep in as to whether or not this move was actually going to happen. Peter had already disappeared to the toilet to ring Kate and make sure the spare room was made up ready, just in case. There was no need, James finally received a call to confirm all was completed and the keys were ready to be collected. Peter and Millie went on ahead and waited whilst James went to fetch the keys from the estate agent.

"He shouldn't be too long, the solicitor's no more than ten minutes from here." Peter offered the statement as small talk as they took in the sight of the shabby property made to look worse by the over grown garden that clearly hadn't been tended to through the summer months. Peter wanted to quiz her over her intentions towards James, but checked himself. Peter and Kate were becoming almost parental over James, and Peter was having to make a conscious effort not to pry.

Millie viewed the property with a critical eye. "James certainly has taken on a project with this one." She was unwavered by the sight of it, unlike many women Peter knew, including his wife Kate who liked everything to be perfect.

In a short while James returned with the keys. Unpacking wouldn't be the relaxed affair that time had afforded him earlier. At last they were inside the new house.

"Got your work cut out here then, Tibbs!" Peter offered in a matter-of-fact kind of way. They spent a few minutes walking around the place, taking in its potential as much as any-thing else. Peter piped up again, "Come on, those boxes aren't going to get unloaded themselves." It shook them out of their trance-like state, and no sooner was the first box brought in and Millie was opening it and unpacking, kitchen equipment first.

By 5.30 pm the van was unloaded, but despite Millie's best efforts, there were several boxes that still needed to be unpacked. Peter and James got the van back in the nick of time, saving James from any potential fines for late return. James then ran Peter back home afterwards.

"Look Tibbs, I don't mind, I'll come back and help unpack, Kate will even come and pick me up."

"No, you've been a great help, but it's Friday evening and I know how much you two cherish your Friday evenings together."

He was right, their Friday nights were a kind of ritual for them and James wasn't about to break it. "We'll be round tomorrow anyway as Kate is dying to see the place."

"Ok, look forward to seeing you both tomorrow, hopefully it will be in less disarray."

Millie was still hard at it by the time James had returned. In his eyes right then and there she was an angel. He took the liberty on his way back to grab some fish and chips. "Come on Millie, have a break. Look, I know it's not the Ritz, but I took the liberty of grabbing some grub on the way back, I hope you like fish and chips. "

"Right now, I can't think of anything better. I'll get the kettle on for a cuppa as well," Millie's voice echoed back from the kitchen.

They settled down on the sofa with the coffee table nearby where Millie put two cups of tea and a bottle of ketchup. They both tucked in ravenously and their hunger was quickly sated. Fatigue had set in with James and the heavy toll of food on his stomach colluded to drag him into a slumber. After all, he hadn't had a wink of sleep in over twenty-four hours.

Millie watched on in amusement at James' nodding head. She watched his eyes drop and the mug of tea start to slip from his hand. She quickly grabbed it. James's eyes flickered open for a moment and then he was gone to the land of nod. She cleared up, washed up and carried on for a little while longer, but it was becoming increasingly difficult to place things without James's attention and tiredness was catching up with her as well.

She found some bedding and made up the mattress which, at this time, was laid directly on the floor, the bed frame still in bits taped together, leaning against the wall. She laid James down on the sofa, lifting his legs curled up to meet his chest, resembling a sleeping baby, then she took herself off to bed.

James woke in the early hours, a little confused, and with a crick in his neck. It was like those times when you drift off to sleep on the sofa after a heavy night drinking, but not a jot of alcohol had passed his lips on this night. He mustered up the energy to make it upstairs to the bedroom. By the moonlight, he could make out the outline of the mattress on the floor. He threw back the duvet off his bed only to reveal the top half of Millie's naked back.

She awoke with a start. "Shit, sorry, I didn't realise." He apologised and quickly pulled the duvet back to recover her. He went to turn to retreat away.

Millie quickly reached out and grabbed his hand. He stopped and turned again. Millie looked him in the eye. "Its ok." She threw the duvet back for him to get in alongside her.

"Are you sure you're ok with this?"

She didn't respond with words, instead, she grabbed his hand and pulled him down to her then she kissed him softly on the lips.

James responded more ardently and passionately embraced her, her naked breasts pushing against him only separated by his thin cotton t-shirt. She began to lift it up and he completed the task by lifting it over his head. Their torsos now skin-on-skin and kissing each other passionately once more, her erect nipples pressing into his chest, exciting Millie equally as much as it did James.

James's firm cock was begging to be released from its prison. Once more Millie initiated events, unbuttoning James's waistband, allowing him to push down his jeans. Millie's soft warm hand slid past the elastic waistband of his briefs and lifted it away and down to release his throbbing member from its prison. She gently cupped it in her hand and began caressing it.

James's hand reached down, his palm gently gliding up her firm but soft and silky inner thigh, meeting her lacy knickers which were wet as he buried his hand into her crotch. He pulled her knickers down and she assisted by arching her back slightly.

She rolled over on top of James and straddled him. She grasped him, guiding the tip of his penis on to her wet hard clitoris. She moaned lightly as she teased herself, finally allowing James to slowly push through into paradise. She gyrated her hips back and forth, seeking out pure pleasure with every movement until she squealed once more and froze into a statue of ecstasy.

The vision before James was so intoxicating that he needed no other physical stimulation. He reached the edge and he wanted to stay there, but his body wouldn't let him and he erupted inside her, one intense wave after another.

Fate had restored its true order as it should have done over two decades earlier. This time Millie and James were to awake as a couple. James woke up to the smell of frying sausages and bacon. He negotiated his way around a few unpacked boxes to the kitchen, only to find Millie standing in front of the cooker wearing one of his t-shirts meeting the top of her thighs and barely covering her bottom. She was completing the final touches ready to serve up two plates of a full English breakfast. "Oh, hello sleepy head, I was going to bring these up, but seeing as you're here, let's eat in the living room."

As he approached Millie, he noticed a frosted pack of Mars bars on the worktop counter. Millie watched on amused at the way he was distracted by it.

"You must have been really tired last night. Those fell out of the freezer when I took out the hash browns."

James picked them up and put them back in the freezer and Millie looked on with a confused expression on her face.

"You can't tell me you've never sampled the delights of a frozen Mars bar."

"You are kidding aren't you? I don't relish the thought of a visit to the dentist with a broken tooth either."

"That's just it, Millie. How long does it take to eat a Mars bar at normal temperature? About a minute tops, right? Well, times that by ten. Why not actually savour every bite from the initial bit of chocolate you can nibble from the sides to the chunk of ice berg you can manage to snap off if you dare."

Millie watched him doubtfully and wondered what other eccentricities he might be harbouring. Then she checked herself. Who's to say that she didn't have any unusual habits that to her are a normal routine of her daily life?

The sun was high in the sky, as it was actually late morning. Millie had already opened the backdoor to clear the smells and to let the morning sunshine into the house. James's eyes were still dry and gritty from the exhaustion of the day before.

"I'll tell you what, I'll get a couple of chairs and we can sit outside and enjoy this in the sun." He found two chairs and one of the bigger boxes which he set up as a table where they enjoyed each other's company while eating their first breakfast together in the warming sun.

Chapter Nineteen
Family

Sunday 5th June 2016

Over the weeks that followed Millie became indispensable—she wasn't aware of it herself, but interior design came naturally to her. She took the lead as they shopped for paint and wallpaper alike. She established his budget for the major upgrades that were needed to the bathroom and kitchen, and negotiated avidly on his behalf. Even details such as lighting, fixtures and fittings would not escape her.

James loved her a little bit more everyday as he watched his tired unloved house blossom into a beautiful, stylish new home. For Millie, this was effortless. She loved seeing the awe and astonishment on his face as each little phase came to an end.

Giles and Mary couldn't keep away from James's little project either and accepted Millie into their lives as eagerly as they had Jess. They saw something more in James this time. He seemed more relaxed. He wasn't having to try in this relationship, it seemed to move along naturally. Somehow with Jess it had been as if there was a tooth missing in a precision clock movement, where every now and again it would need to be corrected to keep the right time. Rolex or Cartier couldn't have done a better job this time. However, parents being parents, they still harboured a worry about their son. Sometimes things can be too perfect.

On the other hand, apart from meeting Millie's sister at Jess's wedding, James hadn't met anyone else from her family. He had enquired with her a few times, but she was adept at avoiding such matters and changing the subject.

Millie finally relented—her brother had invited her over for afternoon tea. They were close to each other and confided in each other often. Vanessa, on the other hand, was the wild card of the family—she did as she pleased, when she pleased. Millie drove them out into the Oxfordshire countryside, entering the gates into a large old Georgian style house set in a few acres of land.

James wondered what other secrets she had been hiding from him. He suspected that she had a wealthy upbringing; after all, she had a penchant for the finer things in life. He had noticed some designer labels in her clothes and more than one Louis Vuitton handbag, but this was more, it eluded to nobility.

Things started to make sense.

He presumed she was ashamed to introduce a mere commoner into the inner workings of high society. The reality was quite the opposite, she was actually ashamed of the arrogant elitism that had been bread into them generation upon generation. Her brother had found some middle ground. Millie ignored it as much as possible and Vanessa simply rebelled against it. Until she needs bailing out of a bad debt or a bad situation, in which case she would come running back to Mummy and Daddy.

As they drove up to the house the slight apprehension she contained within turned into uncontained anger. They pulled up behind a new Aston Martin Vantage. "Stay here," she ordered. Apart from being a little shocked by the outburst, he did as he was told. She marched up the steps, but, before she got to the door, it opened, and a man stood in the doorway. James assumed him to be her brother. They had an intense conversation rather than a full-blown argument.

James wasn't close enough to pick up the whole conversation, but he heard the odd snippet here and there, including, "What the hell are they doing here?"

"Honestly sis, they literally just turned up out of the blue." The first couple of lines more vocal than the rest of the conversation: "Not ready . . ." and "there is no right time . . ."

She came back down to the car, thrust the keys into the ignition, and started the engine. "Whoa, what's going on?" James questioned.

"My mother and father are here. They just turned up apparently. My arse they did!" She was fuming.

"Hold on a minute Millie, look, we've come all this way and you can't avoid this moment forever. It might as well be now."

"You don't understand, she'll drive you away, as she has done with every other man I've introduced. She's got some out-dated attitude that aristocratic blood can't be diluted with common blood. Unless you are a Lord or a French Barron, you simply won't do."

"This is different, I don't care Millie, I promise you I won't let go. Look at me—I PROMISE YOU."

She had heard it all before, no one in the past had ever stayed around for more than a couple of months after meeting her mother. She turned the ignition off and pulled the keys. "I'm going to regret this." She sat staring at the windscreen, hesitating for a moment, and got back out of the car.

James took this as his prompt to get out as well. The front door was on the latch and she entered freely, followed by James. They walked through to the kitchen which was empty. "I'll just go and see if they're outside," she offered and disappeared through another door from the kitchen.

"Now my dear Missy, where's this young man you've been hiding from me?" Her mother finished the sentence just as they entered the room.

James recognised the voice, but for a split second he couldn't place it. As his brain rewound time, searching for the memory bank that would complete the puzzle, the instinctive side of his brain was already foretelling him that this wasn't going to be a welcome moment. Just as the door swung open it came to him and he was taken back to his journey in the wedding car en route to Commerton Hall. He now had a vision of the thread of conversation of Lady Rossford whilst she was on the phone and it rang out in his ears once more. 'Really Missy, I'm fine . . .'

"Shit." His angst, uncontained, vocalised itself involuntarily at the consternation that unfolded before him. Millie's mother's face contorted with a little shock which could have been mistaken for the expletive that James had just used. James knew that she had recognised him from her own kitchen, and again the irony was lost on them both. James pretended to sneeze, trying to make it sound like the initial faux pas to disguise it. "Sorry, hayfever," James offered as an explanation.

"A little late in the season, Old Boy." Millie's Father was just a couple of steps behind.

"I've always had it, I get it around harvest time I'm afraid."

"More likely an allergy to dust, dear chap, you have my sympathies all the same, it can dog your life if you let it."

Millie's brother appeared. "We're about to have strawberries and cream on the terrace, care to join us?" His voice was instantly recognisable as the voice on the phone that booked his wedding car a few months earlier. It was offered as an invitation, but there were no other options.

"Sorry, how rude of us, Millie you must introduce us to your friend here," Millie's father requested reproachfully.

"Yes of course, sorry, this is my brother Johnathan and as you must have guessed my mother and father, Veronica and George, oh and Johnathan's wife, Stephanie." Who had also just appeared at the door. By this time, a Yorkshire terrier was now reacquainting itself with James's shoes. "Oh, how silly of me, and last but not least, this is—"

"Princess," James blurted the name out. He had momentarily forgotten himself.

"How strange, how on earth could you have known my little pooches name?" Stephanie quizzed.

"Pure coincidence I'm afraid, it's just a term of endearment," James responded.

They had digressed a little and Johnathan brought them back to the matter at hand. "Now then, what about these strawberries and cream, they won't eat themselves?"

"Strawberries, I'm sure the ladies would love some cream with theirs, what say you, Veronica?" James had relaxed by now and was feeling a little cheeky. He couldn't help himself.

The conversation that continued over strawberries and cream was highbrow: current affairs, world markets and the inner workings of the government. James was lost, he watched on intently as George and Johnathan rallied their conversation, but inside he was wishing that the earth would open and swallow him up.

Of all people, Lady Veronica threw him a lifeline. "Come now James, will you walk with me in the gardens? If you are going to be friends with my daughter, we really must become better acquainted."

He was, in fact, trapped now; the black widow had spun her web and he had one foot stuck in it. He had little choice but to allow her to scurry away with him. Millie offered to walk with them, her intent to protect the unsuspecting fly caught in her mother's web. Lady Veronica dismissed her, not wishing to disturb her from the strawberries she had yet to finish. James quickly realised that it wasn't a lifeline which she had offered, it was the toll of a death knell for his relationship with Millie.

As they walked away she feigned interest in the flora and fauna that surrounded them, but as soon as they were out of earshot she cut to the chase. "You know this can't last, don't you, dear boy?"

"We love each other and as the old saying goes, love conquers all."

"How do I put this politely? You are not from the right stock and you won't survive in the world she lives in."

"And you seriously believe she is happy in your world? She's a free spirit, she needs to be allowed to live the life that she chooses, not the one you think you have cut out for her."

They contested each other, calmly and fiercely for a little while longer, neither side prepared to yield. Then the bombshell hit. "Oh, this is ridiculous, how much do you need?"

"What the hell are you talking about?"

"Well, everybody has a price, don't they?"

"You can't buy me off, Lady Veronica."

"Oh, you don't understand, I have connections. £25,000 will pay for a nice clean contract killing. I'll give you £30,000 to remove yourself from my daughter's life within the next eight weeks, otherwise I'll be paying somebody else to do it for me?"

"Let me get this right, you're threatening to kill me if I don't leave your daughter?"

"Oh, my dear boy, it's not just a threat, it's an absolute certainty."

"Aren't you forgetting your rather un-lady like behaviour from a few months ago? What's stopping me going to the press, or even telling Lord Rossford himself?"

"Your naivety is beyond reproach. Where's your evidence? Anyhow, if you destroy Lord Rossford you will destroy your relationship with Millie, they dote on each other you know, and then of course I would have to destroy you anyway. Besides, he knows I have carnal desires that he can no longer fulfil. As long as we are both discreet, there is no harm done." As all good spiders do they store up their prey ready for consumption later. No sooner had they returned to the party than Millie made their excuses to leave and Lady Veronica intimated to her that she liked James, ensuring that when the moment came for the relationship to end it couldn't be traced back to her.

The mood of each of them in the car on the way back contrasted. Millie's was more up-beat with all of her other conquests her mother had been overtly aggressive, but on this occasion she seemed to warm to James. In Millie's eyes, it was a promising start.

James's mood on the other hand was more reflective. The only thing that mattered to him in the world right now was Millie, and unless he could muster some kind of ingenious inspiration, he was going to lose her, whether he liked it or not. For the time being, whatever was to be the case, he wanted to cherish every moment that he had with her and he found it hard to do that whilst plotting against her mother. He resumed his attention back to Millie and asked a question to distract his mind, "Why does she call you Missy?"

"I don't know for sure, obviously my full name is Millicent so I guess Lissy was an option too. Maybe she couldn't decide and ended up with Missy. It can come across as a little patronising sometimes, in the way she uses it."

"What about your Father, then?"

"Oh, I'm his little Millie all day long."

He had Millie's company for that night and most of Sunday, but by Sunday evening she had to head home in readiness for work the next day.

Once she had gone, he settled down to hatch a plan. The only weakness that he already knew about Lady Rossford was that she was a little sexually promiscuous and may have a food fetish or some kind of need for escapism, to serve someone rather than be served upon. He had managed to glean other useful bits of information during his various conversations with Millie. Her mother and father were socialites attending numerous high-end parties and gatherings, out of diplomatic duty as much as enjoyment. Her mother found most events utterly boring, but she honoured her duty without complaint, other than to those closest to her.

Wednesday 8th June 2016

Lady Veronica's bombshell had consumed every waking moment of James's time, he looked forward to a moment of distraction with his friends at the quiz night. James was at a loss as to how he could even consider the prospect of getting back at Veronica from his diminutive position in comparison to her high self-preserved class. He entered The Bakers Arms glad of some distraction. Jack was at the bar. "Come on Tibs, what you having? I'm getting the rounds in tonight."

"Gees, you feeling alright, Jack?" Jack was renowned for timing his entry into the pub just after a round had already been bought. It was an in-joke with the rest of them and happened too frequently to be but a mere coincidence.

"Yeah of course, I've come into some money, that's all."

"Oh, where's that come from mate, a long lost Aunt died or something?"

"Never you mind, I've got it and I'm going to spend some of it." He was tipsy and a little melancholy at the same time. James took his pint of cold fresh crisp lager over to the table and dragged Jack along with him.

As they sat at the table, James couldn't help noticing that Mike was bristling with pride, the kind of way you act when you have a grand announcement to make. James wondered if he was about to announce that Jess was pregnant, as ridiculous as it seemed, but he asked anyway. "Don't tell me Jess is pregnant?"

"No, I've been appointed as the Musical Director for what is probably the grandest event of the year, or perhaps even the decade."

"Come on then, enlighten us." Mick was keen on allowing Mike to get his Andy Warhol moment out of the way to continue with the rest of the evening.

"It's for the Queen, they're having a Royal Gala to celebrate the Queen's 90th birthday, but it's not only that, I've managed to bag myself and Jess, of course, a seat at one of the tables for the meal beforehand. What a result? I can't believe it."

"Sounds fucking boring to me mate." The usual kind of response from Jack. Anything that was from outside his remit of comprehension was as he said it 'fucking boring to him', he rarely had the courtesy not to share his thoughts, especially as he was now half cut. Mike had seen him in action on the side lines at many a football match by now, and accepted the comment with a pinch of salt, as did the others that sat at the table.

"Do you reckon you will get to meet the Queen?" Dick asked, as much to distract from Jack's dismissive attitude as anything else.

"I doubt it, I'm not a big enough fish in that pond I'm afraid. However, I'll be rubbing shoulders with the likes of Status Quo, One Direction, Michael McIntyre and the winner of Britain's got talent, no doubt. Oh, and any number of dignitaries who manage to wangle their way in with a 'who you know' ticket. The show should be good, it'd better be, but I am looking forward to the sit-down meal beforehand. I'll warrant that the champagne will be flowing and caviar on tap."

"Even more of a good reason not to go, I hate caviar and I hate champagne." Jack was in full swing, yet again.

"Like you'd expect us to believe that you've tried caviar. Ok champagne maybe, but caviar?" Mick was quick to counter.

"Vanessa keeps it in the fridge. Still, I won't have to eat that shit again, I'm not seeing her anymore."

None of them were surprised when they heard the news, it was an incongruous match and they all expected it to run its course, taking longer than this maybe. Just the week before he'd been bragging about what an animal she was between the sheets and how they were mastering a New York Smooth dance with some intricate technical moves. There was no evidence to suggest that merely a week later they would have parted company.

James downed his pint and immediately rose to get the next round in. Jack stopped him in his tracks, got up and reiterated that he was getting the rounds in tonight, but seeing as James was already up he could help with carrying the drinks back to the table. As soon as they were at the bar James turned to Jack. "She got to you, didn't she?"

"What the fuck are you talking about?"

"Oh, come on Jack, Vanessa's mother. She paid you off to get out of Vanessa's life, didn't she?"

"Who am I kidding? We were never going to work, we live in different worlds."

"Bollocks, she didn't give you a choice. What was the threat?"

"Five big ones, or a nasty accident on the motorbike. I took the 5k, I'd love to have shoved it right up her jacksy though."

"The usual, Jack?" Bill piped up from behind the bar.

"Yeah, and don't forget the poncey drink for the new boy." It's true that Bill did forget on the first couple of occasions, but he was well-versed on the drinks order now and needed no reminding. Jack suddenly realised that if James knew about him then he must have been given the same ultimatum.

"Oh god, sorry mate, I'm guessing she's paid you off too?" The tone of anger had left his voice, it was more conciliatory now. He had sensed that his time with Vanessa had a shelf life but for poor old James and Millie this was the real deal.

"I'm not giving up without a fight, she's got her weaknesses and it's up to me to use them against her. Haven't you worked it out yet? She's the Lady that seduced me on the day I had to ferry the bride's pet dog to the wedding."

"Sugar, never put two and two together, cracking story that one by the way."

James didn't have the heart to tell Jack he'd been offered 30k to disappear. He was obviously perceived to be a much bigger threat to Lady Veronica's plans than Jack. By the time they'd reached the table the quiz papers had already been handed out. Jack turned to catch a glance of Sally dance between the last two tables and disappear behind the bar. "Fuck it! You just made me miss my little bit of banter with Sally."

"Come on Jack, sit down, it's time to concentrate now." Mick was eager to get on with the quiz. They'd had a good run since Mike joined and he didn't want their mojo to be ruined by Jack's bad mood.

As they knuckled down to the quiz, James questioned Mike about his up-coming Royal event. "How long is it to the big day?"

"Got a little while yet. Six weeks on Saturday if I'm not mistaken. Set up on the Thursday before and full-blown rehearsal on the Friday."

James's face changed with a sudden realisation, as if a metaphorical light bulb had been switched on above his head, like you see in cartoons.

"What is it?" Mike quizzed eager to know what was plaguing James's mind.

"Hold on a mo." James lifted a finger at Mike as he grabbed his phone from his pocket and checked his diary. "Well, I guess I'll be seeing you there."

"Bollocks, you're having a giraffe. Do you honestly expect me to believe that? Trust me, you've got be someone special to attend that kind of event. Jesus, the only reason I'm there is because someone at the beeb will need a scape goat if anything goes wrong."

"Who said anything about me being invited. If you must know, I'll be there as part of security. Geoff served at the yard for the best part of his career and he's been asked to provide a crew to make up the numbers, and seeing as I foiled that recent robbery, well the rest, as they say, is history."

"And we all know what a fluke that was." Mike gave the retort unimpressed with James's sudden self-belief.

"Geoff said it was some prestigious event in London and the dates match. It has to be it. Come to think of it, I doubt I will see you there. I should think our lot will be assigned to the bowels of the building, checking out the kitchens and toilets and such like." James's take on the day was obviously far less glamorous than Mike's. Another flash of inspiration entered James's mind and his face lit up once more.

Mike sucked it in and pressed for more. "Oh God, what is it now?"

"Have you got a guest list?"

"No. Why should I? Just an invite like everyone else."

"Okaaay . . . Well, is there any chance you can get your hands on one then?" James's eyes were fixed on Mike like a dog does when they're desperate for a morsel of your food.

Mike took a while to think. "Look, we've got several meetings coming up with the beeb and I'll bet my bottom dollar that whoever is in control of camera positions will have a seating plan to hand. He won't want to waste any camera footage on a bunch of people that nobody knows, that's for sure.

"Oh. So that'll include your table then." James couldn't resist the small quip.

"Look, do you want my help or not? Anyhow, why is this god damn list so important to you?" Mike's demeanour had become agitated and his raised voice and edgy timbre caught the attention of the rest of the lads who had long since lost any interest early on into the conversation.

They all viewed James and Mike expectantly. Dick reinforced Mike's request, even though he wasn't fully in tune with the conversation. "Come on Tibbs, tell us. Why do you need a guest list that doesn't mean anything to any of us?" James wormed around nervously, fumbling with the empty glass in his hands as he contemplated revealing a wildly bizarre half-hatched plan that won't mean anything if the person he's thinking about is not on that list.

"I think another round's in order. I can feel another one of Tibby's incredible stories on its way." And with that Jack made his way to the bar.

"Well, as you're all aware, Millie and I are getting pretty serious and last weekend we . . . actually, I decided that it was time to meet some of her family, her brother to be exact. But when we got there it turned out that her mother and father were there as well and here's the rub." James went silent for a second or two ready for the big reveal. It wasn't intentional, it wasn't designed to provoke suspense, it was just James coming to terms with what he was about to say.

Mick was getting impatient "Well, what the hell is it man?"

"Look, it turned out that her mother is Lady Rossford, the aristocratic vamp that seduced me a few months back."

"Crickey, I bet that went down like a lead balloon, but what's that got to do with this?" It was Dick's turn this time to offer his two-penny worth.

"We recognised each other of course, but remained discreet. Anyway, to cut a long story short she basically told me to back off from Millie or suffer the consequences."

Jack had returned from the bar by this time and finished James's sentence for him. "The evil bitch threatened to top us. Bought me off for five grand not to see her precious daughter again. In fact, that's what I'm using to pay for these drinks."

Mick piped up again. "Am I being dumb or something. So, we've established that she's an evil witch of a woman, but what has this got to do with that damned guest list."

"Look, there has to be a good chance that Lord and Lady Rossford will be on that guest list and, if they are, then we'll be in the same vicinity and if that's the case maybe I can get to her somehow."

"And do what? Bump her off before she can do the same to you? Sorry mate, I think you've lost it this time, this is pure madness." Mick's was always the voice of reason.

"He's right mate, I don't think I've heard so many ifs, buts, and maybes in one sentence." Dick stood stoically in agreement with Mick.

"Firstly, who said anything about bumping her off, and secondly you are all right. I truly don't have a clue about what to do, but I do know that I'm not going to give up Millie with-out a fight."

Chapter Twenty
The Plot Thickens

Tuesday 14th June 2016

James was sat in the garden enjoying a bit of late afternoon sun when his phone pinged. It was sat on the makeshift table next to him which was actually a foldable plastic step from the kitchen. He lazily picked it up and squinted to see who the message was from. His attention piqued once his eyes had focused to see that it was from Mike. It was an image of part of a guest list which included the caption 'Bingo'. There it was in black and white: Lord and Lady Rossford. This was to be his one and only chance.

Over the following days, James stewed things over in his mind and had managed to come up with a half-baked plan. He would need a lot of help and he needed to do even more grovelling to Mike, or moreover—Jess. The plan involved Mike seducing Lady Rossford. Mike's magnetic attraction for the ladies hadn't waned and even Sally would hover around the table a little longer to take in his chiselled looks and catch a glimpse of his crystal blue eyes.

Of course, both Mike and Jess protested profusely. Mike more for the preservation of his marriage than any kind of self-moral high ground. He'd allowed one seductress to drive a rift between him and his one true love and there wasn't a chance in hell he was going to let it happen again. To Jess, the whole escapade was pure madness, but deep down she knew she had to complete her promise to fate which she had cheated so long ago, and besides which, James had a knack for breaking her down, similar to that of a child that harangues its mother until they get the sweets they want.

James was grateful, but couldn't fathom it out. Jess caved far too easily. He was blissfully unaware of the vow Jess had made to herself to put right the wrong she had done all those years before. One other thing was certain: they didn't stand a cat in hell's chance of pulling this off without the help of the rest of his friends.

An emergency meeting was called on the following Sunday at The Baker's Arms. Mike and Jess were in on it, of course, but Peter, Jack, Mick and Dick were, for the time being, completely clueless.

"Ok then, what is it that's so important that you can't tell us over the phone?" Mick broke the ice and led off the conversation. It wasn't unusual it was Mick's way of doing things.

"Ok here goes." James took a breath and continued, "Well, as you know I asked Mike here if he could lay his hands on that guest list and he has, and it turns out that Lord and Lady Rossford are on the list."

"So, what you gonna do about it?" Jack cut in equally as direct as Mick, but not as eloquent.

"Look, I've already spoken to Mike and Jess about this and they've agreed to help me out, and trust me I'm not going to ask any of you to do as much as Mike has agreed to do. Well, apart from Jack that is, but we'll cover that soon enough Jack."

"Now listen mate—"

"Look, just here me out first Jack. All of you, in fact. Please just here me out first and let me know if you're in or out in your own good time. I'm not going to deny that it's not risky, and yes maybe I'm being completely selfish, but I don't know what else to do." James continued to explain his plot to the rest of the gang and the more he went on the more crazy it sounded.

"You're delusional mate. For God's sake, Mike, how did he manage to convince you to go ahead with this? It's shear lunacy and you, Jess, of all people, surely you can see that this is pure madness?" Mick had thrown his spanner into the works.

Mike was on the wane but suddenly Jack chipped in. "I'm in. After what she did to me, that bitch needs teaching a lesson. You're just being chicken. You and Dick here have got the easy bit. You're up for it, aren't you Dick?" Jack didn't give Dick a chance to reply. "If you don't owe James you owe me. Who was it that got the garage to take back that cut and shut death trap you bought a couple of years back? The way I see it you owe me and the rest of your family your lives, so if you won't do it for James you're gonna fucking well do it for me." Of all the people Jack may well have just tipped the balance.

Mick remained silent and coerced.

"What about you, Peter?" James asked calmly, no emotion this time. They all waited patiently for Peter to answer.

"I'm in," Peter answered calmly. This wasn't for James though. This was for himself. This was the necessary jumpstart he needed to restart his flat-lining life. So, from this point forward they were all in on the plot whether they liked it or not.

The first phase of his plan was about to unfold during the set up and rehearsal of The Queen's Royal Gala, carried out a couple of days before the actual event, which was to serve as the opportunity they needed for reconnaissance.

Mobile phones weren't allowed into the rehearsals, so James searched online for a spy equipment specialist and bought a couple of button cameras which Jess fitted onto the cuffs of Mike's and James's jacket.

Thursday 14th July 2016

Mike was shitting himself. In the looks department, he could pass for James Bond, but inside he really had as much backbone as a Jelly Baby. The first part of Mike's exercise was easy, he just needed to capture the uniforms of the serving staff as this would be one of the disguises they needed for the event—after all, there would be a small army of them, most of them hired in and unlikely to recognise each other at any other level than to serve the guests.

James entrusted himself to find an access and exit route for the building. This wasn't difficult, because as he had already suspected, Geoff and his crew were indeed dispatched to cover the toilets and the associated corridors. James expected to find a window in one of the toilets, but once inside his investigation proved fruitless as they were internal rooms and there were no windows whatsoever. No matter how hard he searched through the corridors he couldn't find any way in or out.

Geoff took his job seriously and nobody was allowed to move from their station without strict instruction from himself.

Mike made his way to the toilets for a comfort break. James stopped him with the pretence of a security check and Geoff watched on impressed with his new recruit. "Listen, I haven't been able to work out an entry and exit point and I can't get away from here. Geoff's eyes are on us like a hawk." James's voice was muted and only audible to Mike. "I need you to find us a way in and out for the rest of the crew."

Mike's heart started to race as the adrenalin kicked in. He'd stopped smoking a few years ago, opting for the safer option of vaping. However, these were also banned or confiscated as they could be rigged as an explosive device and, as such, he had resorted back to traditional cigarettes. With the harmless packet of cigarettes, he was merely advised to remove himself to the designated smoking areas.

"We don't want to set the fire alarms off, do we, sir?" was added as an extra precaution to save the huge embarrassment for any individual that ignored the warnings.

He sidled over to one of the attendants at the far end of the dining hall, targeting a chap in his mid-forties in the hope that he was a smoker too. To his relief, he smelt the aroma of stale tobacco on his clothes. He pulled out a pack of cigarettes, explaining that he was gasping for one and did he know where there was a smoking area. The man directed him to the signage at the other end of the hall. "Oh, I'm sorry, I didn't explain myself, you see as far as my company is concerned we have a strictly no smoking policy, and if you don't mind me saying so, there's a few of them here that would only too easily blag me in. Is there anywhere a little more discreet?"

The attendant sympathised with his predicament and, seeing that he wasn't the old-school gentry type, which were actually abhorrent to him, he threw Mike a line. He flicked his head to one side and said, "Follow me, sir."

Mike followed him into the bowels of the building down some steps along a corridor and through the kitchens to a door that was already open to the outside to help ventilate and re-move heat from the kitchens. Whilst outside, Mike offered the chap a cigarette, which he took.

Mike gave his name as a prompt for conversation.

"Henry, sir," the man replied.

Mike explained that they could drop the formalities; while they were out there they were after all equals, he explained. Henry's guard relaxed and they chatted casually and, as the conversation went on, Mike gleaned more and more information about the security arrangements.

They were tight, everybody counted in and everybody counted out, all with ID cards. The good thing about having a camera on his sleeve is that Mike could lift the cigarette to his mouth and pretty much aim his camera wherever he liked, in this case, including a great shot of Henry's ID card.

As they passed through the kitchen, Mike made sure that he got some good footage of the kitchen staff's uniforms. The usual garb—a pair of chequered trousers with a white apron, hair nets and plain black shoes. There were racks full of fresh vegetables, obviously in preparation for the forthcoming event.

As they finished their cigarettes, Mike held back a little and waited for Henry to throw his butt on the floor and stamp it out. Henry turned to leave. "Come on Mike, I'm not allowed to be from my station for too long." He beckoned for Mike to follow. Mike had a moment of clarity and as he turned his back, Mike bent down and picked up a few fag butts, his own still in his hand, and he gingerly nursed the bent ash that was still attached. As they walked passed a rack of cabbages, he flicked them in, his ash spreading nicely across at least four cabbages.

Whilst Mike was conducting his very own Mission Impossible, Jess was at work as usual and completely helpless to Mike's plight. Although the season was late summer and a heatwave was taking hold, the autumn selection of clothing had already gone into production and she had been entrusted to select the winter clothing range.

It's possible that her dark-clouded mood would help her with her task, but it didn't. Mike consumed her thoughts and she was always thinking the worst. For all she knew he could be in some security room somewhere having the living daylights beaten out of him. Her mind raced, imaging all kinds of ridiculous torturing scenarios, an MI6 interrogator ripping the camera from his sleeve, countenancing, "And how do you explain this?" whilst they throw a bag over his head in preparation for waterboarding.

Finally, her phone rang and he was back with her, not in the physical sense but his voice is all she needed to hear. He had actually left the building some time earlier, but he took a few moments in a local coffee shop to calm himself, let the adrenalin wear off, and allow his heart to return to a normal rhythm.

"What took you so long? You told me you'd give me a call at lunch time during your production break? God only knows why I came to work today. You were all I could bring myself to think about. For fuck sake Mike, I've literally been here shitting myself!"

This kind of language was highly unusual for Jess, she's normally composed and articulate, but the circumstances were so fraught that she needed to relieve the angst within, and what better way than a few well-meant expletives.

"Crikey Jess, you weren't the one that just had to complete a fucking James Bond mission!" She guessed Mike needed to verbalise his relief too. "I thought that once you were divorced, you weren't beholden to your ex anymore, this really is beyond the call of duty, surely?"

"Look Mike, it's complicated. I don't know, maybe you're right. Let's just leave it at that, shall we."

In a perverse way, they both felt more alive than they could ever remember. In fact, their highly charged emotional state resulted in a highly charged emotional release later that day. Suddenly, the whole torrid affair became worthwhile.

Later that evening they all met up at Jess's and Mike's to review the footage. It wasn't quite as Mike and James had envisaged it, all perfect stealth-like shots of everything they needed. In actual fact, much of it was shaky and out of focus, but it was good enough and they managed to download some good stills of all the uniforms and that precious ID card.

Jess was charged with the job of sourcing the uniforms. Mick had connections in sourcing the ID cards, apparently they could even fake the hologram image of the kingfisher in the top right hand corner. Dick reckoned he could get some vegetable crates from the market where he sourced all his fresh green organic produce. Peter and James were left to finalise the plan and a couple of alternatives if the necessity arose.

The only thing left to do now was wait, but of course that wouldn't be for long, less than forty-eight hours in fact. Jack sat with them all feeling rather left out. "I feel like a spare prick in a brothel. What am I supposed to be doing?"

"Jack, look, we've spoken about all this, you're the key to whole thing, remember? Without you we simply can't do this, and who knows, if all goes well, you'll get your wish, you really will get a chance to shove that five-grand right up her Jacksy."

"Too fucking late, I've spent £2,000 of it, but I'm still happy to shove the rest up."

"You're going to have to perform some rather ungentlemanly acts on our lady for the cameras, of course." James had gone over the top a little bit buying three more spy cameras that could be secreted in boxes and such like.

Mick was quick to point out that there wasn't a chance in a million years that Lady Rossford would let Jack get anywhere near her. "Have you forgotten already that that's Mike's job. Mike is going to have to seduce her and get her down to the kitchens. Jack will take over from there and do all the dirty work."

"It'll never work. We might as well hand ourselves over to the police now," Mick countenanced.

Jess was quiet, too quiet in fact. She'd been playing scenario's over in her mind time and time again. Finally, she opened up. "I'm sorry James, I've been playing this over in my mind, I don't think I can let you make Mike do it."

"Jess, I promise you, I just need Mike to get her down to that kitchen. Jack will take things over from there." Despite being told so, Jack realised that he was the key to all this after all. He had finally worked it out that he was the only one qualified to complete the entrapment of Lady Rossford by virtue that he wasn't already in a relationship and could freely commit the necessary adulterous acts to blackmail her.

In one fell swoop he'd been elevated from zero to hero with the added bonus of staring in his very own exclusive porn movie.

Mick decided to throw his spanner into the works once more. "There's just one small point, how the hell will you manage to swap Jack for Mike once you've got her down into the kitchens?"

They all eyed James, patiently waiting. "Blindfold," James answered.

Mick couldn't believe his ears. "Oh, come on, this has gotten far-fetched enough, what makes you think she will just go and let Mike put a blindfold on her?"

"Look, she's a thrill seeker, she's a dominant woman who wants to be dominated to release her from the shackles life has placed upon her. She'll do it, trust me!" James's little speech was impassioned, it needed to be to convince them, but deep down in their gut they truly thought the whole plan was madness, and what's more, they were having to risk arrest and God knows what else for this sorry fiasco.

All but one that is—Peter. Peter knew there was something extraordinary about James, especially in the last few months, whatever he had been setting his mind to he had achieved. James needed Peter now, he needed someone to stand in his corner with him. The rest of the group were faltering, apart from Jack who would do just about anything to get back at Lady Rossford and get a shag to boot. What a glorious bonus that would be. Peter was his trump card and he dealt it well.

Peter was pragmatic about it all, explaining that Mike and Jess had nothing to fear, they were bona fide guests and it wouldn't need all of them to complete the mission. However, it may hinder them if they have to bring into play any other plans. When it came to it they only needed Mike, Jess, Jack and one other to pull off plan 'A'. An extra pair of hands to help set up in the kitchen on the other hand would be good. If Mike was to find it difficult to lure Lady Rossford down the kitchens, then they would need to bring into action plan 'B', which would require Dick, who would be disguised as a waiter, to clumsily spill some wine over Lady Rossford.

They all expected that Dick would be perfect to carry out the task with a certain aplomb, as by nature he was quite clumsy. This would provide the opportunity for Mike to step in as a knight in shining armour and take control, leading her down to the kitchens to deal with it personally. If that didn't work they were prepared to resort to one final plan requiring Mick's convincing voice of authority to extract Lady Rossford for a bogus phone call and to add some certainty he would be able to explain that it was from her son, Johnathan.

Mick threw the cards in then and there. "I'm sorry, if it gets to plan 'C' I fear it'll be all over before it's started. I've got you the ID cards and I don't want them traced back to me. It's all just too risky. That's as far as I'm prepared to go with this, I'm sorry but that's just the way it has to be for me."

He made sense, there was no need for all of them to take the risk; James agreed and it was beginning to dawn on him how much he was asking of his friends for his own selfish desires and needs. He was ready to pull the plug on the whole thing himself. Peter asserted that they would all regret it if they didn't at least give it a try and, anyhow, they needed someone on the outside to take control if it all went tits up, and who better to trust than Mick to organise solicitors and lawyers and whatever else they may need.

Chapter Twenty-One
Candid Camera

Saturday 16th July 2016 – Royal Gala Day
It was time for another dress rehearsal, at Jesss and Mike's this time. Mick turned up to help, even though he wouldn't be involved in the main event he still wanted to help out as much as possible, he still wanted them to succeed.

Given the limited time Jess had to source the clothes, she had done a fantastic job. Dick looked resplendent in his waiter's uniform, the rest just as you would expect kitchen staff to appear, although possibly a little too clinical and clean, not marred by the odd food or sauce stain that won't quite fully wash out.

Dick was the only one of the group who wasn't actually apprehensive, or at least he didn't give off that vibe. He kind of drifted through life serenely whilst everyone around him worked their asses off at it. James loved this about Dick, he wasn't self-assured, in fact he was as clumsy as hell, but he was just a guy that was comfortable in his own skin. He didn't need to prove anything to anybody, he was what he was. He was at one with the world and did his bit to preserve it for others to follow and enjoy it as he has.

The rest were mere mortals in comparison, worrying about the smallest things on a daily basis: getting to a meeting, being late for a meeting, paying the bills on time, picking up the kids, where are the kids at, which friends are they with, which park are they playing in, getting to the dentist, making a doctor's appointment, which will turn out to be a waste of time because you'll be better in a week's time when your appointment finally comes around. The list was endless.

Dick actually had three outfits for his part in the mission. He needed to get entry in with the others as kitchen staff and, later on, disappear to the toilets to change into his waiter's uniform, and then a Tuxedo to blend in and make a quick clean exit. The crates were rigged with a false bottom, giving about an inch of space underneath to conceal the extra clothes and camera equipment they would need.

The timing of their arrival as a fake kitchen crew was critical, but at the same time pure guess work. From the rehearsal, they had gathered that food was to be served between five pm and 7.30pm, at which time they were to exit the dining hall to the balcony areas in the main theatre with the show to start at 8pm, finishing at approximately 10.30pm.

The kitchens were to be active from twelve noon—Mike had managed to garnish this much information from Henry a couple of days earlier. They figured that the great joints of meat would be prepared first, ready for a slow roast of approximately three hours. On this assumption, they guessed that the vegetables would be prepared at about 1.30pm.

Jack and Dick went down to the market to source the savoy cabbages and other vegetables identified in Mike's footage which ended up filling six crates. Jack had donated his ill-gotten gains for all the necessary costumes, fruit and veg, and even reimbursed James for the spy equipment he had bought, leaving him with £300 spare in his back pocket.

"This is it, it's now or never," Peter exclaimed as the taxi arrived outside.

James was long gone, already committed to his security duties. His fate now remained in the hands of his friends. James was already in the building, and kept a watchful eye on Geoff and as the eta approached for the arrival of the fresh veg, he made his move. "Geoff, is anyone assigned to the kitchens?" James enquired nonchalantly.

"Dunno, why do you ask?"

"Probably nothing, just a hunch. You know when you get a feeling, an itch you just have to scratch. Forget I ever mentioned it."

"Yes, well, this is our station and if there's one thing I know you don't leave it for no good reason." James had planted the seed. All he could do now was wait to see if it would grow. Peter, Jack, Dick and six crates full of vegetables were crammed into the taxi.

Mick, Jess and Mike helped load up before Jess and Mike scurried back inside to get ready themselves. Mick waved them off with a tinge of guilt and a heavy heart. "Come back safe you bunch of stupid imbeciles," he said to himself as they left. His last words not reflecting his true sentiments. To him they were akin to his one pair of slippers that he had owned for the last ten years, soles worn through to his feet, but he couldn't bear to throw them away because something else simply just wouldn't do.

The taxi arrived at the back security gate. There were two burly looking guards at the gate with ill-fitting uniforms, too tight around the torso and shoulders, and baggy around the midriff. The type that lifted weights all day and probably took some kind of steroids that would help to add two inches to their biceps and lose two off their dicks.

They all stepped out of the taxi, dragging their crates behind them. The guard approached them, clipboard in hand. Peter was to be their spokesman. "Nah, you won't find us on there mate, we're on the reserve list, we're meant to be covering for illnesses and no shows."

"Everyone's here mate, all checked in, I did it myself!"

"Yeah, I know, but we've had an emergency call, apparently the cabbages have been sabotaged. They don't want to take any chances with this being the event that it is. I mean, do you want to see the Queen chewing on a fag butt?"

The guard pulled a walkie-talkie from a holder on his hip and spoke into it. "Anyone near the kitchens to check something out? Over." Carl was head of security and, as such, held rank over the hired help.

The radio request came through over Geoff's walkie-talkie as it did everybody else's, but Geoff's interest was spiked by the mention of the kitchens. He quickly glanced at James and lifted his walkie-talkie from its holster. A crackly voice echoed back from the guard's de-vice "That you Carl? Over." It was Geoff's.

"Yes mate, I need someone to go down to the kitchens and check something out for me. Over."

"Ok, I'm on my way now. Over."

"You two stay here," he barked with an air of authority. "James, you come with me. Let's go and scratch that itch you were talking about." After a minute or so, which actually seemed like five, Peter, Jack and Dick all stood staring into space until Geoff's voice echoed back once more, "Ok mate I'm down here now. Over."

"Ask the chef if he's requested a whole new load of fresh vegetables. Over."

The place was a hive of activity, bodies moving from one station to another in chaotic synchronicity. Geoff and James bustled through, catching the eye of whoever noticed them to find the whereabouts of the Head Chef. When Geoff finally found his target and began to speak to him, the chef cut him short. "I don't know who the fuck you think you are, but if you're not here to prep some food you can fuck right off out of my kitchen." After another minute or so Geoff's reply finally came back.

"Fuck sake mate, it's mayhem down here, he's just told me to fuck off. Over."

The guard looked at the new crew suspiciously now. "Look mate, it wasn't the chef that contacted us. I think it was the Maitre D. Don't take this the wrong way, but if this lot's left any longer it will spoil and the Queen will have nothing to eat. We've got to do something. Get your man to check the cabbages, we've got to keep this lot fresh. They've been in a sweaty taxi for the last hour to get them across town."

Peter was very convincing, it was as if he truly believed it himself and in a way, he did, he really didn't want the Queen chomping on fag ash and fag butts.

"Geoff, come in mate. Over."

"What do want me to do mate? Over."

"You still in the kitchens? Over."

"Yes mate. Over."

"Do us a favour and go and check out the cabbages, will you mate? Let me know what you find. Over."

"Jim, go and check out the cabbages for me, will you mate? Look for anything suspicious."

James pushed his way through to the veg racks. Fortunately, the fag ash and fag butts were in plain sight. James silently praised Mike for a job well done.

"Geoff, you'd better come over here and see this for yourself," James shouted across the room to make no mistake that Geoff would hear him, along with the Chef.

"Fag ash and fag butts galore down here mate. Over."

"Stay there, mate, don't let them use any veg till we get there. Over."

"Ok mate. Over." Carl turned to them. "Right, you lot follow me. Sid, you stay here on the gate, don't let anybody in, pass or no pass."

"Ok boss."

Carl's chest was so puffed up with pride that the buttons on his jacket were ready to pop. They all marched down to the kitchens, crates in hand. Carl was so incensed by this travesty of justice that he had completely forgotten to search any of the crates. "How dare he swear at one of my men, no nothing so and so." He was muttering to himself as they approached the open doors leading to the kitchen. "You alright, Geoff?"

"Yeah, a bit pissed off with the chef though, no need to swear at me like that."

"Leave that with me, give us that cabbage with all that fag ash on it and a couple of those fag butts." Carl made his way over to the chef and stood towering over him. He flicked the fag butts in the chef's face. "What's your game mate? Planning to feed the Queen fag ash and fag butts, are we?"

"I don't understand, I checked it all when it was delivered a couple of days ago."

"That was two days ago, you didn't think to check it again?"

"There's no way we'd have used it once we had spotted it."

"Now listen to me, you're going to chuck that lot in the bins and use this fresh stuff we've just brought down."

The chef directed a couple of kitchen assistants to start removing the contaminated veg to the bins.

"No, I don't think you quite heard me right, I said YOU'RE GOING TO TAKE THAT SHIT OUT AND BIN IT, he can stay here for five minutes while you do it." He had a firm grip on one of the kitchen assistants.

The chef reluctantly left his station, protesting as he went.

Carl hadn't finished. "And while you are at it, you can apologise to my man Geoff here."

At this point, James suggested that it might be a good idea that he and the others conducted a full inspection of the kitchens and oversaw everything. After all, if the veg had been contaminated then God only knows what else might be.

Carl piped up again. "This lot are going to carry out an inspection. If the veg is contaminated then maybe other stuff is too. Don't disturb them, just carry on as you were. Right then, I'm back off up to the gate. Geoff, are you ok leaving your man here with this lot while you cover off your station?"

"Err . . . Yes mate. Jim, you look after this here for the rest of your shift and if there's any trouble from this lot you come and get me. Understood?"

"Yeah of course mate. Leave it with me."

They couldn't believe their luck. They had free reign to do as they pleased. Jack and Dick conducted a thorough search of the kitchens, rifling through all the drawers, checking the chillers, the ovens, anything in fact that would provide a distraction whilst Peter and James got up to the sneaky stuff taking a couple of boxes away for inspection, emptying their con-tents and rigging their natty little spy cameras inside.

They helped themselves to the contents of the secret compartments from the now empty crates laid outside which they carried out with brazen contempt, using their newly bestowed authority given to them by Carl to its fullest extent. James couldn't help thinking to himself that this was all too easy. The chef had recovered his bravery following his humiliation from Carl. "If any of you fuckers notice anything again in my kitchen, you tell me first. You fucking hear me right?"

One of the kitchen assistants leaned into Jack and Dick. "Take no notice, he's prone to his little outbursts, it's his way of dealing with the stress."

"Vicious little fucker," Jack commented back.

The food was being plated up ready to go and the kitchen staff were already into prepping the deserts following a quick clean down. The chef may have been a harsh taskmaster and a bully to boot, but he knew his stuff and his timing was key.

James half thought that once the mains had been sent up that they would take five minutes and chill with a cup of tea but no, they were straight on it, no time to waste. This was good, it meant that none of the kitchen staff would have any time to reflect on earlier events, possibly putting two and two together. Six pm and the first of the deserts were ready, by 6.30pm they would all be complete and the food and prep side would be dormant again. They had a separate room for cleaning the used crockery and cutlery with two large commercial dishwashers, something about removing any chance of cross-contamination.

It was time for phase two of the operation to commence.

Dick changed into his waiter's uniform and mingled amongst the tables, watching and copying the other waiters, which consisted of standing a few feet away from the tables and watching attentively, ready to top up wine glasses as soon as they were empty. He assumed his position at Lord and Lady Rossford's table. He ambled up alongside one of the waiter's already at his station. The waiter leant into Dick and spoke in his ear. "I think you're in the wrong place mate, this position has been assigned to me." The waiter then gesticulated for Dick to move on.

"Yes, but the maître D sent me over, he said he needed some extra hands at the Queen's table and asked for you specifically. He said that you were the best he's got . . . Something like that."

The other waiter duly walked over to the Queen's table, explaining to the others that it was at the orders of the maître D and if they had any beef about it to go and take it up with him directly, which course they didn't. The formalities of dinner were over now and Lord Rossford had been chatting with Brigadier Sanders who he had met a few years back in Afghanistan when there was a delicate diplomatic issue concerning one of the Brigadier's Sergeants and a local married secretarial assistant. "I'm sorry darling, I really must catch up with the Brigadier, I need to find out the outcome of that fiasco a few years back. Fascinating story, I'll tell you about it one day."

"Of course you must, darling," she replied, knowing full well that it was just an excuse to sink a few brandies before the show. She also knew that he wouldn't tell her and he knew that she didn't want to know either. It was just the way they conducted themselves in front of others.

Lord Rossford got up from his seat and Mike took this as his opportunity to meet Lady Rossford; however, as soon as he began to make a beeline for her, another gentleman scurried over and sat in Lord Rossford's seat. It was one of his friends, but in actual fact he wasn't to be trusted at all, he would seek any opportunity to fawn over Lady Rossford. To her, though, he was nothing more than a lecherous old bore.

It was twenty-five minutes before they would be called to leave the hall and Dick waited patiently to stroll up to the table. As he approached, Dick picked up a bottle of red wine and offered it to Lady Rossford's glass, but she covered the glass with her hand. Dick ignored it, splashing the wine over her hand and then flicking it over her dress as he pretended to realise his error.

This was Mike's cue.

Whilst Dick stood over the Lady, apologising profusely, Mike stepped in, pushing the clumsy waiter to one side. "Out of the way, you clumsy oaf. Do you know who this? Are you ok, Lady Rossford? Please allow me to deal with this personally."

"Oh, I'll be fine, but the clumsy fool has just ruined a £1,500 dress."

"Come with me, Lady Rossford. It really is amazing what a bit of bicarbonate of soda can do, but we need to treat it now; besides, I haven't had a chance to thank you for the fantastic charity donation you made for us at the World Animal Centre. Anyhow, you look like you could do with a cigarette and I know the perfect place away from staring eyes."

She was glad of the distraction and a chance to remove herself from the wandering hands of the lecherous old bore.

"Very well Mr . . . ?"

"Oh, please, call me Mike." He placed his jacket around her to hide the stains and led her down to the kitchens through the open doors to outside. He lit a cigarette for her and told her to enjoy it and try to relax while he made a solution of bicarbonate of soda.

She was used to men fawning over her, but they were usually ghastly older men from her generation, acquaintances of her husband, balding, potbellied with smoke-stained teeth. Here before her stood a ruggedly handsome specimen of a man still in his prime. The smell and the utilitarianism of the kitchen were evocative to her for some reason, triggering carnal urges within. She didn't think she could contain herself and was feeling the need to fulfil her gathering urges, her breathing had lifted and her chest was heaving slightly in her shimmering body-hugging dress.

"Come back inside, Lady Rossford, let's see what we can do to remove that stain."

Her cigarette was all but finished and she did as she was told. He cupped his hand on her waist as she did so to guide her in, bringing her urges more and more to the surface at the excitement of his gentle yet authoritative touch. He dabbed at it with a sponge. "Lady Rossford, if I am to do this properly I think we need to remove the dress."

From this moment on she was putty in his hands. "Well, if that's what one must do then we shall have to do it."

Mike came up behind her and slowly but provocatively began to unzip her dress from behind. As he did so, he quietly spoke in her ear. "If you don't want me to do this, tell me to stop at any time." The warmth of his breath danced in her ear.

She didn't respond, she just allowed her body to bathe in his attention. He slipped his hands onto the bare skin of her back and gently prized the dress off her shoulders, allowing the faintest touch of his hand on the side of her bosom.

Jack and James were holed up in the staff toilets next door, watching on a monitor via Bluetooth. "Fucking hell he's good, he's got to have a stiffy surely—no wonder Jess has always got a smile on her face nowadays."

"Yeah thanks for that Jack, you really don't know when to keep your mouth shut, do you? Anyway, pay attention, it's nearly your turn to perform." Lady Rossford's choice of underwear was classic, suspender belt, stockings, lacy bra and knickers, her nipples just visible through the fine mesh of her bra.

"Fucking hell mate, this defies the laws of nature. How can a woman of her age have a body like that?"

James knew it to be true. He had sampled her delights first hand and yes, she was very easy on the eye.

"Oh my god Lady Rossford, you are so beautiful, I simply must have you. Lady Rossford, have you ever been taken whilst blindfolded? Trust me, it heightens your other senses, it's incredibly sensual." He pulled a silk scarf from his pocket, placed it over her eyes, and tied it behind her head.

"There's your cue, Jack." Jack made to rush out of the toilet cubicle "Wait wait, don't forget this." James threw the now infamous mask from 'bunnygate' at him. If this ever needed to be leaked to the press, anonymity was of the utmost importance.

Jack held the mask like it was some kind of trophy. Ever since James revealed the story of Bunnygate the mask took on a legendary status in Jack's eyes. It was nothing short of Excalibur to Jack, but of course to everybody else it was just a grubby old mask. "Christ James, I don't know what to say."

"It's not a frozen Mars bar, but do you reckon it'll cover the debt." Jack stared back at him silent for a few seconds and then he replied. "Fuck off, you're not getting away with it that easily. You still owe me a frozen Mars bar. Right."

"Ahh, ok, worth a try though ehh!"

Like some kind of perverse tag team, Jack silently entered the kitchen and took over from Mike.

Mike left the kitchen and met up with James in the cubicle.

"Bloody hell Mike, I can't thank you enough. That was simply sublime mate. Have you ever thought of taking up acting?" James gushed out the words as Mike entered the cubicle.

"Done some Am Dram in the past, but this wasn't too difficult with a Lady as beautiful as her. Don't tell Jess, but I was starting to feel the effects when that dress hit the floor."

"I know, I'm a sucker for sexy lingerie too. Still, enough said. Let's see how Jack's getting on."

Lady Rossford immediately sensed something different once Jack had taken over, it was less sensual and more animalistic. He swept her off her feet and sat her on the edge of a stainless-steel prep table, the cold metal sending a chill up her spine and her skin momentarily spiked with goosebumps, making her nipples become even more erect, pressing through the fine lace mesh of her bra awaiting the final excitement of consummation.

Jack ran one hand up her stockinged leg from the ankle right up to the bare flesh of her inner thigh. He pulled the lacy cup down from her left breast and allowed it to spring out, he took the nipple in to his mouth and ran his tongue around it, as he did so he moved his hand up to the crotch of her knickers and gently massaged it. She felt Jack's soft furry bunny ears caressing her chest and other breast. She didn't know how he was managing to do it, but it was making her as horny as hell.

James and Mike stood awkwardly in the cubicle together, bent over a little bit and slightly turned away from each other to hide the fact that they were both rather excited by the sexual act unfolding in the other room just a few feet away from them. "God, he's good at this porn stuff," Mike said.

"I think he's missed his calling in life," was James's reply.

Jack slipped her knickers down and threw them onto the floor. He parted her legs and tasted her tangy sweetness as he danced his tongue over her clitoris, teasing the small firm button until her hips began to writhe as the crescendo of nerve endings began to take over her body.

He stopped, he didn't want to take her beyond the point of no return. She lay resting on the edge somewhere between reality and sublime bliss. He placed an unopened condom in her hand for her to open and whilst she was doing this he opened one himself. He took the rest of the money from his pocket, folded it up and rolled the condom over it.

He then held Lady Rossford's wrist and directed her hand to his erect cock, rolling the condom in her hand over it. He gently eased the condom full of notes into her back passage before entering her himself.

It was a feeling she had never experienced before, and it was exquisite. She climaxed immediately. Jack was also lost for a brief moment, and he had forgotten what he was there for, burying his head into her chest as he came inside her. Reality came back to him and he removed himself from her and left the room.

Lady Rossford came back to her senses and after a few seconds of silence she realised that she was alone and lifted the scarf from her head, removing the now uncomfortable condom from her backside. She was confused and disorientated as she took in the empty room around her, as if she had just woken up from a weird, surreal dream.

She had no choice but to gather her senses and she felt the need to quickly get dressed before being found in a compromising position. That simply wouldn't do for Lord Rossford's high standing position, or her own self-respect.

As she made her way back upstairs to the Gala, she noticed that the stain had completely disappeared. The bottle had been rigged by Dick with water and invisible ink from a prank shop. She had no clue as to the contents of the condom that she had extracted from herself when the act was committed, and she actually thought that a courgette had been used. It remained discarded on the floor.

Once she had reached the dining hall, they were calling everybody through to the balconies, and no sooner had she gone from the kitchen than the boys entered the room to remove the cameras and any other incriminating evidence. That is apart from the money-filled condom which none of them wanted to touch as they all knew where it had been.

Ordinarily, Jack wouldn't have batted an eyelid at picking it up and removing the contents, but it was part of a business deal that he had to remain faithful to. The others just knew where it had been and just couldn't bring themselves to touch it.

Mike left to rejoin Jess as soon as Jack had completed his deed whilst the others cleared up. Dick was sent back to give Mike and Jess the thumbs up and Mike ushered him over. "What about the condom, have you cleared the condom?" Mike was fretting over every little detail.

"I'm certainly not touching it, do you know how long those things take to degrade?"

"Tell them to forget about it, I have an idea, I'll deal with it."

"Are you sure Mike?"

"Yes, I've got it covered, just leave it with me."

They stuffed the excess clothing into James's man bag, which he had taken out of retirement for one more ruse and entrusted its safe keeping to Peter. Dick met back up with the others and announced that Mike was going to deal with the condom issue. "How's he going to deal with that from up there?" James asked.

"I asked him and he assured me to leave it with him."

Mike and Jess weren't heading for the balconies, they were to make an exit as quickly as possible and simply disappear. Mike stopped Jess. "Look, I've got one more thing to do." Before she could say anything, he was gone and then she caught a glimpse of him talking to one of the waiters.

"Henry!" Mike called out. The man looked at him quizzically, then realised it was the gentleman he had shared a cigarette with just a couple of days earlier.

"Ahh yes sir, how can I help you?"

"Well, I have to admit that I popped down to the kitchens to sneak a cigarette when I noticed a strange package on the floor. You may want to use some gloves to clear it up but I'm sure there will be a bonus in it for you." He dipped his head and tapped the side of his nose with a knowing look and a wry smile.

The hall was very nearly cleared and Henry made his way down to the kitchens inquisitively. Even if it amounted to nothing he would still be able to sneak a crafty fag for himself. He picked up the package between finger and thumb and placed it on a prep table. He found some scissors in a draw and cut it open to reveal the contents.

Mike's words rang in his ears. 'I'm sure there will be a bonus in it for you.' His eyes widened and a smile came over his face. He glanced over his shoulder, not a soul in sight. He extracted the contents, pushed it into his pocket and disposed of the condom in the bins outside. By this time, the rest of the boys were dressed to the nines and walked straight out of the theatre to freedom, apart from James who returned to Geoff to complete his security duties.

Job done!

Chapter Twenty-Two
Stalemate

The whole film footage was sent to Mick for safe keeping, in fact it was streamed to him as it was being made. Having Mick on the outside was a godsend. It actually worked in their favour on so many levels, but more importantly he would have all the evidence they would need if their final escape failed. There would be no doctoring and no cover up. The full extent of the footage would be released to the tabloids for them to have a field day.

Luckily it didn't come to this. They breezed out of the building easily and away from the scene of the sordid action with their hearts beating heavily and with smiles of exhilaration at their triumphant success.

Mick was entrusted in issuing encrypted copies out to five of their most trusted family members and friends. Within an hour, Mick's part of the mission was complete. He then set upon the edited version, the version that would be sent to Lady Rossford. Mike would be cut from this version and all that would be seen would be an anonymous man wearing a furry bunny mask having his wicked way with her whilst she actively encouraged it.

Sunday 17th July 2016
Jess was desperate to see the footage. She needed to see that Mike's faithfulness had remained intact. She scrutinised the film, looking for any slip or weakness on Mike's part. She soaked in the imagery of her husband casually undressing what must be said was a beautiful strange lady. She found herself being surprisingly aroused by it all as the events

unfolded bit by bit on the screen in front of her. How could something so sordid make her feel this way? She felt her face flush and was feeling like a naughty teenager back in her bedroom all those years ago wondering about boys. "Did you just cop a feel then, Mike?"

"Not that I recall, I may have done by accident, I think I may have brushed against the side of her breast as I removed the dress." Strangely she wasn't upset, in fact by this time she was feeling down right horny and insisted that he complete the full roleplay with her back in their own kitchen, except when Mike slipped Jess's dress from her shoulders, on this occasion he cupped and squeezed her breasts and whispered in her ear, "This is what I call copping a feel."

She turned to him and kissed him passionately, her heart racing. Mike lifted her onto the kitchen work top and claimed his reward which Jess gave him willingly, again and again.

Wednesday 20th July 2016

Lord and Lady Rossford sat whilst breakfast was served and the morning news was on the television in the background. "And again, back to breaking news about the E. coli break out in the restaurant of The Queens Royal Theatre. The head chef is helping the police with their enquires at Scotland Yard. It's been alleged that traces of faecal matter have been identified on one of the prep surfaces along with a pair of contaminated scissors. The head of security, Carl Pilkington, who has also been helping the police with their enquiries, has now, we believe, been released." The news reporter lifted her hand to her ear briefly and fell silent. "I can now confirm that we are going live over to Scotland Yard where our Royal correspondent, Morag Morewiny is about to get an exclusive interview with Mr Pilkington."

"Hello, I'm Morag Morewiny and I'm outside Scotland Yard with Mr Pilkington, head of security for the Queens Royal Theatre. Mr Pilkington, what can you tell us about the alleged contamination in the kitchens?"

"I can confirm that a member of my team identified contaminated food produce on the day of the Queen's Gala celebrations and I acted personally to ensure that it was disposed of safely and replaced with fresh produce."

"We understand the head chef is also helping the police with their enquiries, do you think there is any significance in this?"

"At this stage I can neither confirm nor deny his involvement. Just suffice it to say that he was less than helpful on that particular day when we were conducting our own enquiries into the contaminated produce."

"Can you tell us what contamination you found?"

"In our instance, it was cigarette ash and cigarette butts mixed in with the fresh vegetables. I must stress that none of this contamination made it onto any of the plates in the food hall. It was all replaced with fresh produce, I saw to it myself, and I think you will find that there haven't been any reported incidents from the night of the Queen's meal. Only from those meals consumed the following day."

"This is Morag Morewiny at Scotland Yard, now back to you in the studio."

"I say darling, jolly good thing that fellow was there to save the day for us the other evening. For all we know we could have been sitting on old Tommy Crapper for the next fortnight, or worse, on a drip in a hospital relieving ourselves into a bed pan. Can you imagine the embarrassment?"

"Oh, really George, I'm sure it's just over-exaggerated poppy cock."

The doorbell chimed in the background. "The delivery is early for the kitchens," George mumbled.

A maid entered the dining room carrying a bouquet of flowers. "These are addressed to you, Lady Rossford," she said handing them to her.

"Who are they from? They are beautiful," said George.

"I'll just check, there's an envelope stamped from The Queen's Royal Theatre." Except there was something different about this envelope, it was thick, padded as if it contained something more than just a card. George sat opposite, waiting with anticipation for her to open the envelope to reveal the card which she held for a while, curious as to what else may be concealed within it.

"Well, come on darling, are you going to open it or just sit gawping at it?" George wasn't a patient type.

"I can't see the point really, it's only going to be another one of those ghastly insincere little cards. I'll pop it in my handbag and open it later when I have more time, besides I've promised to accompany Polly to Clarridges this morning and I'm already late getting ready, she'll be here soon."

"Oh, come now darling, what difference is a few seconds going to make now?"

The more she held the envelope the more suspicious she became of its contents. She knew how to handle George and gave him short shrift whilst she left to get ready for her shopping trip.

Once she was in the safety of her bathroom she made sure to lock the door behind her before she opened the envelope. She pulled out a letter and as she did so an SD card dropped to the floor at her feet.

My dearest Lady Veronica, I'm so sorry I forgot to ask you to smile on Saturday evening, because yes, believe it or not you were filmed on our very own candid camera. Well, two to be exact. We've taken the time to edit it for you and I think you will find it truly entertaining. Several encrypted copies have been distributed throughout the country and even internationally. So, what's the purpose of all this I hear you ask? Well, it's my insurance. If anything out of the ordinary should happen to myself, my friend Jack, or any of my close friends in fact, then the encryption codes will be released and your sordid little secret will be released to the press, destroying your husband's career, your respected status, and the trust and love of Millie. She means the world to me, and I will not stop seeing her unless she stops loving me. I love her and am prepared to keep one eye over my shoulder at all times. So here we have it, stale mate!!

Yours,
 James.

With that, Lady Rossford coolly and calmly wrapped the SD card in a small ream of toilet tissue and flushed it down the toilet, thus removing one piece of evidence against her. It was a start. She moved over to the dressing table and sat for a while staring at herself in the mirror, contemplating her next move. "Poor deluded fool. If it's chess he wants to play then it's chess we shall play," she spoke to her reflection in the mirror as she began to apply her make up. She pulled her mobile from her clutch bag and pulled up a contact she hadn't seen or spoken to for at least three years and called him.

"Stanley, how are you darling? It's Veronica Rossford."

"I'm fine Lady Rossford, for what do I owe the honour of this call? How's George, I haven't seen him in a while?"

Stanley was a bank manager, but he was in actual fact a ghost. Not the supernatural type, of course. His true identity of head of MI6 remained shrouded in mystery to all but a few people.

"I'm sorry to have to land you with this but I've been rather silly. It's a rather delicate matter. Are you available to meet me in person?"

Stanley wouldn't normally give the time of day to a request like this, but suspecting the worst for his old friend George and wishing to avert a national scandal, he felt compelled to meet Lady Rossford. "Of course, where would you like to meet?"

"How about lunch at Claridges? My treat."

He was already checking his schedule and his day was, on the whole, clear apart from a couple of meetings with his subordinates, which he could have cancelled at the drop of a hat anyway. "Great, shall I see you there at one?"

"That would be lovely. Thanks so much for making the time to meet with me."

Stanley sat back in his chair looking forward to his distraction later in the day, and he was already savouring a fine lunch.

Lady Veronica entered the study where George was working. "There's been a slight change of plan. Polly can't make it this morning after all. I'd still like to go, I've rather set my mind to it."

"Of course you must, darling. Look, I'm not using the car, would you like me to get David to take you and wait?"

"Oh, you are such a dear. That would be lovely."

George picked up the phone and called his driver and, at a moment's notice, the car was sat outside the front of the house awaiting Lady Rossford.

Lady Rossford was shown to a table and sat sipping at a glass of sherry whilst she waited for her companion. She was soon joined by Stanley at one o'clock on the dot. No sooner was he shown to the table than the waiter was pouring out a glass of red wine for him to sample. "I took the liberty of ordering for you Stanley. I hope I'm not mistaken, but 'Rothschilde' isn't it?"

"Spot on Lady Rossford." Stanley lifted the glass, swirled the wine around, and lowered his nose in before taking a sip. He nodded to the waiter to express his approval and the waiter duly went on his way.

"Please, I think we can dispense with the formalities. Call me Veronica, I insist."

Stanley perused the lunch menu and Lady Rossford sat patiently. She was a regular patron, there no need to scrutinise the menu, she knew it by heart. Stanley ordered his lunch time treat, took in another sip of his wine and settled down to business. "So, what is it I can help you with Lady . . . Veronica?"

Lady Rossford went on to explain how she had been duped into being led down to the kitchens and her ensuing embarrassment, however her story was by this time subject to some rather serious editing. "I'm sorry, but I can't fully explain what happened in the kitchen. It's all very hazy. I think they may have spiked my drink beforehand."

"Rohypnol," Stanley interrupted. "It's a dating drug. It's not uncommon. Most can't remember a thing that's happened to them, but obviously all the symptoms are present the day after. Is this why you're here La . . . err . . . Veronica, do you think you may have been raped?"

"Well, of course there is that, but they filmed it and they're threatening to go public. I can't believe I've been such a fool." She raised her napkin to her eye and gently wiped away a tear she had managed to muster.

Stanley reached out a hand to comfort her. "Do you have the ransom note? Is there any evidence to verify that you were actually filmed? They could be bluffing."

"Oh, I can't believe how foolish I've been. I panicked and flushed it down the toilet. They sent a note and an SD card which I flushed away. I couldn't let George find it. It would crush him."

The damsel in distress act was very believable and Stanley was certainly swayed to her dilemma. "Do you have any idea who could have done this to you, Veronica?"

"No, I'm afraid I don't. Will you help me Stanley, if not for me, for George's sake? He doesn't deserve this. He's an honourable man. I simply can't allow him to tolerate such an indignation as a result of my misgivings. Drug induced or not." Lady Rossford knew that there was no need to implicate James into the equation. She knew that the ensuing investigation would quickly close in on James, along with his friends.

All the time Stanley was weighing up the story put before him. Ordinarily, he would have thanked Lady Rossford for the lunch and walked away as it would not have been in the national interest to pursue the case, but in reality there was very little going on in the way of national security and he needed to keep his department on their toes, and what better way than a short investigation to allay a minor scandal from the tabloids. So, he took it.

Lady Rossford entered the car. "Driver, take me to Harrods. I think a little retail therapy is in order." Her mood had lifted. "Checkmate!" she pronounced to herself smugly.

Chapter Twenty-Three
Out-Foxing the Fox

Thursday 21st July 2016

Stanley briefed his crew, wound them up and let them go. There was no physical evidence to go with, but these were experts and had access to all but the most personal details of every guest that attended The Queen's gala. They didn't need it, of course, Mike and Lady Rossford were clearly evident on both the camera footage they had commandeered from the TV studio and the security cameras that were dotted about the place.

"This is child's play. I reckon we'll have this sussed soon. What are we going to do for the other seven hours of the day?" one of the operatives boasted to the other. "Let's see where our friend Mike Crosby leads us to next, shall we?" By the end of day one they had linked Mike back to Dick, whose identity was confirmed on the camera footage twice as a waiter and a guest. From this point, it was easy to triangulate back through to Peter and Jack. They were both picked up on camera footage leaving the Gala dressed as guests. Jess, whom they were already aware of as Mike's wife, and Mike were the only two bona fide guests. The rest were imposters.

By mid-afternoon they had reported their findings back to Stanley and he instructed them to carry out a cyber search of all identified, which essentially involved hacking their computers through their own Wi-Fi systems. This was proving to be more time-consuming and far less fruitful.

"I'm sorry mate, we appear to have hit a bit of a dead end with the cyber search. I'm not getting anything suspicious in the slightest."

Stanley paused for a while. He didn't like to waste resources on wild goose chases, but as with a game of poker, he decided to go all in to satisfy his own whimsical intrigue. "Ok, let's step up the game a little bit, put them under surveillance and hack their phones as well."

Within half an hour one of the operatives returned. "I'm sorry, sir. I don't know how we missed it. We found some dialogue between Jess Crosby and Millie Rossford, Lady Rossford's daughter, implicating another man, James Simpson. He's been dating Millie for the past few months. We've taken the liberty of adding him to our investigation. It turns out that he was present at the royal gala evening as a security guard. We didn't pick him up on any camera footage.

"Pass that here, let me see." Stanley took the paper from his operative. "James Simpson. Do you think they're in cahoots together? A neat little scam to relieve her mother of several thousands of pounds? Do some more digging. Find out if there's some history behind these two. See if you can find any skeletons in the closet."

After a few more days his chief operative reported back to him. "I think we've cracked it, sir. There's another man involved, Mick Brownlow. He meets up with them at the local pub for Wednesday quiz night. We hacked into his system. It took a while, everything was encrypted. Jacob soon figured it all out though. We've removed any trace of it and replaced it with an episode of the Tellytubbies. This is the only copy left." He duly handed over a disc. "It makes for some interesting viewing. I went through it several times . . . in the matter of national security, of course."

Stanley looked at him, noting his body language which reflected a certain smugness. Jacob isn't some incredibly intelligent geek, it's actually an acronym for Joint Allied Code Breaker, a computer programme funded by NATO for the preserve of international security.

"What about James Simpson and Millie Rossford, find any dirt on them?"

"We're struggling with that one, sir. We've established a link between his ex-wife and Millie which goes back to their uni days. There's a good chance that Simpson knew Miss Rossford back then, but there's no hard evidence to prove it. As far as any criminal history is concerned, they're both squeaky clean. Model citizens. In fact, James was hand-picked to make up the security guard numbers on the evening of the royal gala."

"Go on. How did he manage to wangle his way into that position? Are we barking up the wrong tree or what? He'd have to be some kind of mastermind to bring all this together. I don't get it."

"I'm with you on that one, sir. We ran the odds through the computer and they came out at five million to one."

"So, are we saying that all this is just a fluke? What did he do to get the in on the security team?"

"He foiled a robbery from the warehouse he worked at even though he'd been tied to his seat, knocked out cold, and taken a beating. His boss was so impressed that he offered James the job at the royal gala performance."

"Hold on a minute, what's his boss got to do with all this?"

"It turns out that he'd done a full term with Scotland Yard and was asked to put together a team to make up the numbers. Just menial duties, of course."

"So, what are the chances that James engineered the warehouse break in to give him credibility to get the job as the security guard?"

"Impossible. Only Geoff knew about the venue, the rest were kept in the dark. Our man at the yard queried him about it. He planted a sensor on him when they met. Measured his heart rate, sweat glands, everything. Completely clear, sir. Sir, how far do you want us to take this? Do you want us to bring him in?"

"Yes . . . No, wait. Better still. Book him for me. You did say that he's a chauffeur, didn't you?"

"Yes sir. Weddings and private hire."

Stanley raised his hand to his chin and thought for a while. "I've got an appointment coming up with Chief of Police in Birmingham about some increased terrorist activity there. Let's reschedule it to a nice hotel. We'll treat him to a slap-up dinner. Book James Simpson as my driver. Get him to pick me up from the bank. Tell him it's for a banking convention. Book me in on the train for my return leg, first class of course."

Tuesday 2nd August 2016
James arrived outside the bank and was about to exit his car to announce his arrival when the rear door opened. "Milbank, I take it you're my car for the day."

James responded his affirmation, although he would have liked to have responded that he wasn't in actual fact a car.

He also assumed that with a name like Milbank that banking had been in the family for a seriously long time.

"Do you know where we're going, driver?"

"I've been told to take you to the Regal Hotel in Edgebaston."

"That's right, just around the corner from the cricket ground. There's no cricket on today so there shouldn't be any issues with traffic and parking for that matter . . . err, the car-park's a bit pokey. Expanded the hotel and forgot about the blasted carpark."

James had already guessed that this wasn't going to be one of those silent journeys. He'd picked up a chatterer. His customer did quieten down for a while, pulling some paperwork from his briefcase and studying its contents. The silence was broken when his passenger's phone pinged to let him know he had a message and the silence was broken again with his passengers agitated voice after he had read its contents. "Damn and blast, every bloody time."

James thought it prudent to enquire whether there was a problem. Had he forgotten something? "Everything ok, sir? Do you need me to go back for anything?"

"No no. It's the damned wife, she wants me to go and visit her mother in Solihull and check that she's ok."

"I'll make the time for you, sir. If that's the issue."

"God no, I'd rather you didn't. She's been nothing but a thorn in my side since the day we met. God only knows how I've tolerated her for so long. I really must love my wife. Of course, she doesn't have half a clue as to how conniving her dear mother can be. Is it just me, what about you, do you get on with your mother-in-law?"

"Ex mother in law, and yes and no. She's been a bit frosty where I'm concerned, but I don't think she held any malice towards me. I just didn't live up to her expectations for her precious little daughter." James was relaxed by this time, cruising on an open stretch of motorway. He'd gotten himself caught up in the conversation.

"Any future mother-in law-on the horizon?"

"God, don't get me started. She's the mother of all mother-in-laws."

"How so?"

"Trust me, she warned me off Millie in no uncertain terms." At last Stanley had him where he wanted him. All he had to do now is continue to push his buttons. "Any reason why she's so dead set against you?"

"Yes, she told me straight. We're not cut from the same cloth. You see, she's high society. She's an aristocrat and I'm nothing more than a commoner."

"At the end of the day what can she do about it? If you want to continue seeing her daughter she can't do anything about that, can she?"

"Jees, you don't know the half of it. If I told you, you wouldn't believe me."

"Try me, by my reckoning we've got at least another hour and I've got nothing better to do. I'm not one of these that can work whilst they're being driven."

"Seriously, I can't see the point. You simply won't believe me."

"Come on, you've led me halfway down the garden path now. You can't leave me hanging. What's the worst thing that can happen?"

"Well, let's put it this way, she threatened to have me bumped off."

"By bumped off you mean killed?"

"Yes, a neat little contract 25k or I could take 30k, leave Millie, and stay alive."

"Cripes, it does sound far-fetched I'll warrant you that. How long ago was all this?"

"About three months."

"And you're still seeing this erm . . . Millie."

"I had to take matters into my own hands. Got myself an insurance policy."

"Excuse my ignorance, I assume this insurance policy is metaphorical." Stanley held his hand up and dipped his forefinger and middle finger as he said it.

"You could say that."

"So, what is it?"

"Ah well, as Tom Cruise once famously said, 'I could tell you, but then I'd have to kill you'. Let's just say that if anything should happen to me, or anyone close to me for that matter, she'll be made to suffer with life changing consequences."

"If it's as good as you say it is, you could turn the tables on her and blackmail her."

"You've got to be kidding. It's not a war I'm looking for, I just want this relationship to have a chance."

"Sounds like the understatement of the century to me. It sounds like you've taken some serious risks."

"You're right there. I have quite literally put my life on the line for her and I've stretched some friendships to the absolute limit. All just for the chance for me to spend some time with another person."

"If anything else, it's certainly an entertaining story you have there. One for the grandchildren, I'll wager."

"We're approaching our turn off. Time to concentrate if you don't mind, sir."

"Of course, forgive me. I won't interrupt anymore." James drew up in front of the doors to a grand well-established hotel. He pulled the catch on his door to open it, but before he could exit the car to release his passenger, Stanley piped up with another question. "I'm sorry to keep going on but you've rather spiked my imagination. Do you think that Millie's mother may have done something like this before?"

"A hundred percent. She got to my friend Jack, he was seeing her other daughter. She paid him five grand. It was either that or a nasty motorbike accident."

"Why only five grand for him and thirty for you?"

"I've wondered about that myself. I can only figure that she saw me as a bigger risk, you see her other daughter's a bit flaky. Jack and her probably wouldn't have lasted long any-way. I'm guessing she wanted him out of the way for debutant season or some such thing. As for me, well Millie's a different kettle of fish. She has a strong will, probably gets it from her mother. As far as I'm concerned, well, call me old fashioned but I love her, and it's as simple as that."

"What about before all this, do you think she's been habitually scaring off unsuitable boyfriends?"

"Can't say for sure, but when we first met her parents it was out of the blue and Millie was pretty upset. She basically said that her mother had put the kiss of death on every relationship she'd ever had. I remember way back in her uni days that within a few weeks of meeting her mother some chap called Gerald just disappeared into the ether. Kept making one excuse after another not to see Millie and the relationship fizzled out."

"Well, if it's any consolation, I don't think it's an insurance policy you need. I think you're going to need a guardian angel."

"Oh great, thanks for that," James exclaimed sarcastically with hint of despair in his voice.

"Look, I feel like I know you now, if you drive for me again feel free to call by my first name."

"Which is?"

"Oh, sorry, yes. Forgive me. Gabriel."

With that, James continued to exit the car and opened the door for his passenger. "Have a good day s—Gabriel"

"I will, thank you, James." With that he walked quickly to the doors of the hotel and dis-appeared.

James watched on with a quizzical expression on his face and began to mutter to himself. "I don't remember telling him my name? Crickey, if he wasn't wearing a suit I could have sworn I was driving Miss Marple." James removed his jacket and tie and placed them on the backseat of the car. Time to relax and head home. He had plans for a special evening with Millie.

Stanley was a little early for his appointment with the Chief of Police, so he ordered a coffee and took a seat in the lobby. Once he'd settled he ruminated over James's story. He was convinced that Lady Rossford was the true villain of the peace and poor old James was having to wrestle with this titan of society. It really was a true-life David and Goliath battle, but there's no way James could win this without some help. A guardian angel. Stanley hated wasting resources on matters that weren't of national security, but he was in too deep with this.

Lady Rossford had tried to play him, and in the long run James didn't stand a chance. He needed a champion for his cause and Stanley was right in the thick of it all. He pulled his phone from his pocket and called his chief operative. "Steven, I need you to clarify a few things for me. Firstly, check out if there's been a transfer of funds into Jack Connolly's account in the last six months. Let me know where it originated from."

Steven came back with the answer that Stanley already knew. It had come direct from Lady Rossford's personal bank account. Stanley got them to do some more digging into Lady Rossford's financial affairs, and over a period of two decades, substantial sums of money had been transferred to various individuals, all male. Even Gerald's substantial overdrafts from his uni days had all been cleared in one fell swoop. Stanley listened patiently as Steven reeled off a list to him.

Stanley cut him off mid-flow. "Ok Steven, I think we've all got the drift. Let's turn the tables back onto Lady Rossford. Watch her accounts and put a tap on her phones."

"Ok sir. Are there any keywords we need to listen out for?"

"The usual stuff in cases like these, hit, target, mark, thousand, cash, grand, and twenty-five would be useful in this case as well. Put Little Willy on it." Little Willy, although pronounced like that, the willy part is actually spelt Willie, and is yet another acronym for a clever computer system, Word Intelligent Liaison Listening Interpretation

Equipment. A sophisticated system designed to trigger an alarm if certain words are used frequently enough.

The original system it was based on was developed in the seventies and took up a whole room. That system was fondly known as Big Willy. Little Willy is far more potent than its predecessor and is capable of monitoring hundreds of phone lines at any one time, developed primarily to monitor suspected terrorists and such like. By now though, Little Willy is the size of a laptop and probably should be called Micro Willy but I don't think the male-dominated domains of the secret service could bring themselves to call it any less than Little Willy.

On the train back, Stanley decided that it was time to give Lady Rossford an update. "It's good news . . . Yes, we've retrieved all of the encrypted material and carried out a thorough search of all premises involved and believe we have all hard copies, but that's obviously more difficult to substantiate. Of course, we have retained a copy on our files as a matter of our investigation protocol."

Lady Rossford was less pleased about that. She wanted every fragment of evidence to be destroyed. "Please Stanley, is that really necessary? Just knowing there's something out there unnerves me; I fear I may have a breakdown over it."

Stanley reassured her that it was perfectly safe and would end up buried in an archive somewhere. She had duped him once, and he wasn't about to let it happen again. He hadn't removed it for her sake. It was for his old friend and colleague, George, which went back to their military days.

Stanley had one last thing to say. "Oh, and one other thing, we'll be monitoring your bank accounts for the foreseeable future for any substantial funds that may be leaving your account. If these people are as unscrupulous as we believe, then they may get to you in another way. A way where you are unable to contact us. Call it an insurance." Stanley had everything tied up in a nice little bundle.

Or did he?

Lady Rossford sat back and pondered over her next move. If only it was a case of calling a hitman and transferring the necessary funds, but she knew she would incriminate herself immediately. A different tack was in order. She picked up her phone and began to ring around her substantial list of friends and contacts. "Hello darling, it's been so long. We really should meet up for a catch up. Did I mention that I've been roped into a charity event . . . Yes I've been asked to raise some money for children in need. It's a bit of a competition and I've been pitted against that ghastly woman the Dowager of Fortminster. It's cash only . . . Yes, they thought it would be fun to see us all turn up with sacks full of cash and top it all off with a publicity stunt."

A little red diode blinked on Little Willie's circuitry.

"How much am I looking to raise? That's a good question. I think twenty-five thousand should see me clear, that's my target." Little Willie's diode blinked some more. Of course, if this were way back in the seventies, Big Willie's room full of monster machines with spools of tape would be whizzing around at fever pitch by this time.

Little Willie did his job and Stanley's team set to follow her every move. They tracked her and watched on as one bulging envelope after another was passed across a table at various lunch time meetings.

Friday 12th August 2016

Another clandestine meeting for Lady Veronica but this time it was different. It wasn't her receiving a package. This time she was the one handing over the package. Two to be precise. Bulging A4 size envelopes. Stanley's operative reeled off several photographs of the recipient.

Stanley browsed through the photographs with Steven. "Have you run facial identification on these?"

"Yes sir. We don't know his true identity. So far, we have ten hits, all the same face but all different names and IDs to corroborate every one of them. There's an assassin out there called 'The Ghost' and we believe it may be him. He assumes the identity of recently deceased individuals before the authorities are fully up to speed."

"Have you got a tail on him?"

"Yes sir, but he's a slippery fish. He keeps disguising himself. We don't actually know what he really looks like. One minute he's fair and fat, the next he's dark and slim or vice versa."

"What's he been up to?"

"Good question sir. He's been tailing James Simpson. Not everywhere, you understand, but he seems to have honed in on his journey to his girlfriend's."

"Do you think that's where he's planning to make his hit?"

"If I were a betting man that's what I would say. Oh, one other thing sir. If this is 'The Ghost', we have intel to say that he specialises in making all his hits look like innocent accidents."

"Check out the route for me. Let me know if there are any accident black spots along the way." Steven checked with the local constabulary and villages along the route. For the most part the journey was rural.

It turned out there was one sharp bend at the end of a long straight that has a name all to itself. Devil's Dyke. There's a drop of about eight foot into a ditch approximately six feet deep of water. If any unsuspecting motorist were to misjudge the corner and leave the road, they would disappear over the edge and out of sight. If they were lucky they would escape and scramble back to the top of the embankment to flag down some help, but more often than not they become trapped and either die of exposure on a cold winter's night or drown in a flipped over car. Only to be found the next day by the local farmer.

Stanley scrutinised the photographs of The Ghost laid out on his desk. There was something familiar about him, something that triggered an old memory. He figured that Lady Rossford possibly knew this individual before he became 'The Ghost', and if she knew him then he was likely to be connected to George, and if there was a connection to George then there would be an equally good chance there would be a similar connection back to him.

He searched back through regiment archive photographs of all those that served with him or alongside him during his service with George. He focused in on five potential, young, fresh-faced individuals, but one pulled at his gut. Harry Hutchinson who specialised in bomb disposal. Stanley couldn't recollect him, but his service history made interesting reading. One minute the hero and next the villain. Known as a bit of a ladies' man, resulting in more than one cover up for his philandering ways. Stanley couldn't be sure, but perhaps Lady Rossford and Harry had enjoyed some extracurricular activities together. His file was closed as missing in action while serving in Afghanistan, which also meant that he could still be out there. He probably became a mercenary. He had the right kind of profile match. The facial match came back at eighty-eight percent. Not conclusive but close enough.

Stanley called Steven in to discuss his findings and work out whether they can make any sense as to how he will carry out his hit on James. Stanley slid the photograph of the young Harry Hutchinson across his desk and under Steven's gaze. "Look familiar?"

"Yes, I can make out a resemblance, but I would be hard pushed to say that he is our man. Have you done a facial check yet, sir?"

"Came back at eighty-eight percent. That's close enough for me."

"Ok, so we think we have a name for The Ghost, how is that going to help us with the case in hand?"

"His speciality back in the day was bomb disposal. So, he has good knowledge of electronic triggers and remote detonation. We also know from what little intel we have that when he makes a hit they can always be put down to a tragic accident of some kind and we think that in James Simpson's case it will happen at Devil's Dyke."

"That's an awful lot of supposition if you don't mind me saying so, sir."

"Yes well, as my wife keeps telling me, sometimes you just have to go with what you feel your guts are telling you. Keep the tail on him and let me know if he goes anywhere near James Simpson's car. Something in my gut's telling me that he's going to rig the car for an accident at Devil's Dyke."

The vigil covering The Ghost was becoming one of monotony. He'd pop out to the shop now and again to get a paper and just general everyday supplies. Steven's men were used to it. Nothing happening for ages, then something.

Friday 19th August 2016
"Aye aye, he's on the move again." They watched him get into his car and expected to follow him to the supermarket as usual, but this time he headed out into the countryside to Little Piddley.

He parked up outside the small shop but didn't go inside. His destination from here was entirely different. The driver of the following car parked some distance ahead and his passenger exited to follow his prey at a suitable distance.

Stanley's man trailed The Ghost a hundred yards behind, carrying a folded paper in his hand as if he'd just purchased it from the shop and were making his way home. The Ghost turned onto Ermine Way, the road of James's abode.

As he turned the corner and disappeared out of view his follower sped up. He rounded the corner in time to make out The Ghost heading into James's driveway and was once more obstructed from view by the hedgerow that fronted the house.

He continued to walk at a stroll in the hope that he might see what he was up to. He was too late. As he drew level with the driveway, The Ghost reappeared and headed back in the direction of his car. Stanley's man radioed through to his partner that The Ghost was heading back to his car and to keep tailing him. It would be too risky for him to follow him back. He'd have to get someone from HQ to pick him up.

"There's been some developments, sir. The Ghost has paid a visit to James Simpson's house."

"Go on, spill the beans."

"Ah yes, well, we can't tell you a great deal from there. He was obscured from view by the hedgerow at the front of the property. Our man watched him enter the driveway then re-appear a minute later. Once he was out of sight, my man did a recky and came up with nothing. No forced entry, no tampered locks, nothing."

"That's because he focused on the wrong thing. It wasn't the house he was interested in, it was the car. I specifically told you to focus on the car."

Steven sensed his boss's agitation but tried to remain cool. "The Bentley's locked away in the garage so he must have tampered with the Corsa. It's his run about car, must save him a fortune in fuel compared to the gas guzzler!"

"When is he next due to visit his girlfriend?"

"He has a regular Friday night slot now. He's made sure it's clear in his rota with the warehouse."

"That's today. When does he make his way over there?"

"He leaves at about seven. As regular as clockwork. Probably waits for the rush hour to clear."

"There's only one thing for it, we're going to have to get that car to the impound and check it over."

"That should be a doddle if we act now. It's still only twelve and he doesn't get up till 1.30."

"Great, well off you go and let me know what you find. Oh, yes, and keep the car. Let the local constabulary know that we've got it and to expect it to be reported in as stolen.

Tell them it's all part of a covert operation. They must not try to apprehend the vehicle while we have it. Make that clear."

"Ok, right you are sir."

Stanley sat back in his chair and looked once more at the photograph of The Ghost. Perhaps all the resource he's given up on this won't be folly after all. He was close to bringing in an assassin who before all this remained buried deep within the foundations of the underworld. Suddenly, his investigations have become part of the national interest and worth-while.

The order was given and James's car was driven away to the compound. There was nothing difficult about it, MI6 had access to all key codes for pretty much any vehicle. They simply blipped a key fob and drove it away. In the meantime, James lay blissfully unaware in the land of nod.

Steven entered Stanley's office with a smug expression on his face and threw a ball of plasticine, about the size of a gobby marble. He then placed a tiny printed circuit board on the desk next to it about the size of a nail on one of your fingers.

Stanley picked up the soft tactile ball and smelt it. "Semtex," he said without any hesitation.

"Yes sir, we found it embedded around the brake line feeding one of the front breaks on the Corsa. The P.C.B was embedded into it. On the back of the P.C.B nestled a small watch battery. The trigger for detonation," Stanley uttered matter-of-factly.

"Yes sir. That's why I handed it to you separately. No harm can be done now. Looks like your hunch was right all along. Blow the brake line on the approach to Devil's Dyke and over you go, and if that doesn't finish him off there's no end of options to finish the job. A blow to the head, broken neck or simple drowning. Of course, if there were an investigation afterwards they'd find a brake line that's been damaged as part of the accident."

"What do you think the range is on this thing?"

"Fifty to a hundred yards tops, sir. It's similar to a remote lock on a car."

"Look, we're close now, whatever you do don't lose sight of this Ghost. We don't know for sure that he'll detonate this thing at Devil's Dyke. Don't lose him." Stanley reiterated his words to drive home the importance of it all. "Better still, put an extra unit on it. Put one on his flat and another laying low at Devil's Dyke."

"Right you are, sir." Things were getting tasty and Steven was starting to savour the thought of the chase.

A black BMW drew up fifty yards away from the Ford Focus which housed the two men that had been scoping The Ghost's apartment for the past three days. The Focus moved off and headed in the direction of Devil's Dyke.

Steven reckoned that his target was likely to have eyes on stalks by now. It would be too risky for him to keep seeing the same car around in various locations.

He was right.

The Ghost peered through his window and the Ford Focus he had been suspicious of had gone. He glanced left and right. The BMW was just out of sight. He'd check again in an hour and every hour until it was his time to leave. The Ghost took one last look out of his windows before leaving for his destination, but this time he didn't leave by the door. He left via a fire escape on the end of the apartment block out of view from both the front and back of the building. He made his way to a row of communal garages with up and over doors. He had one rented—paying cash. All completely untraceable back to him.

The unassuming mark three Golf fired up first time, even though it had been sat dormant for the last six months. Tax, MOT and insurance all up to date under one of his assumed identities.

The occupants of the black BMW were becoming restless, they had been told to expect some movement by 1800 hours. "It's 6:05pm, what do you reckon?" The driver motioned to his passenger.

"I was thinking the same thing. I'll go and give it a quick recky." He quickly returned. "I don't reckon he's in there. There's a fire exit door at the end of the building out of sight, I reckon he's given us the slip."

"What, deliberately? Or do you think he used it as a precaution."

"God knows mate." He went to the boot of the car and pulled out a Royal Mail high vis jacket, a small parcel and an electronic signature pad. It was used as an excuse to get a suspect to answer a door without leading to too much suspicion. They would pretend it was for a neighbour who was out. On this occasion, his knocks went unheard. He went on to pick the lock. His suspicions were confirmed: there was nobody there. He got back to the car with a hurried walk. "Radio through to HQ. He's given us the slip, he's not there."

"Great, that's all we need. The gaffer's going to be livid."

Steven didn't take the news well. His only hope now was to focus on Devil's Dyke. Stanley had been spot on with everything up until now. This had to pan out. He gave the order for his men to head out to Devil's Dyke, but park half a mile before and wait for the Corsa to pass, then fall in behind and scope out the assassin.

James woke up at 1.30pm, his body now well accustomed to it. He threw open the curtains and took a double take. He stared at the empty space on his driveway. His stomach clenched. "What the . . . I locked it, I know I did. This is Little Piddley, nobody steals cars around here."

He ran downstairs to find his keys on the kitchen worktop where he had left them. He checked through the lounge window to make sure that his eyes weren't deceiving him. The drive remained empty. "Oh, no. Surely not?"

An even more worrying thought entered his mind. What if they merely wanted to move the Corsa out of the way to get to the Bentley? He threw on a dressing gown and some slippers, and ran out to the garage door. He opened it and the Bentley stared back at him like an obedient dog.

He went to the end of the driveway and looked left and right for as far as he could see. Still no sign of the Corsa. He looked up the number for the local police station and rang in to report his car stolen.

"It's been a busy day today, sir, but we should be able to get someone around to yours by seven this evening to take a statement." They were given specific orders not to allow James to leave until 7.30 at the earliest.

"Can't you come any sooner? I have another engagement and I need to leave at seven." James felt like his day was going from bad to worse. "I'm sorry, that's the earliest time I can do. It's only a formality sir. We won't take up any more time than we have to. Half an hour at the most, then we'll be able to raise a crime number for your insurance."

"Right ok then, but if you get a chance to come around sooner, I'll be here all day." James resigned himself to the situation. He picked up his mobile and texted Millie that he was going to be late explaining that the Corsa had been stolen from his driveway. A thought occurred to him that if he was going to take the Bentley, then why not make a night of it. After all, he owed her so much for the transformation of his drab house into a des res. He set the rest of the afternoon booking a nice little Italian restaurant and some tickets for the theatre. Tonight, she would be getting the VIP treatment.

Seven pm and another man was assigned to the task of driving the route to Millie in James's Corsa, whilst the two men in the black BMW followed close behind. They were both in radio contact via walkie-talkie. The two others were now on foot in the vicinity of Devil's Dyke, each wearing typical rambler garb and carrying binoculars, trying to assume the identity of bird watchers.

"See anything yet?" one said to the other as he peered through his bins.

"Nah nothing."

"Me neither. Are they sure he's out here?"

"The boss hasn't been wrong yet."

"Yeah well, there's always a first time."

"What about that copse? He could be laying low in there. There's no way we'd be able to pick him out from here."

"Can't get too close, though, or we'll spook him. Look, this is as good a spot as any. The light's fading and I can barely see where I'm putting my feet. You got that ground sheet."

"With you on that one. Make sure your radio's turned down as well. You know how noise travels out in the open."

They laid out low on the ground sheet and focused in on the copse a couple of hundred yards ahead of them and about eighty yards away from Devil's Dyke.

Their hunch was right. The Ghost laid low in a camouflaged bivuac on the edge of the copse facing Devil's Dyke. He'd taken another road which runs parallel, but half a mile apart where there's a track leading down to a fishing lake on the far side of the copse.

The black BMW took the lead, heading up to Devil's Dyke corner and staying a couple of hundred yards ahead of the Corsa. The passenger radioed through to the Corsa. "Right then, you know the score. If we can't eyeball him before you get to Devil's Dyke you're under orders to crash the car there. And remember you can only use the handbrake to scrub off any speed. No brake lights. I repeat NO brake lights."

"Great, thanks for that. You'd better fucking well eyeball him, that's all I can say."

The black BMW approached Devil's Dyke corner.

"You see anything?" the driver asked his passenger.

"Not a fucking thing. It's pitch black out there," he radioed through to the two men out in the field.

A muted voice came through their radio.

"See anything?" he radioed back.

"Sweet FA, mate."

They then radioed back through to the Corsa. "Sorry mate, we've got diddly squat, you're gonna have to ditch it, and remember, no brake lights." The driver mimicked him as he said it as if he were a granny trying to teach him to suck eggs. "And don't forget to discharge your pistol when the red diode lights up."

"Cheers guys, you've really thought this through, haven't you? I've got to fire my gun out of the window in one hand and apply the hand brake with the other. How am I meant to steer this thing?"

"That's the whole point dumbass, you're meant to be having an accident."

"A controlled accident!"

"You'll be fine. Just ditch the gun as soon as you've fired it." The little red diode taped to the dash was set to light up when it received the signal from The Ghost's remote trigger. They'd worked out the frequency from the tiny PCB they had pulled out of the semtex.

The black BMW rounded the corner and disappeared into the distance, pulled up once out of sight and completed a three-point turn ready to head back.

By this time, the Corsa was on the approach to the corner. The Ghost wore night vision goggles and was easily able to identify the shape of the Corsa approaching. As the vehicle got within thirty yards of the corner, he pressed the button on his remote detonation device. As expected he heard the tiny explosive and watched on as the car didn't brake and went over the edge of the bend, crashing into the ditch below. There was only one thing left to do. Make sure that whatever the outcome of the accident that the final result is tragic death.

The driver of the Corsa was carrying more speed than he wanted when he hit the bend at Devil's Dyke corner. He threw the gun into the passenger foot well a split second before taking control of the wheel and hitting the bend. So late, in fact, that the accident wasn't controlled at all. The car launched itself off the raised verge and lurched left and right as the tyres grabbed into the soft soil of the embankment.

The driver's head was swung left and right, hitting the side glass and knocking him out cold. The car finally came to rest at an angle with the left-hand half of the car submerged in the murky water of the dyke and the right side still exposed, with the headlight shining along the length of the dyke.

His walkie-talkie crackled to life, breaking the eerie silence that comes after an accident. "Are you ok? Over."

The question wasn't heard and they received no answer. The driver hung by his seatbelt with his head slumped on the passenger seat. His gun and taser that he was to use to disable his assailant lay in the passenger foot well, gradually disappearing as water from the dyke filtered through, passed the seals of the passenger door, and worked its way up to the driver's head.

His companions laying low radioed through once more. "Stu, I repeat, are you ok? Come in. Over."

Still no reply.

The radio operator turned to his mate. "I think he's out cold. Can you see any activity yet?"

His mate stared through the night vision binoculars, focusing in on the copse ahead of them. "I've got him. He's making his way over to the car. Looks like he's wearing night vision goggles. He seems to be making easy work of it. Damn those fucking government cut-backs, all we've got are these shitty binoculars. Once he gets to the embankment the other side of the bend he'll be out of sight. We'll have to make our move to intercept then. Get ready on my say so."

The Ghost made easy work of crossing the terrain. The agents knew it wouldn't be anywhere near as easy for them as they would effectively be running blind.

"Ok, let's go." They got up and ran in the direction of the shaft of light illuminating the embankment in front of them. Without the benefit of night vision goggles it was heavy going as they lurched over one trough after another. They couldn't use a torch—that would have given the game away. It had to be done under the cover of complete darkness. They got to within fifty yards of the car and heard the door open. It had to be The Ghost.

The Ghost couldn't believe his luck. He found his target hanging by his seatbelt, his head just an inch above the rapidly rising water line. He reached in and pushed his head down into the water.

The freezing cold ditch water brought the driver back to consciousness. Luckily the lap strap held fast and only his forehead and eyes were submerged. His immediate reaction was to lift his head and remove himself, but he couldn't. It took him a moment to realise that it was actually The Ghost stopping him.

Before the water level reached his mouth, he took in a gasp of air and fumbled in the murky depths of the foot well. He knew he was under orders to taser his assailant, but at this moment in time it was life or death, and whichever he found first didn't matter.

One of the field agents had made it to the dyke, jumping as far as he could to cross it. The other had stumbled halfway across the rutted field and twisted his ankle. Despite his best efforts, he was effectively out of the hunt.

The fit field agent followed the shaft of light to the car, but it was too late, he would never make it in time.

The driver's time was up. No matter how many times he swept the foot well of the car he couldn't lay his hands on either the gun or the taser, which was probably rendered useless by the water anyway. His only hope now was to be rescued by one of his companions or drown.

The Ghost was pulled back by what seemed like a mysterious force and the driver was able to raise his head back above the water line. He could make out two dark shadows tussling with each other. A helping hand reached in to support his fatigued body and unclasp the seatbelt buckle which had prevented him from drowning and was now stopping him from escaping his watery prison. He recognised him as one of the agents from the BMW. "You took your time."

"Got stuck in traffic," the other one jested.

The Ghost began to overpower the other agent from the BMW. He was fit, strong, and well used to hand-to-hand combat.

Finally, the third field agent arrived and acted quickly with the backup taser.

The Ghost arched uncontrollably and fell to floor, convulsing and flopping around on the embankment like a fish out of water.

There was no time to waste, they cuffed him and tied his feet and ankles together with cable tidies. They wrestled their wriggling catch up the embankment to the BMW and bundled it into the boot.

The police arrived at James's house at seven and he gave them as much information as he could. They seemed rather officious, which was because they were. They were under instructions to detain him until seven thirty. Finally, once they had left, James rang Millie. Before he could say anything, she answered it and spoke at the same time. "Hi hun, how did you get on with the 'Old Bill'?"

"Jees, don't get me started, they paffed about going over and over the same thing. Anybody would have thought it was the Prime Minister's Jag or something. Anyway, that's why I'm ringing, they've finished with me so I'm about to head out to you."

"Ok, drive carefully and I'll see you soon. Love you hun." She ended the call.

James approached Devil's Dyke corner to be met with blue flashing lights. 'Looks like the Devil's claimed another victim,' he thought to himself as he carefully rounded the corner. He soon arrived safely at Millie's.

She owned a beautifully appointed cottage in the Oxfordshire countryside not too far away from her brother's grand abode. The Bentley looked resplendent on the gravelled drive that fronted the property, but it wasn't to stay there for long, he'd made plans to treat her to a fine meal and take her to see a show later in the evening. He insisted on it, he wanted to thank her for all her help in transforming his house into what is now: a des res. He wanted to treat her as the lady he knew she was.

As she approached the car he opened a rear door. "You're kidding? I'm riding shotgun up front with you," she insisted.

"Oh, very well." He relented, secretly pleased. He loved having her close to him. As they sat for their meal, James's phone rang. He pulled it from his pocket ready to ignore it. He pulled a face in apology to Millie. "It's the police, I guess I should answer it." He accepted the call and listened intently whilst they explained about finding his car.

Millie's inquisitiveness got the better of her. "Well, come on then, spill the beans."

"They've found my car crashed and abandoned at Devil's Dyke corner. They reckon it was taken by joyriders. It's ironic really, I guess I must have driven past my own car crash earlier this evening."

"Crickey, that's a coincidence and a half. I mean for the accident to be on the very same road you used later in the same day."

"Is it a coincidence or do you think there's more to it?"

"I don't know, what are you trying to say, James?"

"Oh, I don't know, maybe it's me trying to be all philosophical. I mean, could all this be down to the great fabric of life?"

"Cripes James, you're not going to get all deep and meaningful on me, are you?"

"Well, look at us Millie, neigh on twenty years ago we were on the verge of something. You have to admit that, yet in the blink of an eye it was snatched away from us for reasons that we will never know and, suddenly, out of the blue, here we are sitting, eating a meal together as a couple."

"So, what you're trying to say is that all this is a part of life's great plan that the fabric of life got torn a little and fate has repaired it to restore order in the world?"

"Do you know what Millie, I don't think I could have put it better myself. I mean Jess even ended up with Mike, and believe me he swears blind that nothing ever happened with that tart at the Halloween party." It became the topic of conversation for the rest of the meal before moving on to the show he had booked.

Following the show, they both jumped into his car, she leant over and kissed him softly, and thanked him for a lovely evening.

"Where to now?" he asked.

Her reply, "Take me home James, besides, I've got a little treat in the freezer for you."

⁂

THE END. WELL, ALMOST

Saturday 20th August 2016

"Morning sir"

"Morning Steven. Congrats on your catch last night."

"Yes sir, thank you, but what exactly do you want us to do with him? We've got him locked up in an interview room downstairs. How do you want us to proceed?"

"Yes, I've been pondering that very question myself, since I first heard you'd brought him in. I think I should like to offer him a deal. Bring him in, out from the cold as it were. Put him on the books."

"Give him a licence to kill?"

"Why not? He's acquitted himself well for more than a decade, possibly two. Sound him out and see how it sits with him. If he doesn't play ball, we'll have to throw him to the lions of the Great British justice system. Oh yes, there's one proviso. He can keep all his assets, but I will need the twenty-five thousand his was promised for his last hit." Stanley sat back in his chair and stared into space for a short moment.

Steven was disappointed that his boss wasn't more excited at the successful completion of their mission. "You ok, sir? You seem a little distracted."

"Blackmail Steven."

"Sorry sir?"

"Have you ever contemplated the act of blackmail."

"No sir, can't say I have."

"It's instilled in us at an early age. Eat your dinner or you won't get any pudding. It's a human thing. Ultimately, it comes down to one thing. You have to have done something wrong. How can anyone blackmail you if you haven't done anything wrong. If you're completely upfront and honest, I mean? The trouble is none of us are, are we?"

"I guess not, sir." And with that Steven left the room.

As soon as he did so, Stanley picked up the phone, scrolled through to a number and rang it. As expected he was connected through to an answer phone. "Hello James, it's Gabriel. I've got a little job for you. I'll call you again later to iron out the details."

Sunday 28th August 2016
After receiving the call, James turned up outside the bank as instructed. It was a Sunday but Gabriel was very specific and who was James to question it. The rear door was opened, but it wasn't Gabriel. It was a younger man carrying a small sack. To all intents and purposes, it looked like a sack full of letters. "Where's Gabriel?"

"Something came up, but he needs you to take this to the carfest at Overton and hand it in at the gate. It's a charity donation. As soon as you've done that you can go home, you'll be paid in full as agreed."

"Right ok, but why," the car door slammed shut, "didn't he get a clerk to do it?" He was shouting to himself now, but he felt compelled to finish his sentence regardless.

He carried on talking to himself. "Why would he spend six hundred quid hiring me when all of that could have gone to charity?" He was annoyed at Gabriel, but for the time being he had a contract to complete. He did as he was duly appointed and drove directly up to the gate, got out, opened the rear door, and handed over the sack full of money to the marshal on the gate.

The marshal was expecting to be met by some VIP of some nature and was a little disappointed to be presented with a sack. He peered into the sack to see that the contents were nothing but twenty pound notes.

"It's a charity donation," James offered as explanation, and with that he got back into his car and drove off as he watched the marshal scurry off to his boss.

Monday 29th August 2016

Lord and Lady Rossford sat for breakfast with the muted tones of radio two for company. Chris Evans was waxing lyrical about the success of his recent event, about the great musical talent that was present and the lengths that people were willing to put themselves through to raise money. The choir that conducted a seventy-two hour singathon without any breaks and a chap that cycled from John O'Groats to Land's End towing a trailer behind him to collect donations, which by the time he had reached Land's End was too heavy to move.

"Oh yes, and one other thing, we had a sky-blue Bentley turn up at one of the gates, and who do you think it was?" His crew threw out one famous name after another. "Sorry. I'm going to have to stop you there. You see it was a bit of a trick question because nobody got out of the car. Well, that's not exactly true either, the chauffeur did. The chauffeur did to open the back door. So, I hear you ask, if there was nobody else in the car, why did he open the back door? It's simple, he pulled out a sack, but this wasn't any old sack. No!

This was a sack full of twenty pound notes and we counted it and who would like to know how much was in it?"

By this time his crew and half the country waited with baited breath to find out how much money was in the sack. His crew started to guess "Ten thousand?"

"Nope, higher than that."

"Fifteen thousand?"

"Well, you're going in the right direction, but I can't wait any longer the director's screaming in my ear right now to get a move on, so I'm going to have to tell you. Twenty-five thousand pounds. Yes folks, you heard it right, twenty-five thousand pounds. Not a penny more or a penny less. His crew pitched in once more.

"Wow Chris, do have any idea who the benefactor is?"

"Not a clue, but if the driver of the sky-blue Bentley is out there listening in, we'd love for you to get in touch and shed some more light on this, or if anyone thinks they know who he is, don't hesitate to contact us. As much as I don't want to drop this, I'm going to have to because it's time for Sally to fill you in on what the traffic's doing out there."

Lord Rossford listened intently until the traffic news came up, which didn't interest him as he wasn't going anywhere. "I say darling, doesn't that fella who's seeing our Millie drive a sky-blue Bentley. He's a chauffeur, isn't he?"

"Oh really, I couldn't say. Is she even still seeing him?" Of course she knew she was, but indifference seemed to be the right course of action. It certainly explained why she was no longer able to contact her hitman and why James was still around, but it didn't explain how James was able to out-fox the most cunning of them all. For Lady Rossford, that would always remain a mystery.

"Well, whoever it is, is most generous indeed," George offered as a finishing statement. A ping chimed from Lady Rossford's handbag and then another and then another. "Goodness darling, you are popular this morning." Lady Rossford's phone continued to ping throughout the morning as messages of congratulations came through for managing to raise the twenty-five thousand for the carfest delivered as promised in a sack.

Chris Evans finished off the show with an update on the mysterious donation. "Well folks, we've had a couple of suggestions phoned through. One insisting that it was a charitable donation from a Lady, but not just any Lady, a Lady married to a Lord no less, and another from a fellow called Jack who insists that his friend James was the chauffeur who de-livered the sack full of notes and that it was donated by a chap called Gabriel. This is the story I like best and it's the one I'm going to stick with because Gabriel, if you're listening, you are well and truly an Angel as far as we're concerned. Well, what can I say to finish the show? It's easy really, the Lord really does move in mysterious ways.

THE END. FOR REAL THIS TIME.

Acknowledgements

My thanks go out to my long-suffering wife for tolerating being ignored for lengthy periods of time whilst I indulged myself in the writing of this novel. The rolled eyes said it all when yet again I would be pleading for help to negotiate my way around the workings of a laptop computer. In fact, much of the first draft was handwritten and it was left for my poor dear wife to transfer my scrawl into the form it is now.

Of course, without friends, both past and present, the soul of my characters wouldn't exist and I'd like to think that an essence of all of them can be witnessed within the pages of this book. Regrettably two of my good friends from my formative youthful years are no longer mortally tied to the planet. Richard was the rock that anchored me as I drifted through a difficult period of my life, and Paul I respected and revered for his maturity and everything he achieved in his life. To that end, and with respect to the loved ones they've left behind, I dedicate the following poem.

Finally, my thanks go out to my editor, Eanna Roberts for her gentle guidance and support in helping me to complete the novel.

The Station

I have to go to the station,
I know you'd like to come,
I know that its not fair,
But your work here isn't done.

I know that you can do it,
The job we've laid to bare,
But I have to go to the station,
I can't be there to share.

In many ways I will be,
In our children, a smile or a distant stare.
Take solace in those moments,
And know that I am there.

And when your work is over,
And all is said and done,
I'll meet you at the station,
And I promise you my dear sweet fair maiden,
Our journey has only just begun.

Printed in Great Britain
by Amazon